Treasures
&
Pleasures

A Collection of Romantic Novellas

Bobbi Smith

13Thirty Books
Print and Digital Editions
Copyright 2016

Discover new and exciting works by Bobbi Smith and 13Thirty Books at www.13thirtybooks.com

Print and Digital Edition, License Notes

ISBN: 0-9977912-1-7
ISBN-13: 978-0-9977912-1-1

DEDICATION

For all my Fans. Hope you enjoy these Novellas.

CONTENTS

Eden's Gate

Chapter 1	8
Chapter 2	17
Chapter 3	29
Chapter 4	34
Chapter 5	47
Chapter 6	58

Something Blue

Chapter 1	70
Chapter2	75
Chapter3	81
Chapter 4	88
Chapter 5	94
Chapter 6	101
Chapter 7	109
Chapter 8	118
Chapter 9	125
Chapter 10	132

Lottery Of Love

Chapter 1	136
Chapter 2	144
Chapter 3	151
Chapter 4	157
Chapter 5	166
Chapter 6	172
Chapter 7	181
Chapter 8	187
Epilogue	193

Time Stolen Love

Prologue   196
Chapter 1   197
Chapter 2   202
Chapter 3   206
Chapter 4   210
Chapter 5   217
Chapter 6   226
Chapter 7   238
Epilogue   247

About The Author   249

EDEN'S GATE

1

Spring, 1993

"The story of Eden's Gate Plantation is a sad and mysterious one," Jane Martin, the tour guide, told the group of travelers standing with her on the deck of the River Queen as it slowed and prepared to pull into the landing at Eden's Gate. "It was built in the late 1830s by the Hampton family, who'd come here from Virginia, and it prospered until the spring of 1860, when tragedy struck."

"What happened?" a petite, gray-haired, elderly lady asked eagerly as she stared up at the white, three-storied, pillared home that had just come into view. Atop a low rise about a half mile back from the river, the elegant house was framed by huge, moss-draped oaks and lush green lawns.

"That was the year Jonas Hampton, the widowed owner of the place, lost his only son, Bradford, in a steamboat explosion. Bradford's body was never found."

"How horrible!"

"It was truly a tragic loss. Bradford Hampton was a man of vision, a man ahead of his times. He was university educated and had made his grand tour. Instead of coming home a spoiled, arrogant young man, though, he returned convinced that changes had to be made to the Southern way of life. His revolutionary ideas didn't sit well with his contemporaries, and this is where the mystery comes in. There were rumors that his death had not been an accident. There were also rumors that he hadn't really been killed in the explosion, that he'd been seen alive at least once after the day he supposedly died."

"Why would anybody have wanted him dead?" another tourist asked.

"According to the gossip of the times, Bradford Hampton was involved with the Underground Railroad. There was never any definitive proof as far as we've been able to ascertain; but in those days, rumor alone was enough to make neighboring slave owners nervous. That was right before the war, you know."

"What about those other rumors? What happened to the family, to the plantation?"

"Diaries we've read chronicled Jonas' grief and his anger at Bradford's death. It seems that after a period of mourning, Jonas suddenly freed his slaves and gave them each a parcel of land in exchange for a promise to work the plantation fields as they'd done before. Before he could do much more, well…"

"So there's no proof that Bradford Hampton ever came back?"

"None. The guides who'll be taking you through the house will read to you some of the passages from Jonas' diary, about how he missed his son and longed for him to return. It was all very sad."

"Who owns the house now?"

"After Jonas died, it passed to several other families until it finally fell into a terrible state of disrepair. The local Historical and Restoration Society bought the property about twelve years ago and have now refurbished it to its original glory."

"Thank heaven," another tourist put in, touched by the heartbreaking tale.

"Indeed," Kacie Cameron murmured in agreement as she stood slightly apart from the group.

"Did you have something to add, Ms. Cameron?" Jane Martin asked. Then, addressing her group of tourists, she explained, "In case you haven't met her yet, ladies and gentlemen, this is Kacie Cameron."

"Kacie Cameron of K.C.'s Paradise Boutiques?" one impressed lady asked, as everyone turned around to regard the slender, fair-haired, beautiful young woman.

"That's right. Ms. Cameron in one of Eden's Gate Historical Society's most ardent supporters," Jane told them enthusiastically. "For those of you unfamiliar with Ms. Cameron's work, let me say that she's a marvelous fashion designer. But you can tell that just by looking at her, can't you?"

Kacie blushed prettily at her praise, while the crowd eyed with interest the dressy-casual, pale-yellow sweater and stretch pants outfit she wore from her own collection.

Jane continued to heap accolades upon Kacie, gushing, "Ms. Cameron has opened boutiques in New York, Chicago, Los Angeles, and Miami, and they're tremendously successful because her styles are so fresh and different. Why, anyone who is anyone on stage, screen, or in the social world shops at the Paradise Boutiques. She's got fans in all age groups, because there's something for everyone in her shops."

"I remember reading about you in one of my business magazines," one man in the group spoke up. "The article was about how you achieved such a great deal of success at such a young age and about how your boutique franchises are right up there with Blockbuster Video and Domino's Pizza in terms of desirability. You're only thirty, aren't you?"

"Yes," Kacie answered, smiling.

"The article mentioned, too, that all the profit from one of your designer lines goes to the plantation fund. Is that true?"

"It's your 'Garden of Eden' lingerie line, isn't it?" Madge Patterson, a cheerful, middle-aged woman from Milwaukee, cut in before Kacie could say anything more. "I've bought several of your nightgowns, and I just love 'em!"

"Yes, it is that line, and thank you. I'm glad you enjoy them."

"Oh, no, my dear. Thank *you*!" Madge replied with a bright smile. "You just can't imagine how exciting it is to get to meet you. Why, my husband here just loves your work!" She laughed, while her husband looked decidedly uncomfortable.

"In addition to her business acumen, Ms. Cameron has studied all the documents available on Eden's Gate and has become a scholar on the family's history and on the home itself." Jane looked to Kacie. "Is there anything you'd like to offer before we leave the boat and go up to the main house? The ladies from the Society are waiting for us."

"I'd just like to tell everyone that Eden's Gate is probably the most accurately restored plantation in the deep South. From the plaster crown moldings to the wallpaper, every item has been carefully reproduced so the house looks almost exactly as it did in

1860."

"Wonderful. Are you here for just a short visit, Ms. Cameron, or will you be staying for a while?" Jane inquired, knowing that the designer was disembarking at the plantation and would not continue on with the tour of the plantations along the Mississippi.

"Actually, the Society notified me that the long-missing Hampton family Bible has been recovered, so I've come to do more research."

"I hope you discover some exciting new information."

"So do I."

"Shall we go now?"

The walkway had been lowered, so the guide led the group from the ship. As they reached the landing, Madge left her husband, who went with the crowd, and waited excitedly for Kacie.

"Ms. Cameron."

"Yes?"

"My name's Madge, Madge Patterson, and I was wondering if you'd mind my walking along with you?"

Kacie had hoped to enjoy a quiet stroll, but the other woman's enthusiasm made it hard to refuse. "Of course not, Madge. Please join me. By the way, please call me Kacie."

Madge was thrilled. "Tell me, how did you get so involved with Eden's Gate? Are you related to the Hampton family?"

"No, I'm not," Kacie answered, though she'd often wondered if there wasn't some distant, obscure connection somewhere in her family tree. "I first read about the plantation in the newspaper when I was only eighteen. I fell in love with the place just from what little information was in the article. I was so fascinated by the family's story that I began saving as much money as I could so I could come and see the house for myself. As soon as I graduated from high school, I made my first trip here."

"Was it as wonderful as you thought it would be?"

"Absolutely. In fact, it was better. It's breathtaking," Kacie replied, lifting her green-eyed gaze to the mansion in the distance. Once again, as happened every time she returned, a tremendous sense of longing welled up inside her, and she wondered how she could have stayed away this long.

Kacie didn't tell Madge everything about her first trip to Eden's Gate. She didn't tell the woman about her reaction to seeing

Bradford Hampton's portrait for the first time. She'd been almost frightened by the power of the feelings that had swept through her at the sight of his handsome features captured for eternity in that painting. Kacie had been filled with a sense of loneliness, a devastating sense of loss. It hadn't made sense to her, but there had been no denying it.

Kacie had never before experienced anything so intense or so unsettling. Having always prided herself on being an intelligent person, she'd attempted to reason away her confusion. She'd told herself it was crazy to react that way to a portrait of a dead man, but the gut-wrenching emotions that had churned within her as she'd stared up at the dark-haired Bradford Hampton's compelling features hadn't disappeared. She'd known an almost uncontrollable desire to reach out and caress his lean, hard cheek. She'd wanted to touch him, to see him smile. She'd wanted to hear him laugh. She'd known it was crazy. She'd told herself it was just a picture, that the man was dead, but all the rationalizing in the world hadn't eased the turmoil in her heart and in her soul.

Kacie had reminded herself that there were a lot of good-looking men alive right now and that she didn't react this way when she saw any of them. Seeing Mel Gibson never evoked this kind of response from her; neither did gazing at handsome Tom Berenger or seeing Gregory Peck in his younger days when he'd starred in movies like *The Big Country*. She'd thought the strange and powerful feelings would fade with time, but during all of her visits, her reaction to seeing Bradford's portrait had been the same. Kacie knew her feelings bordered on being obsessive, but she figured as long as she wasn't hurting anyone, there was nothing to be unduly concerned about.

"Eden's Gate is lovely." Madge sighed, distracting Kacie from her thoughts.

"It's the most beautiful place in the world," Kacie commented. "I'm so glad to be back."

Eagerness filled Kacie as she thought once again of the note she'd received a week ago from Doris Hoyle, the Historical Society's director. The missive had informed her that the Hampton family Bible had finally been found in a secret hiding place in a grotto wall and that Kacie was invited to view the Bible at her convenience. Kacie had been planning to take the riverboat tour later in the spring, but after getting the letter, she'd booked her trip right away. Now that she was finally back on the plantation, she wondered how she'd ever had the strength to leave it.

As they came to the side path that led off to the Historical Society's office, Kacie excused herself from Madge's company and went in search of Doris Hoyle. Kacie's spirits were soaring, and for the first time in months, she felt truly alive. It seemed she'd done nothing but work lately. After her relationship with her last boyfriend had fizzled out from a lack of interest and enthusiasm on both their parts, Kacie had devoted all her energies to creating her fashion line for the following winter. She'd had no time for another relationship, and now, as she headed for the office, she was glad she had no binding ties to distract her from her purpose. She was there to learn everything new she could about Eden's Gate and the Hampton family. Kacie hoped her efforts would help her understand more about her fixation with the place and with Bradford in particular.

The director was waiting for her when she entered the office. A dark-haired lady of impeccable manner and dress, Doris Hoyle was the epitome of Southern womanhood. Soft-spoken yet firm in her convictions, Doris had been the driving power behind the restoration of Eden's Gate, and she had deeply appreciated all of Kacie's support—financial and otherwise. Their reunion was a warm one, the camaraderie that existed between them genuine.

"The house has been rented out for a reception tonight at eight o'clock, but the guests are restricted to the main floor, so you shouldn't be disturbed," Doris told Kacie as she escorted her to the main house. "As usual, you're in the back bedroom."

"Thanks, Doris." Kacie smiled. The master suite and Bradford's room were included in the tour, but the other bedrooms were part of the bed-and-breakfast plan and were rented out to guests. Kacie had stayed in the same bedroom on every visit, and she adored it.

"Since it's already so late," the director said, glancing at her watch to discover it was after five o'clock, "why don't we plan on meeting first thing in the morning? We can have breakfast together and then begin our study of the Bible. How does eight o'clock sound?"

"Eight sounds wonderful. Have you had much of an opportunity to look through it yet?"

"I went through it quickly last week, right after I wrote to you, and I found some very interesting things in it. I think you're going to enjoy looking at it."

"I know I am," Kacie agreed. "Where are you keeping it?"

"It's in Bradford's bedroom under glass for now so nothing can happen to it. You can take a peek at it tonight if you like."

"Thanks."

"I've made arrangements for an early dinner to be brought to you in your room around six-thirty. You should have a relatively quiet evening as long as none of the guests at the reception gets lost and wanders upstairs where it's off-limits. I'll be around all evening if you need anything else."

Kacie thanked her again as they entered the main house by way of the back entrance and used the rear staircase to reach the second floor. Doris accompanied Kacie to her room and then bade her good night. Alone at last in the spacious, beautifully appointed bedroom with its antique furnishings, imported wallpaper, marble fireplace, and over-long gold velvet drapes, Kacie drew a chair to the window and sat down to look out across the perfectly manicured lawns and flowering gardens.

When dinner arrived, Kacie ate on a small table by the window, enjoying the view as she savored the hot, delicious food the cook had prepared. Knowing that the servants would still be working to ready the house for the reception that night, she decided to wait until later to see the Bible. Kicking off her shoes, she shed her clothes and changed into a comfortable pair of shorts and the one-of-a-kind T-shirt she'd designed her herself in honor of Eden's Gate. She stretched out on the comfortable canopy bed, meaning to rest for a little while.

Kacie hadn't thought she'd fallen asleep, and she wasn't exactly sure what woke her, but she came awake suddenly and sat up in bed to discover that it was already after ten. Annoyed with herself for having wasted precious time by sleeping, she jumped out of bed, anxious for her first look at the Hampton family Bible. She checked her appearance in the full-length mirror, then quickly ran a brush through her sleep-tousled blonde hair to make herself look presentable just in case she ran into anyone in the hall. Dismissing shoes as unimportant, she hurried barefoot from her room down the dimly lit hallway to Bradford Hampton's bedroom.

Kacie could hear the music and revelry going on at the reception below, but paid little attention to them. Parties held no interest for her when she was about to get her hands on the book she'd been hoping to read for years.

Entering the bedroom, Kacie flipped the wall switch, and the period lamps, now wired for electricity, lit up the room with a warm golden glow. She closed the door behind her and paused for a moment to let her gaze sweep the room. The dark furniture was massive and heavy, and spoke of a purely masculine presence. Her gaze fell upon the wide four-poster bed that had belonged to Bradford Hampton, and she felt a flush of heat rush through her. Wistfully, she wished things had been different, that he hadn't died so violently, that he'd married and had children and lived a long and happy life. His death had been such a waste. Men like Bradford Hampton were hard to come by.

With an effort, Kacie turned her eyes and thoughts away from the room's first occupant. She spied the Bible on the dresser and hurried to see it. Removing the protective glass case, she opened the Bible almost reverently.

Kacie concentration was fierce as she leafed slowly through the thick, leather-bound book. Reality faded as she became entranced by the family birth and death records in the front. They covered every Hampton for generations, but ended with Bradford's birth and that of his mother's death a few years later. Kacie stared down at the page with Bradford's name written on it, thinking how odd it was that Jonas Hampton never entered the date of his son's death, April 6, in the book. She wondered if Jonas had held out hope that somehow, one day, his son would return to him.

Kacie flipped carefully through more pages and then turned to the back of the Bible, hoping to find something more there. She was disappointed, though, for there were no further references to Bradford anywhere. She was about to close the book when she noticed that there was a carefully made slit in the back binding. Kacie touched the tear as if she hoped to heal it and was surprised to discover a lump beneath it. Curious to see what it was, she gently slipped her fingers inside and, with utmost caution, drew out a sheet of paper.

Kacie's hands were shaking as she unfolded the brittle paper, and her eyes widened in excitement as she stared down at the map she'd discovered. A chill ran down her spine, and her heart actually skipped a beat as she studied it. There was no mistaking the handwriting. She'd studied Bradford's letters and papers often enough to be able to recognize his powerful male script. Her thoughts were flying. What had she found? It was a map of some sort, and she wondered if this had anything to do with the Underground Railroad. The rumors had said that he was involved, but no real proof had ever been found. There were notes written at the bottom of the paper, but they were so faded she could barely make them out. All she could really decipher on the fragile, yellowed sheet was the name signed at the bottom.

"Brad," she whispered.

Suddenly as she said his name out loud, a terrible light-headedness came over her. Wave after wave of dizziness crashed through Kacie until she thought her knees might buckle. She braced herself against the dresser, one palm on the open Bible, as she fought to regain her equilibrium. It didn't help. Her senses intensified to an almost painful perception. The faint, delicate perfume of the magnolia blossoms just outside the bedroom window became cloying and suffocating. The music from downstairs that had been only a faint melody moments before assumed a throbbing, haunting pitch. The room seemed to swirl and tilt before her.

Half-dazed, Kacie told herself that if she could just sit down, she'd be all right. In desperation, still clutching the map, she stumbled toward the bed. Grasping one of the bedposts for support, she sank down on the mattress, wondering what was wrong with her and hoping that the dizziness would pass.

Kacie heard the door open. With great effort, for her head was still spinning, she looked up to see who it was. There, standing in the doorway, was none other than Bradford Hampton.

2

BRADFORD *Hampton? It couldn't be…* Kacie blinked, thinking he would disappear. When she opened her eyes and he was still standing there staring at her with an amused yet puzzled look on his face, she blinked again. She opened only one eye this time and found that he hadn't moved. Her less than trustworthy senses were telling her that a tall, broad-shouldered, darkly handsome man who looked exactly like Bradford Hampton was standing right in front of her, a mere six feet away.

Kacie couldn't help herself. She smiled. She knew it couldn't really be Bradford, but whoever he was, he was a gorgeous hunk of a man. If she had to be rescued from her momentary dizziness, it might as well be by a good-looking Prince Charming like this guy. He was certainly dressed for the part of a romantic hero in his fancy suit with its brocade vest that looked like something straight out of *Gone With The Wind*. Kacie hadn't known that the reception tonight was a costume party, but it didn't matter. This man made the clothes; the clothes didn't make him. He could have come to her rescue in grubby jeans and a sweatshirt, and she would have smiled the same ridiculous smile.

"I didn't know it was a costume party tonight, but you know you really shouldn't be in here," Kacie confided, thinking he was a guest who'd wandered away from the reception downstairs.

"Oh?" He sounded surprised. "And why is that?" His voice was deep and mellow, and sent shivers of awareness up her spine.

"Because the second floor is off-limits to party guests," she explained, wondering why he hadn't been told.

"Well, since I'm not a party guest, I guess it's safe for me to be here. What about you? Should you be in here?" As he spoke, Brad took a step into the room, closing the door behind him.

"Oh, yes. I have permission," Kacie answered with authority.

"Really?" Brad couldn't quite believe what was happening. There in the middle of his bed sat the most beautiful woman he'd ever seen, and she was practically naked! His gaze was hot as it raked over her. He had no idea who she was, but he intended to find out. "And just who was it who gave you permission to wander around my house dressed... or... er, should I say undressed like that?"

"Ms. Hoyle did, but..."

"Who?" Brad's tone sharpened, for he knew no one by that name, and he was growing suspicious.

"The director." Kacie's smile faltered, then vanished, and her eyes suddenly narrowed as she realized what the man had said a moment before. "Did you say 'your house'?"

"That's right, my house. I'm Brad Hampton, in case you didn't know, and this is my house and that's my bed you're sitting on."

He sounded so convincing that Kacie couldn't help laughing out loud. "Yeah, right, you're Bradford Hampton and I'm Madonna."

"I'm afraid you bear little or no resemblance to the Madonna," Brad answered tightly, not understanding why she thought his identity was particularly funny.

"Not *the* Madonna," she corrected. "Madonna." At his blank expression, she went on, "Never mind. Look, I have to admit you do look a lot like Bradford Hampton in the portrait downstairs in the study, but whoever you are, don't you think you're taking this whole costume thing just a bit too far?" Good-looking though he was, this guy was beginning to sound pretty weird, and Kacie thought it might be best if she got the heck out of there. She rose to her feet.

"At least, madam, I have my costume on," Brad countered, his heated regard sweeping from the thrust of her full breasts against the tight shirt she was wearing to her long, shapely legs and bare feet.

"Yeah, right. Look, I'm feeling better now, so why don't you just go on back to your party. I won't tell anyone you were up here." Realizing she'd left the map lying on the bed, she quickly retrieved it and started to move past him.

"That's very kind of you," he said in a wry tone, "but not so fast. I want to know who you are and what you're doing here." His demand was made in the imperious tone of a man completely confident of his position.

Kacie sighed in exasperation. "Not that it's any of your business," she countered with equal arrogance, "but my name is Kacie Cameron, and I'm here because I was looking for and hoping to find something like this." She indicated the map that, peculiarly, she suddenly noticed wasn't so brittle or fragile anymore. She frowned as she continued, "Now, Brad, why don't you head on back downstairs and tell Mrs. Hoyle that I need to see her right away. She's going to be very interested in the information I just found."

"What the hell!" Brad reacted to the sight of his map in her hands without thinking. Storming forward, he snared Kacie by the upper arm and grabbed the document that could mean life or death to so many.

"What do you think you're doing? Be careful! That's old and it might…" Kacie protested frantically, trying to break away from his steely grip. She didn't know who this guy was, but it seemed to her his elevator didn't go all the way up.

"I want answers, and I want them now!" Brad snarled, glaring down at her. "Who are you working for? How much do they know?"

"The only thing that I know for sure is that you're crazy! Let me go!"

Using a trick she'd learned at a police-held self-defense class, Kacie stomped hard on his booted foot while violently jerking her arm. He gave a yelp of pain and loosened his grip just enough so she could break loose and make her escape. She darted for the door.

Brad stood there, his foot aching, unable to believe what was happening. Whoever this woman was, she was a wildcat! He started after her, but stopped cold in his tracks when he saw the writing on the back of her shirt. He could only stare at her back as she threw open the door and charged out into the hall. Befuddled, he paused where he was, trying to understand: *The heavenly South will rise again… Happy 160ᵗʰ Birthday, Eden's Gate, 1832-1992."*

Kacie ran out into the hallway. The sounds of music and laughter swelled around her, reminding her of the celebration going on below. She didn't want to go down the front steps and risk ruining the party, for the society earned a lot of money from such festivities, so she raced down the hall in the direction of the back staircase.

Kacie didn't feel she was in any real danger. She figured Doris was somewhere nearby and all she had to do was find her and let her know what a weirdo the Bradford impostor was. When Kacie heard Brad emerge from the room behind her, she quickened her pace. Rushing on, she turned the corner at the end of the hall, thinking she was almost home free. To her great and utter dismay, she came face to face with an elderly man on his way upstairs. He was obviously part of the reception, too, for he was dressed in a period costume much like Brad's.

"Excuse me, sir," Kacie decided to brazen it out. She started down the steps, trying to move around him, but to her surprise the man didn't budge. He stood there, blocking her way, staring at her with an openly shocked expression.

"My dear young woman, where are your clothes?" the silver-haired man asked as he stared at her legs.

"I'm wearing my clothes," Kacie snapped more than a little irritated. The way this old geezer was gawking at her, she could almost believe he'd never seen a girl in shorts and a top before. "Now, if you'll excuse me..."

"I can't let you go downstairs looking like that, my dear," he told her, refusing to get out of her way.

"Excuse me?" she countered, her hands on her hips, her eyes flashing at his condescending tone. "What you do mean, *you* can't let me go downstairs?"

"It wouldn't be proper," he explained. Then, at the sound of footsteps in the hall, he looked up and smiled. "Ah, Brad, my boy, would you mind telling me just what's going on?"

"Father..." Brad was relieved to see him. He'd paused in his bedroom only long enough to fold the map and put it in his jacket pocket before coming after Kacie and he'd feared she might have eluded him. "I'm glad you caught her."

"Caught her?" Jonas glanced from his son's very serious expression to the defiant, nearly naked young woman standing before him. "What are you talking about? Who are you, young lady?"

"I'm Kacie Cameron, a paying guest here, and I demand to see the director at once!"

"A paying guest?" Jonas looked up at his son and frowned. "Bradford, what is the meaning of all this?"

"We'd better talk about it in my room. Bring her upstairs."

Though her path was blocked going down, Kacie knew she

still had a chance to get past Brad. Deciding to play submissive for a minute in the hope that the men would let their guards down, she turned quietly and made her way back to the second-floor hall. She knew a moment of success when Brad didn't take hold of her again, and she walked past him with great dignity, her head held high.

Brad stayed right with Kacie as she moved coolly down the hallway. Hellion though she was, his curiosity was piqued. He knew he wouldn't rest until he found out who she was and what she'd been doing in his room. If her intent had been to find the map, and she'd obviously done that, then why had she stayed and risked being found? And why had she been sitting on his bed so scantily clad? Had she stayed with the intention of seducing him in the hope of getting more information? The idea seemed farfetched, considering there was a house full of people below, and it was doubtful he would have returned to his room any time soon that night. Brad scowled. He didn't know what her story was, but he certainly meant to find out, especially since she'd nearly crippled him. His foot was still sore, and he was glad she hadn't been wearing shoes. If she had, the damage undoubtedly would have been much worse.

Brad cast Kacie a sidelong glance and noticed how grim her expression was. He wondered if she was cold since she was wearing so little, and thought it might be a good idea to offer her a blanket once they were in the room. He knew it might prove difficult for him to have a serious conversation with her looking as she did now. She certainly was a lovely woman, though. It was too bad she was so treacherous.

Kacie was ready. They were going to walk right past the door to the master bedroom suite on their way to Brad's room. With any luck at all, she could run in there and make it out onto the balcony where she could yell for help. Surely one of the men the Society hired to park cars at the parties would hear her cry and come to her aid. With fierce determination, she didn't let any emotion show on her face as they neared the doorway. Then, in a flash, she bolted through the open door. She slammed it shut behind her and ran full speed toward the balcony doors.

"Damn it!" Brad rarely swore, but this mysterious woman was driving him to distraction. He fumbled with the doorknob, then finally sent the door crashing open. Leaving his father to follow, he gave chase.

Kacie was certain she was going to get away. She ran for the French doors, threw them wide, and darted outside. But her cry for help died on her lips as she stopped dead and stared at the view from the balcony. There was no paved driveway below, parked bumper-to-bumper with cars. Instead, there was a shell-lined drive full of horse-drawn carriages!

Kacie stared about her in bewilderment. Carriages? Horses? What was happening here? She heard the men coming after her and started to run along the balcony, hoping to reach the back bedroom where her things were.

Since she knew the house by heart, Kacie found the room without any trouble. As she burst through the French doors of her bedroom, she discovered that it was completely different from when she'd left it less than a half-hour before. The furniture was gone, and only a settee and a few tables remained. There was no trace of her luggage or clothing. The room was devoid of any trace of her presence.

"What...? But... where...?" Kacie stared about her in complete and utter confusion.

"I don't know what kind of game you're playing, young lady," Brad declared as he caught up with her, "but I mean to find out right now." Taking her by the shoulders, he swung her around to face him.

After the chase she'd led him on, Brad was surprised when she offered no resistance. He gazed down at her in the low light and was startled by the look of abject panic on her pale, strained features.

"Who are you?" Kacie whispered hoarsely, unable to believe the unbelievable.

"I told you who I am. I'm Bradford Hampton, and I want some answers from you. Who sent you?"

"Nobody sent me. I came down here because the director notified me that the Bible had been found..."

"Found?"

"We'd been looking for it and—"

"You've been looking for our family Bible?" Jonas spoke up as he joined them. "Why?"

"Because it's been missing since before the turn of the century, and we were hoping it would give us some more information about Brad's activities."

"And just what did you hope to learn about my activities?"

Brad demanded tightly.

"You…, no…, not you… Bradford Hampton. The real Bradford Hampton."

"I assure you, miss, this is the real Bradford Hampton," Jonas said carefully, wondering what kind of terrible delusions this woman was suffering from. For all that she was a pretty young thing, her state of undress and obvious mental confusion convinced him that she was not right in the head. He didn't know who she was or where she'd come from, but they had to do something about her and fast. They had a house full of guests! "Perhaps Miss Cameron needs to see a doctor? Perhaps some medication to calm her down would help?"

"Look," she bit out sarcastically, wondering about these two loonies. "I don't need any calming down. When I find my overnight case, I'll take a couple of aspirins for the headache you're giving me. Right now, all I want to do is locate Doris Hoyle. She told me she'd be here all night. I'm sure she can straighten everything out to your satisfaction."

Brad exchanged a worried look with his father. "Miss Cameron, why don't we go back to my room? It will be more comfortable there, and we can talk."

"Look, buddy, we can talk just fine right here. All I want to know is what's going on around here? Where is everybody? What happened to all the cars?"

"Cars?" Brad and his father looked perplexed.

"Yes, cars, and where are my things? Who hid them? If you think this is some kind of joke, I'm not laughing."

"No one hid your things, miss." Jonas tried to sound conciliatory, for the woman was obviously deeply disturbed.

"Of course they did," she argued. "When I left this room less than half an hour ago, all of my clothes and—"

"Miss Cameron, you couldn't have left the room a half-hour ago. This is my mother's sitting room. Since she died eight years ago, no one comes in here."

A wave of dizziness threatened Kacie again, and she was almost glad for Brad's strong hands holding her. "What are you talking about?" she asked, feeling more and more lightheaded.

"I'm talking about your delusions… or your lies, whichever they are. I've never seen you before in my life, and yet I find you in my room, nearly naked, stealing some of my personal papers."

"Stealing? I had permission! Besides, I wasn't going to keep it. I just wanted to study it," she protested weakly.

"I'm sure you did. Who's paying you?"

"Paying me? What are you talking about?"

"I think it's time you stopped answering my questions with questions of your own. This is 1860, and even though you are a woman, you were caught stealing—"

"What did you say?" Kacie stared at him, her eyes widening with a crazy mixture of emotions.

Suddenly the horse and carriages outside, the men's period clothing, and the changes in the furnishings swirled maddeningly, tauntingly, though Kacie's consciousness. Everything sharpened to a crystal clarity, and she knew! Her head began to pound as she forced herself to ask again, "What year did you say this was?"

"It's 1860."

The dizziness intensified. There was a loud ringing in her ears, and her legs suddenly seemed incapable of supporting her. As a blessed peace claimed her, Kacie murmured the words she'd said so many times before in jest.

"What?" Brad asked in surprise as she mumbled something. He was even more shocked when, without warning, she collapsed into his arms. "She fainted," he told his father incredulously.

"What did she say?" Jonas asked, thinking there might be a clue in her words.

Brad looked bewildered as he answered, "It didn't make any sense. She said, 'Beam me up, Scotty.'"

3

"Beam me up, Scotty?" Jonas repeated. "Who's Scotty?"

"I have no idea, but I think you'd better find Warren and send him up to my bedroom," Brad told his father as, carrying Kacie, he started out onto the balcony on his way back to his own room.

Jonas hurried from the sitting room to seek out Dr. Warren Coleman, their longtime family physician. Jonas knew Warren could be counted on to handle the situation with discretion and a minimum of questions.

When Brad reached his bedroom, he gently laid Kacie on his bed, then quickly drew a blanket over her. He remained standing there, studying her perfect features and wondering at her part in all this. She'd mentioned only two people—a woman named Doris Hoyle, whom she called the director, and someone named Scotty. He'd never heard either of those names before and that worried him. He thought he knew all the people involved in trying to destroy the Underground Railroad, but obviously he didn't.

As Brad considered his options in dealing with Kacie, he thought again of the writing on her shirt. He'd never known anyone to wear clothes with writing on them, except for the poorer folks who made their garments out of flour sacks and the like. The writing on her shirt had definitely not been labeling from a flour sack, though. *"The heavenly South will rise again."* What did that mean? And the reference to 1992. That was over a hundred and thirty years in the future. He thought of her reaction when they'd told her what year it was, and he frowned.

There was a soft knock at the door, and Brad opened it to find Dr. Coleman standing there. "Brad? Your father said you needed me." Warren Coleman was a gray-haired, kindly looking old man, whose knowledge of medicine and life went unchallenged. He glanced from the tall, handsome young man he'd delivered thirty-two years ago to the young woman who lay unconscious on the bed.

"Please, come in." Brad held the door as the doctor strode toward the bed.

"What happened?" he asked as he gazed down at the beauty.

"She fainted."

Warren's eyes met Brad's, and when he saw his closed, guarded expression, he knew better than to ask anything more. He threw back the blanket and was startled by the clothing she had on. He conducted his examination without comment as Brad looked on from across the room. When he'd finished, he covered Kacie again and turned to Brad.

"There's nothing wrong with her as far as I can see."

Just as he spoke, Kacie gave a low moan and began to stir. "My head..." Feeling completely exhausted, her head throbbing, Kacie opened her eyes to find a strange man hovering over her. "Who are you?"

"I'm Dr. Coleman. It seems you fainted."

"I guess I did." Kacie managed a weak smile, thinking everything that had happened had been a bad dream. "I'm sorry if I caused any trouble."

"No trouble, my dear. It's always a pleasure to come the aid of a beautiful young woman."

"Is Doris here? I'd like to talk to her, and I really ought to get back to my own room..."

"Doris? No, there's no Doris here, but Brad is," he answered, motioning for Brad to come forward.

Kate's eyes grew round as Brad stepped into her line of vision. "I don't believe this! I wasn't dreaming... You really are here."

"Of course," the doctor soothed. "He's been here the whole time. He's been very concerned about you."

"I'm sure he has. Listen, Doc, I have to get out of here."

She started to sit up, but Dr. Coleman would have none of it. He pressed her back down on the bed.

"I'm afraid you're not going anywhere, young lady. You're very weak, and until we know exactly what caused that fainting spell, the best thing for you is to stay in bed."

"You don't understand. I don't have time for any bed rest. I have to figure out what's going on here."

Warren looked to Brad in confusion.

"She's been very upset, even to the point of being a little irrational. You see how she's dressed. She was wandering the halls that way," Brad explained.

"Perhaps a dose of laudanum would help?"

"No…" Kacie tried to put in her two cents' worth, but the men ignored her as if she didn't exist.

"Please," Brad agreed. "Maybe if she gets some rest, she'll be more like her old self."

The doctor said no more as he prepared a dose of the potent medicine.

"If you think I'm going to take any medicine, you've got another think coming!" Kacie declared with open hostility.

"It's for your own good," Brad told her, moving to sit on the bed beside her.

When Kacie would have bolted, Brad caught her and pinned her against his chest. Squirm though she might, he held her easily with one arm. Gripping her chin with his free hand, Brad kept her still so the doctor could give her the medicine.

"Doctor, you've got to listen to me!" Kacie tried to fight Brad, but he was too strong. To her fury, she was forced to choke down the hated laudanum.

"Now, now, my dear. I trust Brad knows what's best. Just rest for tonight, and I'm sure by tomorrow morning you'll feel much better."

"You don't understand," she continued to argue as Brad released. "There's nothing wrong with me."

The physician gave Brad a sympathetic look, and Brad stood up to speak with him before he left the room.

"She must have hit her head. I'll keep a close watch on her tonight."

"Good idea, my boy. You can't be too careful with this kind of thing." Though Dr. Coleman was curious to know who she was and what she was doing in Brad's bed, he did not ask. "She'll sleep for a little while with that dose, but I can't say for how long."

"Thanks."

Knowing there was nothing more he could do, the physician quietly left the room. Brad turned back to where Kacie was sitting up, trying to get out of bed.

"What do you want from me?" Kacie asked slowly, amazed that a peaceful languor was stealing over her already. She wanted to leave, and she wasn't afraid to fight this man who was calling himself Brad, but for some reason she just couldn't get up the energy to keep moving.

"The only thing I want from you is answers, and I'm not letting you go until I get them," Brad answered as he stopped before her. "Now tell me, who sent you and how much do they know?'

"Sent me? Don't you get it? I wasn't *sent* here, not the way you mean."

Brad stared at her, perplexed. "And just what is it you think I mean?"

"You think I'm here to steal your map or something, but I'm not. I don't even know why I'm here. I don't even know how I got here, but I'm here."

She gave a faint chuckle as she gazed up at him. This Brad Hampton was one very attractive man with his dark hair, dark eyes, and firm jaw. He was absolutely, positively gorgeous—as gorgeous as the portrait downstairs. At the thought of the man in the portrait, Kacie sighed. She'd been in love with the Brad in the painting for years, and though the man standing before her was just a wild fantasy her poor little brain was cooking up, for now she was going to pretend he was real and just enjoy it.

"You don't really exist, you know," Kacie murmured, feeling quiet lethargic as the medicine took stronger hold of her senses. She lay back on the bed, suddenly too tired to keep struggling. Comfortable against the pillows, she added more to herself than to him, "I can't believe I'm talking to a dead man. You're a ghost."

Brad stiffened, thinking her words were a threat from whoever had hired her to spy on him. "I assure you, Miss Cameron, I'm very much alive, and I intend to do everything in my power to stay this way."

"Nope. You're not alive. It's 1993, and you've been dead for over a hundred and thirty-two years. You died in the spring of 1860," Kacie told him sorrowfully. She drifted farther and farther down into forgetfulness, murmuring, "I just wish I coulda stopped it…"

"What!" Brad was honestly beginning to believe she was insane.

"I'm just dreaming is all." She gave another soft laugh. "As crazy as it is, I have to admit that this is probably the best dream I've ever had. I've wanted to talk to you forever. You're just so handsome." She sighed again as she felt herself falling asleep. "If you were real, I'd be the envy of everyone at home."

Brad didn't know what to do or say. Stunned, he stood staring down at a sleeping Kacie. His mind raced. She thought she was from the future—from the year 1993? She had to be crazy! But even as he almost believed that, he couldn't help wondering how she'd come to be in his house and in his bed.

Brad reviewed in his mind everything she'd said. She'd talked about wanting to learn more about his activities, about wanting to study his map—the map revealed the stations on the Underground Railroad. No one else even knew he had the map, yet this woman had made her way into his home, had gone straight into his bedroom, and had located the hidden map without anyone catching her. That was virtually impossible. There were servants everywhere, and yet not one had seen her enter. She'd told him, too, that he was going to die this spring. The thought sent a chill of caution through him, but he shook it off, dismissing it as totally ridiculous.

Needing time to think, not to mention a stiff shot of bourbon, Brad rang for a maid. When she arrived, he instructed her to stay in the room with Kacie and not to leave under any circumstances. He saw the curious look on her face but offered no explanations. With one last glance at his mysterious sleeping beauty, Brad left the room.

Brad rejoined the party and danced with several of the single, young ladies in attendance. Pretty though they were, Brad found his thoughts never strayed from the beautiful young woman upstairs in his bed. Again and again he asked himself who Kacie could be and why she was here. He found himself paying particular attention to all the guests at the party, thinking the people she'd mentioned might be there, but he found he knew everyone in attendance. There was nothing amiss.

An hour later, after having made the rounds of the ballroom, Brad couldn't stay away from Kacie any longer. Haunted by the mystery of her appearance, he returned to his bedroom, and after dismissing the maid, settled in a chair near the bed to keep watch.

The candlelight bathed the room in a soft glow. The slumbering Kacie looked even lovelier in the gentle light, and Brad found himself fascinated by her. Question after question besieged him as he remained by her side. Who was she? How had she come to be there and why? What did she want from him? There were no answers to his questions, though, and so Brad remained by her bedside through the long, dark hours of the night, waiting and watching and wondering.

*

Jonas stood in his study with a small group of men from the neighboring plantations.

"I tell you, Jonas, this is not just a case of a few runaways! I've lost three slaves in the last two months!" complained Daniel Lawrence, a big, dark-haired, mean-looking man as he tossed down a straight shot of Jonas' best bourbon. "This is an organized effort! It's probably one of those damned agitating emancipators from the North down here stirring up trouble!"

"How can you be so sure?" Jonas asked. "We haven't had a problem here at Eden's Gate."

"I'm sure because the runaways couldn't have disappeared so completely without help. Used to be that the hounds could track them down in a day or two. Now it's almost as if they've disappeared off the face of the earth."

"Daniel's right," Frank Riley, another neighbor, agreed. "I've lost two myself. Whoever's running this operation knows what he's doing."

"What do you plan to do?" Jonas asked, not greatly surprised to hear that their slaves were fleeing. For years, he'd known and disliked these men. They were the kind who took pride in being brutal to their slaves.

"We've got a few leads, but nothing substantial yet," Daniel answered. "When we find out what's going on and who's behind it, we're going to take matters into our own hands."

"Is there anything Brad or I can do to help?" Jonas offered.

"We'll let you know."

It was after two in the morning when the last guest had

departed. Jonas' thoughts were troubled as he made his way upstairs to retire. He knocked quietly at Brad's bedroom door and was pleased when his son quickly came out into the hall.

"How is she? Warren told me he gave her some laudanum to quiet her."

"She's still sleeping. I'm going to sit up all night with her, just in case she wakes up."

"You'll be all right?"

"I'll be fine."

Jonas nodded, then told him about the conversation he'd had earlier in the study. "Daniel and Frank were angry tonight. It seems they've had quite a few runaways lately. They seem to think there are outsiders at work here, helping them escape. They said when they find out who's behind it all, they're going to put an end to it in their own way."

Brad smiled thinly. "I'm sure they'll try if they get the chance."

"Brad, you know I've never tried to interfere or stop you from doing what you believed was right, but I know how vicious those men can be. This isn't a game. They're deadly serious. Are you sure you want to continue?"

"I'm positive," Brad answered firmly. He was convinced slavery was wrong, and he was willing to put himself at risk to do what he could to stop it.

"Then be careful, my son," Jonas warned him, their eyes meeting in understanding.

"I know," he agreed grimly, the memory of Kacie's reference to his death hovering around the edges of his mind. "It's hard to say how much they know, but there's too much at stake not to take them seriously. And then there is the girl."

"Did she say anything else?"

"Only that she thinks the year is 1993."

"*She what?*" Jonas had never heard anything so outrageous in his life.

"She thinks she's from the future. Of course, she'd already taken the laudanum when she said it, so she was probably just hallucinating."

"Yes, it must have been the medicine talking."

"I'm sure it was," Brad agreed.

"What do you intend to do with her?"

"I'm going to keep her here until I find out who she is."

Jonas agreed with his decision. They had to take every precaution. "If the occasion should arise where someone asks, we'll tell them she's one of your mother's relatives visiting from up North."

"I almost wish she were," he said, hating the thought that she might be a spy and dismissing as ridiculous the idea that she might be who she said she was.

Somewhat reassured that his son would take care, Jonas said good night and went to his room.

Brad returned to his bedside vigil to find Kacie still sleeping soundly. He thought that asleep she appeared the picture of innocence. From the tumbled mass of her golden curls to her faintly flushed cheeks and delicate, perfect complexion, she was a beauty beyond compare. But it wasn't only her loveliness that drew him to her. There was something else about her, something he couldn't quite put a name to. He wanted her to be as innocent as she looked. He wanted to delve into her reasons for being here and find a pure motive. He wanted to believe that if she had been sent here to spy on him, it was because someone was using her to get to him. He wanted to...

Unable to stop himself, Brad reached out and gently touched her cheek. His caress was light against her silken flesh, and he was shocked by the feelings that shot through him with just that simple touch. He withdrew his hand as if he'd been burned.

"Brad..." Kacie whispered his name in her sleep.

It was a soft, sweet murmur, as gentle as a summer breeze, and a heat of sensual awareness shot through him. He wanted to take her in his arms and hold her close. He wanted to... Brad backed away from the bed. Exerting his iron-willed self-control, he sat back down in the chair. As the minutes, then the hours passed, Brad kept watch and wondered what he was going to do with her in the morning.

*

"Well, Daniel, what do you think? Is Brad involved?"

Daniel looked thoughtful as he contemplated the question

that had been nagging him for days now. He and Frank were sitting together in the privacy of his library, having just returned from the party at Eden's Gate. The servants had all retired for the night, so they knew they could talk freely.

"I'm still not sure."

"But the slave we caught was screaming 'I'll never reach the Promised Land… I'll never see Eden' right before he died."

"Too bad he died. We might have been able to get a real answer out of him if he'd hung on a little longer. I had to make an example out of him for the others, though. I've already lost three slaves; I'm not going to lose any more. If scaring them that way works, I'll do it." Daniel felt no remorse at having whipped the runaway to death.

"Do you think he was praying when he was talking about Eden, or do you think he was talking about some connection with the Underground Railroad? He kept saying if he could get to Eden, the Lord would save him. I can't help thinking he meant Eden's Gate."

"I wish I could be certain, but I'm not… yet. We both know there's been talk about Brad Hampton's views on things, and his mother was from up North, even though she's been dead all these years. Still…"

"What do you want to do?"

"Give it a little more time. We've got to be sure before we do anything, and I've got a plan that just might work…"

4

Kacie came awake but didn't open her eyes. She lay perfectly still, trying to remember all the details of the wild dream she'd had. In her fantasy, Bradford Hampton had been alive and well. A smile crept over her face as sleep-drugged recollections of her conversation with Bradford came to her. In her heart, Kacie almost wished it had been real, but in her mind she knew it was impossible. It had been just a dream.

Stretching lazily, she finally faced the fact that she should get up. She opened her eyes, and with a jolt, realized it was still night and that she was in a strange bed. Kacie turned quickly, intending to hurl herself from the bed, and it was then that she saw Brad, standing at the open French doors with his back to her, gazing out into the darkness of the night.

Stopping in mid-motion, Kacie muttered, "Oh, boy." It really had happened. She really was with Brad in 1860. But how? And why? The questions tormented her, but she had no answers.

Brad heard her moving and turned. For the last several hours, as he'd waited for her to awaken, he'd been debating how to treat her. Finally, he'd decided to be cautious until he'd figured out why she was in his house and what she was planning to do. But in spite of all his good intentions, as he looked at her now and saw how beautiful she was, he found himself smiling at her. Her golden hair was loose and tumbling about her shoulders in a mass of untamed curls. Her eyes were still heavy-lidded and her cheeks were sleep-flushed. She looked sensual, completely and utterly desirable, and Brad cursed his body's strong reaction to her.

He had known many beautiful women in his life, but none of

them had ever had such a powerful effect on him. With an effort, he gave himself a fierce mental shake. He reminded himself to concentrate on the reason she was there, not on how beautiful she was.

"Good morning," Brad greeted her, his smile never fading.

"Is it?"

"It's dark now, but it's after five already. The sun should be up in just a few minutes," he explained.

"Have you been in here all night?" Kacie didn't know why she thought of Brad watching her while she slept made her feel shy, but it did.

He nodded. "I was worried about you and thought it would be best if I stayed with you. How do you feel this morning?"

"I'm fine." She rose and moved to stand by him at the window, looking out across the gardens to fertile fields beyond where the field hands were already hard at work. If she'd harbored any doubts about what year it was, they disappeared as she stared out at the activities going on outside. She was back in 1860; 1993 had vanished.

Faced with the undeniable but wild truth, Kacie tried to figure out how to deal with it. Girding herself, she decided to handle it as she did everything in her life—head-on.

It was obvious that Brad still had doubts about her, and rightly so. So the first thing she knew she had to do was convince him that she was no threat and that he could trust her. Kacie knew it wouldn't be easy, but she was determined.

"Brad? Are you really involved with the Underground Railroad?" she asked boldly, without preamble.

He was shocked. "What?"

"In the research I was doing, there were rumors that you had been, but no one has ever been able to prove it."

"Perhaps they couldn't prove it because it wasn't true," he answered evasively.

"Then why was the map hidden in the Bible, and why was it so important to you? It looked to me like a record of the stations. If you aren't involved, why did you have it? And was your grotto really where messages were relayed?"

"Where did you hear all this?" Brad demanded. There were only three people who knew that the grotto was the message drop. If she was a spy as he suspected, why was she telling him what she knew? And if she wasn't a spy...

His hand on her shoulders, he turned her to face him. Beneath his hands he could feel how terribly fragile she was, and he reminded himself that she was just a flesh-and-blood woman. His dark eyes searched her expression for some clue to her motivation, but he saw no guilt there, no deceit.

Kacie met his gaze without fear. "I don't know why I'm here, but I am," she answered softly, very aware of the heat of his hands on her and of his big body so near hers. She felt the urge to reach up and press her lips to his. Her heart told her that this was Brad, the man she'd dreamed of; the man she'd been waiting for all of her life; the man she loved. She wanted to cast aside her fears and doubts and live for the moment, but the knowledge that Brad had died in 1860 was still with her.

At the thought of this vital, handsome man dying, Kacie made her decision. She didn't know how much time she had, but she was going to save him, to somehow find a way to keep him from boarding that ill-fated steamboat. "Brad? What did you say the date was?"

"It's 1860," he replied, feeling an unbidden desire to draw her to him and hold her close. He dropped his hands away from her shoulders as he focused his thoughts on how she'd come to be there in the first place.

"I know, but what day?"

"March 3."

"Good."

"Oh? Why?"

"I was just wondering, that's all." Relief swept through her. There was still time. The explosion wasn't going to happen for over another month. She had until April 6 to convince him of her sincerity.

The eastern sky was brightening now as pale pink-and-gold streaks etched their way across the canopy of darkness. Kacie stared at the dawn of the new day, her first day with Brad, and offered up a silent prayer that somehow she would succeed in helping him.

Wanting to act as normal as possible by his standards and not hers, she asked, "Are there any clothes around that I might borrow while I'm here with you? I know you find my things a little strange, and I don't want to embarrass you by wearing them."

"I'll have one of the servants check," he answered, surprised by her request.

"I was wondering, too, since I am dressed like this, if breakfast could be brought up here to the room?"

"Of course. Would you like to freshen up first?"

"Sounds wonderful."

"Feel free to use the water closet." He gestured her toward the small room. Eden's Gate was one of the most modern homes on the river, boasting inside facilities and running water from a storage tank on the roof.

"Thanks."

Kacie tended to her personal needs, while Brad rang for a servant and gave her his instructions. That done, he waited for Kacie to rejoin him, his thoughts centered on what she'd said the night before as she'd fallen asleep. He knew he had to solve the mystery of her unexplained appearance in his life.

When Kacie emerged from the bathroom a short time later, she found that they were alone. Brad was waiting for her, a pensive loon on his face. Plates of biscuits, hot eggs, and grits were already on the small table that had been brought into the bedroom for them to use. It was set for two, and at the center of the table was a bud vase with a single, exquisite blossom in it. Enchanted, she bent to the flower and cupped the fragrant, delicate bloom in her hands.

"This blossom is lovely," she told him.

"It's from my mother's garden. Flowers were her passion," he explained as he drew out her chair for her.

Kacie sat down, giving him a smile of thanks for his courtesy, and then met his dark-eyed regard squarely as he took the seat opposite her. "And gaining freedom for everyone is yours."

His expression sharpened at her reference to his secret activities. "And what about you, Kacie? What do you care about?"

Her heart lurched at the intensity of his gaze. She hadn't meant to let their conversation get so serious so fast, but she had no idea how much time she would actually have with him. She had to do what she could while she had the opportunity. Unable to stop herself, she reached across the table to touch his hand. "You, Brad. I care about you."

The touch of her hand was electrifying, and he was stunned

by the power of his reaction to that single, simple gesture. "Why, Kacie? You don't even know me."

"I know you, Brad. I know you're a fair and honest man. You're the kind of man who believes in righting injustice wherever it exists. You're a visionary."

Her fervor in singing his praises amazed him. "Who are you?"

"I'm your friend, Brad. I know you're finding this all a little difficult to believe, because I am, too. But I believe I'm here to help you. I'm here to keep you safe."

He gave a short laugh as he turned her hand over so it was resting palm up in his hand. He gently touched her palm, marveling at its softness. "You're going to keep me safe?" he repeated incredulously, remembering how delicate she'd felt when he'd taken her by the shoulders earlier. "It's a man's job to protect a woman, not the other way around."

Kacie's breath caught in her throat at his sensual ploy. "Sometimes it can work both ways," she countered, finding his chauvinism endearing.

She fell silent as their gazes met and locked. It seemed as if he were judging her, searching for truth in her eyes. After a long moment, she forced herself to pull her hand away from his mesmerizing hold.

"Shall we eat?" Brad finally said.

Kacie was glad to be distracted and she helped herself to the assortment of hot, delicious food set before them. They ate in relative silence. When she finished the last bite of the fluffy, flaky biscuit she'd spread thickly with golden butter, she could no longer restrain herself from asking, "What do you intend to do with me?"

It was a question that Brad had been asking himself. He was troubled. She was a stranger to him, yet he found that he almost instinctively believed and trusted in her. That bothered him, for trusting someone he didn't know could very well prove disastrous. "You may have free run of the plantation. Just don't try to leave."

"You don't have to worry. I have no intention of leaving. I'm going to stay right here so I can..." she almost slipped and told him about the explosion, but quickly decided this was not the time.

"So you can what?" Brad was surprised by her answer, but before he could get any more out of her, there was a knock at the door. "Come in."

A maid entered the room, followed by a male servant carrying a big trunk. "This was in the attic, Mr. Brad. It has some of your mother's things in it."

"Thanks, Clara." Brad directed the servant to leave the trunk by the bed. Frustrated because he couldn't continue their conversation in front of Clara, he got up from the table to open the trunk once the male servant had gone.

"We packed away some of my mother's things. There might be something in here you can wear."

"You're offering me your mother's clothes?" Kacie was breathless and wide-eyed with wonder. She'd been a student of fashion all her life, and she was thrilled to think that she was going to get a chance to wear clothing that up until now she'd seen only in pictures or museums.

"Clara will help you with whatever you need." Brad started from the room, but Kacie's call stopped him.

"Brad?"

"Yes?" He glanced back to where she stood looking so wonderfully provocative in her short pants and tight shirt. He wondered distractedly why he'd had the clothes brought down to her. Honor, he reminded himself. Honor. Still, her legs were incredible and...

"Thank you."

"You're welcome."

With that, Brad was gone, and Kacie was left to do something that she'd only dreamed of until now. She was going to try on antique clothes. Of course, they weren't antiques now, but one day they would be.

Kacie almost laughed with delight as she delved into the trunk. She felt like a child at play and thought that maybe she really was in paradise.

It took some time and effort, but with Clara's help Kacie managed to don the correct undergarments, a suitable day gown, and a few accessories. The dress she chose was a high-necked, long-sleeved creation that fit her perfectly. Kacie had had her doubts about wearing the clothes at first, for she'd imagined that most Southern ladies were built like Scarlett O'Hara, but it turned out that she and Andrea Hampton, Brad's mother, were about the same size. Kacie had felt comfortable and free in her modern clothes, but in this hoop-skirted garment, she felt positively, magnificently feminine. The skirts swirled about her as she walked and she loved the feel of them.

Twirling before the full-length mirror in the room, Kacie smiled at her reflection. The deep-turquoise dress looked as if it had been made just for her. Clara found a brush in the trunk and untangled Kacie's hair, then styled it up, away from her face. The style brought emphasis to her eyes and to the graceful line of her neck. Kacie was impressed, for she looked every bit the polished Southern belle. She found herself hoping that Brad would think her pretty.

After Clara had gone, Kacie took one last look in the mirror and, satisfied that Brad would find no flaw in her appearance, she went eagerly in search of him. As she descended the staircase, she heard the faint murmur of men's voices coming from the study, and knocked lightly on the door.

"May I join you?" Kacie asked as she opened the door and entered the room at Jonas' invitation.

Brad had been seated opposite his father at the desk, but at the sound of Kacie's voice they both rose. Brad's eyes widened in pleasant surprise at the sight of her in appropriate clothing. He would have thought it impossible, but the full-skirted turquoise gown had transformed her into an even greater beauty. He couldn't stop himself from crossing the room to her.

"You look wonderful," he said, his dark eyes aglow with open male approval.

"Thank you." Kacie smiled up at him. Glancing at Jonas, she said, "Good morning, Mr. Hampton."

"Good morning, Miss Cameron, and please call me Jonas."

"I'm Kacie."

Lovely though she was, both men remained suspicious. She knew far too much about Brad's activities for them to let their guards down.

"I have a few things I have to do around Eden's Gate today. So I'll be gone for quite a while," Brad told her, intending to leave her safely in the house with his father.

"May I go with you? I'd love to tour the grounds and see how the plantation works," she said. She wanted to spend as much time with him as possible.

Having her with him would make it easier for him to keep

40

track of her, so Brad readily agreed. "Fine. Father, we'll be back in time for dinner."

Brad led Kacie from the house, carrying a luncheon basket the cook had prepared, and as they entered his carriage, he placed the basket in the back. They drove down the shell-lined path that wound its way through the lush gardens. It was a warm, perfect day. The sun was shining, and the air was perfumed with the scent of flowers and blossoming trees.

Kacie was very much aware of Brad beside her, and she found herself thinking of Adam and Eve and wondering if their Eden had been so perfect. The garden the Historical Society had re-created in the future was lovely, but it was far from the real thing. Kacie caught sight of the bush that had borne the blossom that had been on their breakfast table, and she asked Brad to stop so that she could admire it. They stepped down from the carriage, and Brad watched her, entranced.

"This one belongs here," she told him, cradling one of the treasured blossoms in her hand.

"Why's that?" Brad asked, thinking that she, not the flower, belonged there in the garden surrounded by nature's splendor, for she was far more beautiful than any blossom.

"Because it's glorious. Your home was aptly named, you know. I can think of nowhere on Earth more perfect... more of a paradise." At the mention of paradise, Kacie thought of her boutiques and of the business that had been her whole life. Sadness filled her as she realized that it might be lost to her forever, that she might never see her family and friends again. But then she looked at Brad and her unhappiness vanished. She had no answer as to why she was there, but she made up her mind from that moment onward to take each day as a gift and not question the destiny that had brought her to him.

"My mother chose the name Eden's Gate," he was saying.

"I know. She named it after her family's home in Virginia."

Again she startled him with her knowledge, and caution tempered the feeling of enchantment that had held him. "You seem to know so much about me, while I know very little about you."

"What do you want to know?"

"Everything." His reply escaped him before he even realized he'd said it.

41

"I'm thirty years old."

His eyebrows rose at her revelation. He would never have guessed her to be that old. "You're an old maid," he said with a chuckle.

"I'm single because I choose to be," Kacie countered with a defiant lift of her chin. Still, even as she defended herself, she remembered how she'd felt as all of her friends had married and started families and she'd remained alone. "Besides, thirty isn't old. You're thirty-two."

"But I'm a man."

"So? Maturity is what counts, not age," she told him with dignity.

"If you say so." Brad was grinning and his eyes were sparkling as he urged her to continue, "Please go on. I really am interested."

Kacie couldn't help smiling at him. She hadn't known of his sense of humor, and it pleased her. "I live by myself in Chicago, and I drive only American-made cars."

"Drive? You mean carriages?"

Kacie was still smiling as they got back into the carriage and started off down the path once more. "Sort of. I own a Mustang GT. It's red and very fast." Kacie imagined Brad driving her car, his big, strong hands sure and steady on the steering wheel, and knew he'd look wonderful in it.

"So you ride a Western roan?"

"You could say that," she answered wryly, knowing it would be fun to talk to him about cars and their names. She wondered what he'd think about Vipers, Broncos, Cougars, and Thunderbirds, or about being able to drive sixty-five miles an hour, but she didn't want to disturb the temporary truce they seemed to have declared. "I make my living by designing clothes, and I'm happy to say that I'm fairly successful, which allows me to make trips to Eden's Gate several times a year. What more do you want to know?"

"Did you design what you were wearing when you arrived?" he asked, thinking it strange that she could make a living as a seamstress if the clothes she'd been wearing earlier were samples of her wares. Still, he couldn't complain about the way she'd looked. He remembered all too clearly how the pants she'd worn had hugged her hips and how shapely her slender legs had been.

"I designed the T-shirt," she told him, suddenly wondering

what he would look like wearing one, the soft cotton hugging his wide, strong chest. The more she thought about it, the more she decided he'd look even better without a shirt of any kind.

Brad nodded, and then knowing he had to have the answer to the question that had been worrying him since he'd left her in the bedroom that morning, he broached the subject. "Earlier, you said you were going to stay right here so you could do something, but you never said what. What are you planning, Kacie? What is it you think you're going to do?"

Kacie's smile faltered, as did her light-hearted mood. She didn't want to ruin the beauty of this moment. This was her dream come true. She was here with Brad just as she'd imagined so many times before. Yet, Kacie knew if she deliberately avoided answering him, his distrust of her would grow. "I know you don't believe what I've been telling you, but I want to stay to convince you that you're in danger." She lifted her worried gaze to his.

He saw how concerned she seemed to be, and he wanted to take her in his arms and tell her everything would be all right, but he didn't. He held back, knowing he had to have answers to his questions before he could even think of touching her. "How can you know I'm in danger, if you're not involved in some way?"

"Does it matter? All that matters is that I *am* here. Can't you just trust me and believe that I'm here to help you and protect you?"

The sincerity in her eyes truly touched his soul, and again the instinctive feeling that he should trust her filled him. He almost allowed himself to believe, but then reality returned. He told himself that he had found her in his bedroom with the map in her hands. She'd told him things that were impossible for her to know, yet she remained with him, and her presence meant more than all the logic and reality in the world. She hadn't tried to escape or contact anyone with the vital information she knew. She said she wanted to protect him. He smiled at the thought, for he seriously doubted she'd be much help if it came down to a battle. Deciding to humor her for now, he replied, "You're not very big and certainly not very strong, but feel free to protect me all you want."

At his answer, Kacie realized she'd been holding her breath as she awaited his reply. She almost sighed in relief, but her tone was deadly serious when she spoke again. "Brad, if you really believe me, then whatever you do, don't get on any steamboats next month."

"I'll make it a point not to."

They fell silent, each assessing what the other had said. His response had been too lightly given for Kacie's complete peace of mind, but at least she had the satisfaction of knowing that she'd warned him and that she still had enough time to try to convince him further—she hoped.

As they continued their drive, Brad reached out and gently took her arm. He drew her to his side and, looping her arm through his, brought her hand to rest on his forearm and covered it with his own, holding the reins with his other hand. It still filled him with a sense of wonder that she thought she could defend him, and a great surge of protectiveness swelled within him. She was so delicate and feminine. He was the one who should be protecting her.

The unexpected intimacy of Brad's actions startled Kacie. She cast him a sidelong glance as they moved along, but found that his attention seemed to be completely focused on the path ahead. Without a word, she allowed herself to be swept along with him, and she found herself leaning into him, savoring his nearness and the new depth of meaning his gesture gave to their relationship.

As they rode farther away from the house, Kacie suddenly recognized the narrow, secluded path that led to the grotto.

"That's the path to the grotto, isn't it? It looks a little different, but not too much."

Brad hoped that eventually she would stop surprising him, but it hadn't happened yet. "Yes, the grotto's there."

"I have to see it. Can we please take a look? The grotto was... is my favorite place here. There were times when I would sit for hours, just thinking about everything that had happened. Remembering..." She wanted to say "Remembering what I'd read about you and your father," but she stopped herself. Brad reined in the horses and they got out of the carriage. Kacie started down the path, and Brad followed.

Reaching the entrance, Kacie went inside. The small, manmade cave was cool, dark, and peaceful. It pleased her to discover that the Society's restoration was accurate. A crucifix and two candles stood on the small altar at the front, and two kneelers had been placed before it. When she'd visited it, she'd thought it a sad place, filled with tragic emotions from the past. But now the grotto felt serene and quietly blessed, and she couldn't resist taking

44

the opportunity to pray for help to save Brad's life.

Brad stayed at the opening of the cave to watch her as she knelt down, and he was touched by the genuine nature of her reverence. Still, he was careful not to glance at the place where he kept his important messages hidden. After a moment of quiet reflection, Kacie rose and walked up to the altar. She reached out and touched several of the stones in the wall.

"Is this where the secret chamber is?" she asked, remembering where the director had told her it was located. She was amazed at how perfectly it was hidden.

He was again stunned by her revelation. "How did you know that? No one knows about that chamber but my father and me."

"I know, because that's where the director told me the Bible was finally found. They'd been looking for it for years."

She knew she'd shocked him again, so she went to stand beside him in the sunlight.

"Brad, please, trust me." Kacie put a reassuring hand on his arm, and she could feel the tension in him. "I would never do anything to hurt you."

Brad gazed down at her, spellbound. He could see only honesty and openness in her eyes. In the distance, a songbird called out its soft melody, and a gentle breeze stirred the leaves on the trees arching overhead, dappling the ground with a kaleidoscope of sunbeams. The warmth of the day wrapped them in an intimate embrace, and the moment seemed magical. They were alone in a world where time and reality were suspended. There was only the two of them, together.

If this was a dream, Kacie decided she was going to live it to the fullest. She took a tentative step closer to Brad, and as his strong arms enfolded her and brought her against him, it seemed her soul cried out with a joy so intense that it was almost painful. The contact was electric, and she knew as his lips sought hers that this was where she belonged—in Brad's arms.

Brad told himself it was crazy, but then the whole situation was crazy. He thought about the repercussions of what he was doing, but suddenly they didn't seem to matter. Nothing mattered except holding Kacie and kissing her. As his mouth moved over hers, all rational thought fled, and there was only Kacie—and the magic of her kiss.

Kacie clung to Brad's broad shoulders, savoring the heady thrill of his lips on hers. How many times had she imagined herself in his arms? She didn't know why this was happening, and she didn't care. She only wanted to enjoy him. His embrace was bliss, and she knew beyond a shadow of a doubt in that moment so sweet that she loved him and that her love was strong enough to endure anything.

5

Brad and Kacie broke apart, each stunned by what had passed between them.

"I had to travel over one hundred thirty years back in time to find you," Kacie told him, her emerald eyes aglow with happiness, "but you were worth it. I've been looking for you all my life."

Brad lifted a hand as if to caress her cheek, but then changed his mind and let his hand drop. The feelings surging through him were far too powerful to ignore, yet far too dangerous to act upon recklessly. He needed time to think.

Kacie read the uncertainty in his expression and understood. She'd had years to discover her love for him. He'd known her less than twenty-four hours. She smiled and broke the tension by asking, "Were we going to the stables next? I did want to see your horses. I've heard the bloodlines were superb."

Brad was glad to have a reason to move off down the path away from the intimacy of the grotto. Over the next several hours, after having shared their picnic lunch, he showed Kacie the plantation at work. He told her with pride of his plans to expand the stables, and raise the finest horses in the state. He also told her he intended to free all the slaves when he took over the plantation and that he would give them each a parcel of land of their own to work in return for their staying on at Eden's Gate as laborers.

Kacie's admiration for Brad grew even more as he explained his firm belief that free men worked harder than "owned" men, that giving a man an incentive to do well paid dividends, whereas punishing him with whippings and brutality did not. Kacie found that Brad's dream of the future held opportunity and justice for everyone.

This affirmation of his true character deepened her love for him. He was everything she'd imagined he would be.

It was late afternoon when they returned to the house. Brad went to discuss the business of the day with his father, while Kacie retreated upstairs to freshen up for dinner. While she'd been gone, the maid had moved the trunk of clothes and Kacie's few things into a guest bedroom just down the hall from Brad's room. The maid showed her to the new room now, and after drawing her bath and laying out a gown suitable to wear to dinner, she left Kacie in peace to soak and enjoy the quiet of the moment.

Kacie sighed as she rested in the hot, perfumed bath water. It had been an incredible day. The memory of Brad's kiss alone was enough to bring a smile to her lips. Being with him had been wonderful, and she wanted never to be parted from him.

But the bliss of the moment turned to horror as the real future broke into her thoughts. Not only was war on the horizon, but unless there was some way she could stop it, Brad would be killed next month. Panic jolted through her, and it took all of her willpower to curb it. She told herself that she would find a way to save him, but the fear that she would be whisked back to her own time before she got the chance cast a dark, threatening shadow on her happiness.

Her heart was suddenly as chilled as the bathwater she was sitting in, so Kacie climbed from the tub and began to dress for dinner. She donned the clothes the maid had set out and was pleased with the fit of the long-sleeved, high-necked emerald gown. She brushed her hair and left the room to find Brad.

She was descending the staircase when she saw him in the parlor talking to his father. Her heartbeat quickened as she paused half-way down the steps to watch him. Brad was the most devastatingly handsome man she'd ever seen. He had obviously taken the time to change for dinner, too, and he looked more wonderful than ever in his black pants and white shirt. She longed to run to him, to throw her arms around him and kiss him, but as much as she wanted to, she knew she couldn't. Ladies in 1860 just didn't do that kind of thing.

"Brad?" She called his name softly as she came to the parlor door.

"Kacie." His smile was warm and inviting. "Come in."

As she entered the room, Brad thought she was absolutely

lovely. The green of the dress highlighted her sparkling eyes and fair complexion, and he could barely take his eyes off her. While he'd been talking with his father, Brad had tried to convince himself that her kiss hadn't really been as incredible as he'd thought, but seeing Kacie now after only a short time apart, he knew he was wrong. The kiss had been perfect, just as she was. If only there wasn't that remaining doubt about her…

"Shall we dine?" Jonas spoke up, breaking the sensual reverie that existed between the two young people.

The men escorted her into the dining room, and Brad seated her at his right at the table. The meal was a sumptuous repast. Kacie took great care to keep her conversation light yet interesting. She wanted to avoid anything that might be construed as controversial.

Jonas enjoyed the banter and realized with some surprise that this mysterious woman who called herself Kacie Cameron was well-read and intelligent. Brad had asked him earlier to put his suspicions about her aside and let him handle the situation, and Jonas had agreed. Though he still did not trust her completely, by the end of the evening he had to admit he did like her.

Brad walked Kacie to her room that night. "I hope you find the room comfortable."

"It's fine, thank you," she answered, very much aware of him beside her. They stopped outside her bedroom door, and as she opened it, she turned to him. "Thank you for today. I enjoyed being with you."

He stared down at her in the muted light, entranced by the strength of the attraction between them. "I enjoyed being with you, too." He said the words before he'd realized it. Then, puzzled by their whole situation, he couldn't stop himself from asking, "Who are you, Kacie? Why have you come into my life?"

Kacie, too, was caught up in the intimacy of the moment. She lifted her gaze to his as she answered, "To love you…" Her voice was a whisper as she raised her hands to frame his face. The moment was Elysian, and she drew him down to her, unable to resist the temptation to kiss him once more. "Only to love you."

In the deserted quiet of the hall, their lips met and paradise was theirs. Brad wrapped his arm around her and held her close as his mouth moved over hers. He sought and found the bliss that had been his earlier at the grotto, and the power of it sent desire pounding through him.

Kacie didn't know whether to laugh or cry. That was ecstasy! She'd found her heaven! Yet even as she exulted, she realized that at any second she could be torn from Brad's arms forever. Anguish filled her. She wanted to be with him. She wanted to love him. Did she dare risk it? Kacie knew the answer even as she asked herself the question. She would willingly surrender to the desire that promised her sweet fulfillment. Returning Brad's kiss with even more fervor, she pressed herself tightly against him and reveled in the contact.

Brad felt her willingness, and as much as he was enjoying every moment of holding her close, he knew he had to stop. There was too much at stake for him to give in to his own passion. Desire Kacie though he did, he had to be cautious. He ended the kiss and held her from him. He could see the confusion in her eyes, but knew he had to end it before things got out of hand.

"Good night, Kacie," he said softly, kissing her gently.

"Brad…" She sighed his name.

"I'll see you in the morning," he told her, ignoring his own desire that urged him to throw caution to the wind and make love to her.

When Kacie had gone into her room and closed the door, Brad retreated to his own bedroom. The night passed slowly for him as sleep proved elusive. His thoughts were of Kacie, and try as he might, he couldn't seem to put the glory of holding her out of his mind.

Kacie's own emotions were in turmoil, and she was up all night, too, trying to figure out what to do. Her heart told her she loved Brad and that she should take her happiness where she found it, no matter how crazy it seemed. But the painful truth of knowing that at any moment she could be torn from this place and year and returned to her real life in 1993 filled her with fear. She spent the night weighing her love for him against her fear of losing him forever, and by dawn she knew there could be no hiding from the truth of her feelings. She loved Brad, and she would celebrate that love for as long as this twisted quirk of fate allowed.

The days that followed passed in a whirlwind of activity. Kacie and Brad spent as much time together as they could, laughing and growing in their understanding of each other. Simple touches, soft smiles, and gentle kisses all took on a deeper meaning. Without spoken words, each seemed to understand the ultimate outcome of their carefully controlled desire.

They tried to ride together every day, and Kacie found that she loved riding down by the river. She enjoyed watching the Mississippi flow by and often imagined that the occasional steamboat they saw churning its way up or downstream was the *River Queen* on a tour. It was there one afternoon that they reined in their horses for a rest.

"Do you want to sit on the bank for a while?" Brad suggested.

"That would be lovely."

Ever the gentleman, he dismounted and hurried over to help her down. Kacie appreciated his help, and she rested her hands on his broad shoulders for balance as his hands found her waist to aid her in her descent. Her body brushed full-length against him as she slid to the ground, and the contact was his hard body left her breathless and glowing. The days she spent with Brad were the happiest she'd ever known.

"Thank you," she said as she gazed up at him, her eyes shining with love.

"My pleasure," Brad answered, and he meant it. He thoroughly enjoyed having Kacie in his arms.

"Do you want to sit under the trees?" she suggested as she moved regretfully away from him.

"Fine." He followed her to what was becoming their favorite place. It was a secluded, grassy spot that offered them a panoramic view of the river.

They sat there together, sharing soft kisses and watching the river flow by on its way to the gulf.

The river's timeless, you know. There's really no end to it and no beginning," Kacie told him thoughtfully. "Just like what I feel for you."

"And just what is it you feel for me?"

"You know I love you, Brad. I always have and I always will, no matter what happens."

"Nothing's going to happen," he reassured her after seeing the shadow of worry that shone momentarily in her eyes.

"I wish I were as certain as you are. The trouble is I know what might happen…"

"Kacie, we've never really talked about this…" He paused as if searching for the right words. "But do you really believe you were sent here from the future?"

"I know I was. One minute I was standing in your bedroom in the year 1993 and suddenly it was just like Scotty beamed me—"

"Scotty? You said that name before. Who's this Scotty?'

Kacie couldn't help laughing now that she remembered sighing Scotty's name when she fainted that very first night. "Scotty's a character in *Star Trek*." At his confused expression, she quickly explained, "In my time, we have television and movies. They're pictures that move and talk."

"Right, and what else do you have a hundred and some odd years from now?"

"Well, that Western roan I told you about is really a car. That's a carriage with a motor instead of horses. And then there are airplanes and the space shuttle. You know we've even put men on the moon."

"That's impossible," he denied.

"So is my being here, but I'm here. The most important thing I think you'd like to know is that in my time, everyone is free. There is no slavery in the United States in 1993."

I think I would like your times," he agreed, still refusing to completely believe that what she was saying was absolutely true, but having more and more trouble denying it. "What other inventions are there?"

"There's air conditioning that keeps houses cool in the summer, and paved expressways where cars can travel coast-to-coast quickly. There's electricity that gives us light indoors with the flick of a switch, and microwave ovens that cook dinner in less than five minutes."

"It sounds fascinating. I think I might like to visit your time and see all these things."

"I know you'd like my Mustang," she told him with a smile. "If I ever have to go back, I'll take you with me."

He slipped an arm around her shoulders as he drew her against him. "I hope you never go, Kacie, but if you do, don't go without me."

His words touched her deeply, and she turned to him and kissed him passionately.

"I don't ever want to leave you, Brad."

Their lips met again as if to seal that vow between them.

As the month of March ended and April began, Kacie's concern over the explosion grew. Although Brad had not been off the plantation in all that time, knowing that the critical moment was only a few days away filled her with dread. She loved Brad with all her heart and soul, and was desperate to keep him safe. She knew that if she could just keep him with her until the seventh, everything would be fine.

On the afternoon of the fifth, while Kacie and Brad were having lunch, a messenger delivered a letter to Brad requesting his presence at an important business meeting. When he said he'd be back that evening, she didn't worry, but she did miss him terribly. The hours passed slowly for Kacie. She felt alone and lost without him.

As darkness fell and Brad still did not return, Kacie's imagination ran rampant. She dined alone with Jonas, her appetite gone as worry consumed her. When at last she heard him come in the front door, she was tremendously relieved. There was no hiding her pleasure at seeing him as he came to stand in the dining room doorway to greet them.

"You're back," she breathed, her face alight with happiness.

"It took longer than I thought it would," he explained, his gaze on Kacie. He hadn't realized how much he enjoyed being with her until he'd been forced to leave her today. He'd been as eager as a schoolboy to return to her and had nearly run his horse into the ground on the way back.

"Is everything taken care of?" Jonas inquired from where he sat at the head of the table.

"It's all worked out," he answered, his expression growing shuttered at the mention of the meeting. He strode into the room and settled in at the table, pouring himself a cup of coffee from the silver service.

"Good. Are you hungry? Do you want some dinner?" Jonas asked him.

"Coffee's fine," he answered, drinking the hot, strong brew.

They fell into conversation, discussing what had happened that afternoon while he'd been gone, but while they talked of mundane things, his thoughts were far from ordinary. His meeting had been with his contacts in the Underground Railroad, and the news had not been good. Word was out that a raid was planned on several of the stations north of Eden's Gate. No one knew how the identity of the people on the Railroad had been discovered, and right now, no one cared. The important thing was getting word to them so they could be ready.

The possibility that Kacie might have been involved nagged at Brad, but having kept such a close watch on her for the last month, he refused to believe it. As he gazed at her now, he saw only beauty and innocence. His body stirred at the thought of holding her and kissing her, and he excused himself from the table. He couldn't afford the distraction.

Brad's departure was so abrupt that Kacie was hurt by it. She turned her attention back to the meal and finished dining with Jonas, acting as though nothing was bothering her.

Brad paced his bedroom. He needed to concentrate on the trip he had to make, but try as he might, he couldn't banish Kacie from his thoughts. He could think only of the honeyed taste of her lips, the sweetness of her body pressed against his. He knew this was not the time, but all the logic in the world did not ease the need in him. He loved her. It was as simple and basic and right as that. He'd tried to deny it, had tried to tell himself it was a purely physical attraction between them, but leaving her today had convinced him. He did love her.

The memory of her warning not to travel by steamer slipped into Brad's thoughts as he stood in the middle of his room debating his next move. He could make the trip upriver in half a day by boat, but as insane as it sounded, he knew he would travel by horseback in the morning. He didn't question the sense of it. He would just do it.

His thoughts moving back to the woman he loved, Brad knew he could stay away from her no longer. When he left at dawn, he would be gone for several days. He wanted to take the memory of her love with him. Tonight, he would go to her. Tonight, they would be together.

Brad left his bedroom by way of the balcony. He used the outdoor steps to reach the gardens, for there was something there he wanted to give to her. A moment later, he was back upstairs, standing outside of her still-empty bedroom.

Her room was dark as Kacie entered, and she paused just

inside the door to light the lamp on the dresser. A soft, muted glow illuminated the room, and she turned to start getting ready for bed. It was then that she saw it—the single, delicate blossom on her pillow. Kacie's breath caught in her throat. She glanced up and saw Brad standing outside the open French doors at the rail of the balcony, his eyes upon her. Kacie's heart sang. She didn't say a word as she picked up the flower and moved to the door.

"Brad…"

Their gazes locked, his dark, intense, and questioning, hers open, loving and shining with invitation.

"Kacie…" Her name was a groan on his lips as he crossed the short distance between them in two strides and swept her into his embrace. He'd wanted her for so long, and tonight he would have her. His mouth sought hers in a blazing kiss as he crushed her against his chest.

Kacie let the blossom drop as she wrapped her arms around Brad and returned his embrace full measure. She'd loved him forever and would no longer deny her need to be one with him.

They came together passionately, each starved for a taste of the other's love. When Brad lifted Kacie into his arms to carry her to the bed, she looped her arms around his neck and kissed him. He laid her upon the softness, then followed her down, his big body covering hers in a heated brand.

Kacie gloried in the sensuousness of his body on hers, and she reached for him hungrily, craving this closeness with him, reveling in the wonder of it. Brad was there with her, loving her. As he caressed her, she responded openly, knowing this was what she'd always wanted.

Driven by desire, Brad unfastened the bodice of Kacie's gown. He parted the fabric and slipped her chemise lower to bare her breasts to his heated kisses. Kacie was mindless with pleasure as Brad's intimate touch sent shivers of excitement through her.

"Love me, Brad," she told him huskily as she began to move restlessly, invitingly beneath him.

Eager to be rid of all barriers between them, Brad drew slightly away from her as he helped her to undress. She felt a bit shy before him, but the warmth of his gaze soon eased her nervousness.

"You're beautiful," he declared, his dark gaze wandering over her slender figure. From the lush fullness of her breasts to the gentle curves of her hips, she was delectable.

"So are you," Kacie responded, unbuttoning his shirt and pushing it from his shoulders to bare his hard-muscled chest to her caress.

They lay back together, exploring each other and arousing each other to a fiery pitch. His hands were never still, skimming over her satiny flesh, cupping and molding, teasing and pleasuring her until she was aching for more.

"Love me, Brad... please..." she whispered, her mouth seeking and finding his in a passionate exchange.

When at last he stripped away the rest of his clothes and came to her, Kacie opened to him like a flower to the warmth of the sun, and when he moved to possess her, she welcomed him eagerly. Brad kissed her as he began to move, pressing deep within her past the proof of her innocence. Made one by the act of love, they knew paradise. With tender touches and soft words of love, they luxuriated in the rare glory of their joining. Then, unable to hold back any longer, Brad moved in the timeless rhythm of love and possession.

It was all new to Kacie. Though she'd had many boyfriends who would have been more than willing to take her virginity, she'd never wanted to be with any of them. Brad, however, was different, and Kacie knew this was what she'd been saving herself for. She loved him and wanted to give all of herself to him.

They moved together, surging to new heights of passion, each kiss and caress taking them higher and higher until ecstasy burst upon them. Their legs entwined, their bodies still one, they lay in each other's arms enjoying passion's peaceful afterglow.

"I love you, Kacie," Brad professed in a husky voice.

"I love you, too," Kacie responded, kissing him desperately. She was thrilled by his declaration, but the fear of losing him was always with her. Having known the beauty of his love now, she shivered at the thought that at any minute it could all end.

Brad felt her shiver. "What's wrong?"

"I'm afraid," she whispered, her eyes clouded with worry as she tightened her arms around him.

"There's nothing to be afraid of, Kacie."

"You don't understand, Brad." There was real anguish in her voice.

"Yes, I do, love." He reached down and lifted her chin so

their eyes met. "I love you, Kacie. As long as we have each other, nothing can come between us."

Kacie wanted to believe that. She wanted to believe with all her heart. "But there are things that could happen, things that could tear us apart."

He interrupted her with a soft kiss. "No, love. As long as we love each other and have faith, everything will be all right. You trust me, don't you?"

"With my life."

"As I trust you with mine. We'll be fine, Kacie. Nothing will separate us. Nothing."

"I hope you're right," she whispered.

They lay quietly together. The languor of love stole over them, and Brad drifted off to sleep first.

The turmoil of her emotions kept Kacie awake. She was filled with love for Brad, yet terrified of losing that love. As she nestled behind him, she swore that she would do everything in her power to save his life. If she accomplished at least that much, it would all have been worth it.

6

"Whatever you do, son, be careful," Jonas warned. It was an hour before dawn, and Brad had just told him that he was leaving to deliver the warning about the raid to the next two stations. "Will you be back tonight?"

"No. I'm going by horseback. I won't be back until tomorrow."

Jonas was puzzled. "Why ride? You could be back tonight if you went by steamer."

Brad wasn't sure how to explain his decision so that it would make sense to his father. He knew it was crazy, but he trusted Kacie. "Kacie seems to think that something terrible will happen if I go by boat."

"You believe Kacie? Something just might happen if you follow her advice! She could be setting you up! You'll be riding alone—"

"Kacie's not setting me up," he denied firmly, no doubt in his mind.

"How can you be so sure?"

"I've fallen in love with her."

"You're in love with her? But what about that wild tale of hers about being from the future?"

For a moment, Brad's expression reflected the confusion he felt over her claims, but then the truth of his love shone through. "I don't know where she came from, and I don't care. All I know is that I want her with me always. When I get back from this trip, I plan to ask her to marry me."

"You do?" There was no denying that Jonas was stunned.

"I love her, and I trust her."

"You two are very different, you know," he cautioned.

"So were you and Mother," Brad countered with a grin. "She was a Yankee, too."

They stood together in silence, their gazes meeting in understanding. Jonas knew his son's mind was made up, so he went to him and put an arm around his shoulders. "I want only your happiness."

"My future is with Kacie. I want to spend the rest of my life with her."

Anxious to leave so that he could return that much sooner, Brad left for the stables. He wanted to be well on his way by sunup. As he rode off toward his rendezvous, his thoughts were with Kacie and the love they would share once he returned.

*

In the darkness, Arlin Gates, the man hired by Daniel Lawrence to keep an eye on Bradford Hampton, watched and waited. His lonely vigil was rewarded when he saw Brad ride away from Eden's Gate just before dawn. Knowing the man who'd hired him would be pleased, he followed Brad.

*

Kacie awoke slowly. The glory of Brad's lovemaking the night before still filled her. Expecting to find Brad slumbering peacefully beside her, she smiled as she rolled over to face him. It surprised Kacie to discover that he had left her, and the realization jarred her fully awake. After a moment's reflection, though, she thought she understood why Brad had gone. It certainly wouldn't have been proper for him to have spent the entire night in her bed. Her happiness returned, and she got up and dressed quickly, eager to see Brad again. She wanted to make sure that last night had really happened, that it had not been a wonderful dream.

A short time later, Kacie was standing in the dining room at the foot of the table, facing Jonas where he sat at the head. Her expression mirrored her terror. She couldn't find Brad anywhere, and it was the sixth of April. Frightened, she asked, "Where's Brad?"

"He had to leave early this morning to take care of some business in town."

"Will he be back today?"

"No, he thought it would be late tomorrow before he could return."

Brad was traveling and this was the day of the fateful explosion! Kacie was in a panic. She was afraid to ask, but she had to know. "How did he travel?"

Jonas heard the very real concern in her voice. "He told me about your warning, and that's why he went on horseback, Kacie. It's a short trip by steamer, but almost a full-day one by road."

"Thank God," she murmured in tremendous relief at the news.

"Kacie," Jonas began slowly, completely confused, "I don't understand any of this."

"I love Brad, Jonas. That's the only thing any of us needs to understand," she told him. "I love him more than you can imagine, but I'm afraid for him, too."

"Why would you be afraid for him?" he demanded, trying to get the truth of her background.

"I will not betray you and Brad, Jonas. You have to believe that. And you have to believe that Brad's never betrayed any confidences to me. It's just that I have a feeling I know what he's doing, and sometimes he can be too brave and too self-sacrificing for his own good. When he believes he's right, there's no stopping him, and I just want to keep him safe. I don't want anything to happen to him."

"But how can you know any of this if Brad hasn't told you?"

Kacie's gaze met his and he found no guile or deceit there. "You have to trust me as Brad does."

For a moment, time was suspended as Jonas chose whether to believe in his son's judgment of this woman or to cling to his own doubts and fears. Finally, the pleading look in her eyes convinced him. He would trust her.

"He'll be back tomorrow, and I'm sure he'll be on horseback."

*

Brad rode at a steady, ground-eating pace. He had an uneasy feeling about the trip and took extra caution as he traveled. He sensed that someone was following him, but he never caught a glimpse of anyone and finally decided it was his concern for secrecy that was making him suspect the worst. These were dangerous times, and his foes were deadly, cunning people who would stop at nothing to put an end to the Railroad.

It was late afternoon, almost dark, when Brad reached the small upriver town where he was to meet his contact. He entered the bar where messages were passed and sat down to wait. The place was relatively quiet, and had he had the time, Brad would have waited until there was a crowd, for it was easier to blend in that way. Today, however, it was important that he not delay. No one knew exactly when the raid was to take place, and he had to warn his compatriots right away.

Shortly after he'd entered the bar, while he was waiting to give the news to his contact, Brad noticed a man enter. There seemed nothing out of the ordinary about him, so at first Brad paid him little attention. When Brad's contact arrived, he quietly passed on the warning to the man, who was known to him as "Saint," identifying himself as he always did by his own code name, "Adam." Brad waited a few minutes after Saint had departed, then paid his bill and left, too. He knew it was late, but he had one more stop to make that couldn't wait.

Arlin had been silently observing everything, and he knew his boss was going to be pleased with what he'd discovered. Lawrence's hunch had been right: Brad Hampton was involved with the Underground Railroad. Rather than head back right away with the news, Arlin decided to trail after Hampton just a little longer to see if he could find out where the next stop was. Lawrence had told him there would be a big bonus if he brought back any other information he could use.

Brad saw Arlin come out of the tavern shortly after him. He thought the man was acting a bit strangely. Deciding to be cautious, Brad chose not to continue on to his next rendezvous. Instead, he walked down toward the river, just to see what would happen. It did not surprise him when the man came after him on foot.

Brad trusted his instincts, and at this moment his instincts were warning him of danger. Stepping into a deserted alley, he waited until the man had come even with him and then surprised him by grabbing his arm and yanking him around to face him.

"I want to talk to you," Brad seethed, his grip on Arlin threatening.

"Me? Why do you want to talk to me?"

"I want to know who you are and why you're following me."

"I wasn't following you…"

"I know better," Brad told him with undisguised menace, giving him a shake.

Arlin paled as he realized this man knew he was lying. He didn't know how Hampton had spotted him, but this wasn't the time to worry about it. He had to get away. Reaching down with the smoothness of one used to fighting with knives, Arlin drew his knife out of his boot and slashed at Brad, cutting his upper arm.

Brad was livid, and his temper erupted. They grappled until Brad finally managed to overpower Arlin and knock the knife out of his hand.

"Who sent you after me?" Brad snarled, slamming Arlin up against the side of a building.

Momentarily defeated, Arlin answered, "Lawrence sent me… Daniel Lawrence."

"I should have known. And what about Cameron? How is Kacie Cameron involved in this?" Brad had to know, he had to find out.

"Whoever this Casey Cameron is, he ain't involved," Arlin answered quickly. "Lawrence hired me and told me to watch you and report back to him."

Brad's relief was immense at the discovery that Kacie was as innocent as he'd hoped. In that instant, Brad let his guard down, and Arlin knew it.

Though not a brave man, Arlin was a survivor. He made his move the moment Brad wasn't expecting it, jerking free and diving to grab his knife. He pounced on Brad as he turned to do battle and managed to pin him to the ground. He grinned down into Brad's face, showing uneven, blackened teeth.

"Once I tell Lawrence what I know, you're dead, Hampton, and so is your family. Hell, I might as well save them the trouble and end your miserable life right now!" Arlin was ready to cut his throat in a single wicked motion, but Brad wasn't about to give up the battle.

With all the strength he could muster, Brad threw Arlin off. They struggled together, rolling over and over on the ground, fighting for supremacy. As they grappled, Arlin managed to get on top. He raised his arm to stab Brad, but Brad reacted instinctively and grabbed his arm in a viselike grip. Brad forced Arlin's arm downward with all his might, twisting it as he did so the knife was pointing away from him.

In the face of Brad's unrelenting pressure, Arlin's strength failed him. His arm buckled, and his knife drove deep into his own flesh. He collapsed and lay still, wounded on his side. Brad's own bleeding arm was aching and he was exhausted by the fight. He pushed Arlin's limp body away from him, got to his feet, and staggered over to lean against one of the buildings.

Arlin's agony was unbearable. The stab wound was like a burning flame in his flesh, but he was not about to give up. As Brad leaned against the building, his back to him, Arlin lurched to his feet and with what strength he had left, he hit Brad from behind. Brad fell, dazed, as Arlin fled on foot, heading for the riverfront, desperate to escape back to Lawrence so he could tell him what he'd learned.

An older steamer, heavily laden with merchandise, had already raised its gangplank and was pulling out on its way downriver as Arlin reached the levee. In one last frantic effort, he leaped onboard. In the darkness, no one saw him.

Brad had been momentarily stunned by the man's unexpected assault, but he recovered quickly. He ran after Arlin and made an even more desperate leap to the boat's deck. It was close, but Brad managed to get a tenuous hold on the railing. He hung there precariously for a moment while he struggled to catch his breath. Though his arm hurt, Brad finally hauled himself onboard. He, too, went unnoticed in the night.

Once he'd regained his footing on deck, Brad looked around. The deck was stacked high with crates and merchandise, making it a jumbled maze. Ignoring his throbbing arm, he began to search for Arlin. It took over an hour, but he finally found him, barely conscious, in a remote corner near the livestock pen. He bent over him and took him in his arms.

"You may have stopped me," Arlin gasped, "but you won't stop the raid."

"The hell I won't," Brad vowed. "You're going to die if you don't get help soon. Give me the exact date of the raid and I'll do everything I can to save you."

A flicker of hope shone on Arlin's face. "The ninth," he whispered, then went limp in Brad's arms, his head lolling to one side. He was dead.

Distraught over the man's death, Brad moved away to the rail and leaned heavily on it. He was deeply troubled by Arlin's death, but at least now he knew exactly when the raid would take place. He thought of Kacie then, and of what Arlin had told him. Hearing that Kacie hadn't betrayed him had filled him with joy. Everything she'd said had been the truth.

The steamer gave a mournful whistle, and the realization hit Brad. He was on a steamboat in the middle of the Mississippi. His hand gripped the rail. If Kacie had told him the truth about so many things, had she also told him the truth about the steamboat explosion? His stomach lurched sickeningly as he realized the date. It was the sixth. He was on a steamer. Suddenly he heard an ominous rumble and felt the ship tremble.

*

Kacie was beside herself with worry all day. Though Jonas assured her that Brad had made the trip on horseback, she knew she wouldn't rest until the sixth of April had ended and he was back safely in her arms. Hour after hour she wandered the halls of Eden's Gate trying to distract herself, but everywhere she looked there were memories of Brad. Nothing worked. She prayed that his love for her was true and his trust was unshakable.

Night fell, and Kacie's fears grew. There were only a few hours left of the terrible day, yet she had never known time to pass so slowly. Each minute seemed an eternity.

At Jonas' insistent invitation, Kacie joined him for dinner. Her attempt at pretending normalcy was an abject failure. Her conversation lagged, and despite her best effort to eat, she tasted nothing of the food placed before her.

"If you don't mind, I think I'll say good night," she said.

"I'd really enjoy it if you'd stay and keep me company for a while." It was as close as Jonas could come to admitting that he, too, was concerned about Brad.

She read the unspoken worry in his expression and realized he was just as upset as she was. "Of course."

As they went into the parlor to have their coffee, Kacie glanced at the clock. It was almost nine. Just as they took their seats on the sofa they heard a distant yet terrible roar that shattered the tense quiet of the night.

"Oh, God…" She came to her feet. The delicate china cup she'd been holding slipped from her fingers, and she jumped as it shattered on the floor. The horrible thought that the steamer had just exploded and that she hadn't changed anything assailed her. Brad had said he was going to ride. He had told his father he wouldn't take the steamer, yet there was still the chance… Heartsick with fear, she gathered up her skirts and ran from the room.

Jonas followed her and they raced down to the river landing. Over the tops of the trees, the glow of the burning steamer turned the upriver night sky a harsh orange-red. People were dying and there was little they could do.

"Wait at the house!" Jonas ordered Kacie. "I'll take some men with me and we'll see if we can help."

"I want to come with you!" she protested.

"No, you'll only slow us down! Now do as I say! I'll be back as soon as I can!" He barked out orders to the men who had joined them at the landing to watch the spectacle, and within a few minutes they were riding across country toward the disaster.

Kacie's nerves were stretched taut as she watched them ride off. She felt helpless and very, very frightened. What if she hadn't changed anything? What if, in spite of all her warnings, Brad had boarded that steamer and died?

Kacie bit back a sob at the thought and with tears blinding her, stumbled back up the walk. She didn't even consider going back to the big house. Instead, she went straight to the grotto. She lit the candles and knelt on the kneeler. She clasped her hands tightly before her, and her eyes closed as she prayed fervently to God for His help. The thought of never holding Brad or kissing him or talking with him again was just too much for her to bear.

"Please, don't let Brad be dead! Please, if You didn't want me to save him, why did You send me back here? Oh, God, please…" Tears fell as she pleaded unceasingly for his safety. "I love Brad with all my heart, God, but I'll give him up forever if he's alive and well..."

Kacie remained on her knees, praying desperately through the long, dark night. She tried to tell herself that Brad had not been on the steamer. She tried to convince herself that he would return to her happy and healthy the next day, but always the ugly memories of history as she'd learned it intruded and destroyed what little solace she'd had with those thoughts.

Hours passed and she heard nothing. Still, she did not abandon her vigil. Brad was out there somewhere, and she would not leave the grotto until he was back with her. Over and over, she recited every prayer she knew.

Her maid sought her out to see if she was all right, and Kacie bid her to bring her the Bible. When she did, Kacie clutched it to her as she continued to beseech God with her unending pleas for help. She had been touching the Holy Book when she'd first come to Brad, and she hoped with all her heart that this time it would return him to her.

Dawn came, the rays of the morning sun cutting through the darkness in the grotto. Kacie took little notice. Her entire being was focused on Brad. Not knowing her love's fate filled her with a devastating agony. He had to be alive! He had to!

Kacie was concentrating so hard on her prayers that she didn't hear the footsteps approaching.

"Kacie?"

Only when Jonas said her name was she jarred back to an awareness of her surroundings, and she trembled as she lifted her fearful gaze to him.

"Jonas... Brad, is he... was he...?" she asked in a strangled voice.

"I'm here, Kacie... I'm right here..." Brad stepped from behind his father. His face was battered and bruised and his clothing was torn, but he was alive.

"Brad! Oh, thank God!" Kacie cried as she launched herself into his arms. Her heart sang with joy as she clung to him. He was alive! Alive!

Jonas saw the depth of their love and understood.

"Why were you on the steamer? What happened?" she asked frantically as she held him.

"It doesn't matter, sweetheart. All that matters is that you were right. If you hadn't warned me about the explosion, I wouldn't have known to jump from the ship when I heard the rumbling of the engine, and I'd be dead now. Thanks to you, my work can continue and more lives than you know will be saved." As he spoke, he drew the map from his pocket and slipped it into the Bible, still in Kacie's hands. "I love you, Kacie. I want us to be together always." Brad did not know what forces had brought her to him, but he knew he wanted never to be separated from her. She was his life.

"Oh, Brad… I love you…"

His hand covered hers on the Bible as he drew her to him and kissed her, their lips meeting in a sweet celebration of their future. A dizzying, whirlwind of emotion enfolded them as they embraced. They clung together, one in heart, mind, and soul. Somewhere, as if from far away, they heard Jonas calling their names.

The kiss ended, yet Brad and Kacie did not move apart. Wrapped in each other's arms, they remained standing together until the light-headed sensation that had gripped them passed. For an instant, they had both thought it was their passion and desperation that had filled them with such an unusual feeling, but then they looked up. Jonas was gone, and Kacie could hear the sounds of modern-day living nearby.

"Dear God…" she murmured. The Bible was still clutched in her hand, and she moved out of Brad's embrace to look outside. She saw the gardener at work using a power tool and turned back to Brad, not knowing whether to be happy or scared.

"What is it? Where's my father?" Brad asked, seeing the strange look on her face and going to stand beside her and look out.

"It's 1993, Brad. You've come back with me." She was awestruck by the realization.

"Kacie?" Brad glanced down at her, remembering everything she'd told him about being from the future. He'd doubted her, and now…

"I don't know how or why, Brad. I just know we're here." She took his hand in hers as she stood on tiptoe to kiss him again.

"I have to go back," he insisted. "There are things I have to do. People are counting on me."

She lifted one hand to caress his cheek. "We have no control over this time travel. Don't you think I would have returned home in the beginning if I'd had the chance?"

"Then all my work was for nothing."

"No, no, love. It's better than you're here, safe with me. Your father continued your work, but then the war came."

"War?" Brad tensed, struggling to understand and accept what she was saying.

"The North and South fought, and though the South lost the war, in the long run, my darling, you won."

"I don't understand." He frowned.

"Remember when I told you everyone was free in my day? Well, slavery was abolished. Your work did mean something," she assured him. "Come with me." She took his hand and drew him out of the grotto into the garden.

Brad took a step away from her and stared around in surprise. In the distance, a car was coming up the now paved driveway, and he was fascinated as he watched its progress. A roar high overhead startled him, and he looked up in total amazement.

Kacie was nervous as she watched him. She wasn't sure just how he was going to react to being brought forward to her time, and her heart was pounding with a mixture of fear and hope. When he turned to her after a moment, she waited expectantly for him to speak.

"I was right to believe in you," he said softly, his smile gentle and loving. "Show me the way, love. I'll follow wherever you lead."

Kacie smiled back at him and took his hand once more. "You showed me your world. Now I'll show you mine."

As Kacie led Brad into the sunlight, she gave thanks for the glory of the new day, for the future she knew would be theirs, and for the trust of the man who held her hand in his.

SOMETHING BLUE

1

Saguaro Springs, Arizona Territory

"Are you ready for another drink, General?" Mattie asked the military man as she stopped before his table in the back corner of the Palace Saloon. She'd waited on him when he'd first come into the bar and thought him quite handsome in his blue cavalry officer's uniform. Tall and blond, he had an air of quiet authority about him. She'd been watching him while he'd sat alone, downing the drink she'd served him, and he looked so serious that she'd thought he might be in need of some cheering up.

"It's *Captain*," Philip Long corrected as he glanced up, surprised by her presence. He had been so deep in thought that he hadn't noticed her approach. Not that she wasn't worth noticing. He supposed for a bar girl she was pretty enough, with her dark hair and green eyes, but she was definitely not his type. He hadn't met his dream woman yet, but he was certain she wouldn't be wearing a skin-tight, low-cut, red silk dress and heavy face paint.

"Well, you look like a general to me," Mattie countered with a wink.

"I appreciate the promotion, but I don't think my superiors would approve."

"Pity. I'd follow any orders you'd want to give me," she told him, grinning.

Philip shoved his glass across the table to her. "Then I'll take a double whiskey."

"Right away, sir." She moved off toward the bar.

Philip watched her go and distractedly tried to guess her age.

Not too young; judging by the ample display of bosom her dress provided. He didn't consider the possibility of any kind of encounter with her, though. He had too much else to think about, too much else to worry about.

"Thanks," he said when she returned to place the drink before him.

"You're welcome, and my name's Mattie if you want anything else tonight."

Philip paid her and gave her a good tip.

"Thanks, General," she said, her eyes widening at the generous amount. "Just let me know when you need me.'

Philip nodded but didn't respond as he lifted the tumbler and took a deep drink. It wasn't good whiskey, but it was strong enough to do the trick. Right now, he needed something that would ease his dark mood and help him see things a bit more clearly. Rotgut would do.

The last month had been a hard one for him. His father had passed away back home in Boston, and, as his only son and heir, Philip had had to take a leave from his post at Fort McDowell in Arizona Territory and head east to settle the estate.

In life, wealthy Charles Long had been domineering, controlling, with firm ideas about his sole heir's brilliant future. Father and son had not had a close relationship since Philip had chosen to serve in the cavalry on the frontier. Charles had wanted Philip to remain in Boston, marry a rich, well-connected girl like Dwylah Carpenter, and become influential in political circles. But Philip would have none of it. He had been drawn to the adventure of the untamed West. Though the senior Long had argued vehemently against such a notion, Philip had stood his ground and had become his own man. Now, however, even from the grave, his father was once again attempting to control him.

Philip gave a cynical laugh and took another drink as he remembered meeting with his father's lawyer back in Boston. The attorney had read the will aloud, and Philip had been shocked by the unusual clause his father had inserted into the document—that his only son had to be wed within six months of the reading of the will, and remain married for over a year, or lose every cent of his inheritance.

Clearly, Charles Long had wagered that such a requirement

would make Philip quit his remote frontier outpost for genteel Boston, where he'd find suitable females in far greater supply.

Philip had been furious. He'd wanted to contest the will, but the lawyer had told him it was ironclad. Unless he fulfilled his father's matrimonial requirement, the entire estate would be divided among distant cousins-cousins neither he nor his father had had any use for. His father had been shrewd to add that Philip had to stay married for a year; Charles had thereby sealed up his son's only escape route from the clause. Unless he chose to walk away from his fortune without a backward glance, Philip was trapped.

The thought of abandoning the money had occurred to him. He made a decent living in the military and was basically content with his life. Busy with the demands of his command, he had always believed there would be time later for getting married, settling down, and starting his own family. Evidently, however, his father wanted that time to be now. And Charles had wagered—correctly—that Philip would not stand for his obnoxious cousins to inherit. Conspicuously greedy for Charles's wealth, the relatives had offended Philip by kowtowing in Charles's presence, but belittling him behind his back. Philip despised them for their hypocrisy. He could not step aside and let them claim his father's legacy.

"I said *no*, mister!"

The sound of a woman's frantic protest interrupted Philip's troubled thoughts. He looked up to see the pretty barmaid struggling to free herself from another customer's grip. The man had hauled her onto his lap and was attempting to take liberties with her person.

"Easy there, Mattie girl," the man said in a slurred, drunken voice as he all but salivated down the front of her gown. "You know you love ol' Micah. That's why you're working here, just so you can spend time with me. No, quit fighting me so hard."

"No!" Mattie twisted with all her might to avoid his groping hands. "I'm here only to serve drinks!"

"Well, darlin'. I know something else you can serve me right now," he growled, laughing evilly and trying to reach up her skirt.

The girl's desperation was real, and Philip rose from his table to go to her aid. No one else, not even the bartender, had made a move to help her.

"The young lady said she isn't interested in your attentions," Philip told the man named Micah.

"Sure she is," the lecher sneered, grabbing at her curves.

"Let her go," Philip commanded.

Silence fell over the saloon.

Micah looked up, clearly irritated at being interrupted. "I ain't in the cavalry, soldier, so your orders don't mean a damned thing to me. Go on back to your table, and leave us alone. Little Mattie here is just playin' hard to get. I know she's selling, and tonight I'm buying." He slipped a hand inside her bodice and squeezed her tender flesh.

"Don't!" The girl shoved violently against his chest, hitting out at him blindly, trying to escape his vile hands.

Philip saw the panic and horror on the girl's face and didn't waste any more time trying to reason with the drunk. He simply took charge. In one commanding move, he gripped the lecher by the throat and squeezed until the man released Mattie.

"Why, you…" Furious and red in the face, Micah reeled to his feet and reached for his gun.

Philip was ready for him. He laid the hulking Micah low with one blow to the jaw. "A gentleman doesn't treat a lady that way," Philip pointed out, looking down at the prone figure.

"Mattie ain't no lady!" Micah whined, rubbing his aching jaw. "She ain't nothing but a whore! Everybody knows that!"

"I am not!" Mattie cried, backing away from the table, frightened and humiliated.

All eyes were on her as she turned and ran into the back room. Cal, the bartender, went after her.

Micah stood up slowly and spit blood on the floor. "I'm getting the hell out of this lousy joint," he snarled. He snatched up what was left of his drink, downed it, then slammed the glass onto the table and stomped out of the saloon.

The two men he'd been boozing with, who'd been watching what had transpired, followed him from the bar.

Philip didn't relax his vigilance until they were out of sight. Then he turned to go after the bartender and the girl. He wanted to make sure Mattie hadn't been hurt.

"I know what I told you when I hired you, Mattie, but…" Cal was ranting. He stopped when Philip appeared in the doorway. "What do you want?"

"I came to check on Miss Mattie," he answered, his gaze settling on her as she stood glaring up at the man who was her boss.

"She's fine," Cal said dismissively.

"I'd like to hear that from her, if you don't mind," Philip said calmly but firmly.

Cal glowered at Mattie as she glanced at Philip.

"I'm all right." She quickly dropped her gaze from his.

"You're sure?" Something didn't feel right to him.

"Yes. Thanks." Her voice was flat.

Philip looked at the two of them yet had little recourse but to leave the room. He returned to his table to finish his drink. He'd come into the Palace to relax a bit, but it hadn't turned out that way. Of course, lately nothing was turning out the way it was supposed to.

Philip drained what was left of his liquor as he reconsidered his future. Marrying as his father had ordered, receiving his inheritance in full, and staying on in the military wasn't, he supposed, a bad idea. Except that there wasn't a woman around he'd even consider marrying right now. He wasn't in love; he never even had been.

His thoughts drifted on. He could resign his commission, return to Boston, marry, and collect the money, but he didn't like the idea at all. He was dedicated to his command and didn't want to leave it. And, of course, there was still the problem of the missing bride.

Last but not least, Philip mused darkly, he could turn down the money and continue as he was, allowing the fortune to go to his greedy cousins. That wasn't an option.

Philip frowned and glanced up just in time to see Mattie rush out of the back room, her head down, her manner tense. She fled the saloon without a word. Cal emerged to watch her go, his expression angry.

As much as Philip told himself it was none of his business, he wondered what had transpired in the back room. It was still early in the evening, and yet the girl had left her post. Curious, he got up and made his way from the Palace.

Outside, the night was dark, moonless. Philip looked around to see where she had gone, and it surprised him to find no sign of her anywhere. And then he heard it-one brief, desperate cry for help that came from the alley alongside the saloon. He headed that way at a run.

2

"You shoulda just given me what I wanted inside, girlie!' Micah Johnson leered down at Mattie. He had thrown her to the ground and covered her mouth with one hand to stifle her screams. "You wouldn't have gotten yourself hurt then."

Mattie was fighting for all she was worth, desperate to defend herself. Micah and the other two men had been lurking outside, waiting for her. She'd always known that Micah was a low-life bastard, but until tonight she'd never had to deal firsthand with his ugliness. Now, however, she was really frightened. If she could get one hand free, she might be able to reach the small derringer she kept hidden in her garter. But even if she did manage to get the gun, it was only a single-shot, and there were three men.

Trembling, Mattie made her move. Micah was too busy tearing at her clothing to notice. She offered up a silent prayer as she tugged her weapon free. She dug the gun into her assailant's side as he bit his hand.

"Why, you—!" Micah yanked his hand away from her mouth, swearing violently.

"Get off me, or I'll shoot!" Mattie ordered, pressing the gun even harder against him, wanting to make sure he knew she was serious.

For an instant, Micah was stunned, but then he reacted. He slapped her and managed to knock the gun from her hand in one vicious blow. He drew back, ready to hit her again, when he felt the sting of cold metal against the back of his neck. He went still, his upraised hand frozen in midair.

"I think I already told you once tonight how to treat a lady. I

75

don't like having my orders ignored," Philip said in a soft yet dangerous voice. He glanced over at Micah's two friends, his deadly expression warning them to stay out of the fight.

Cowards that they were, they turned tail and ran.

"Get up," Philip ordered Johnson.

Micah stood and turned to face him, keeping his movements slow and steady. He didn't want to give the soldier any reason to shoot.

"If you ever go anywhere near this woman again, I'll hunt you down. Do you understand me?"

Micah nodded, a cold sweat beading his brow.

"Now get out of here." Philip spoke slowly and quietly, but there was no doubt of the threat behind his words.

Micah didn't have to be told twice. He fled into the night.

Philip slowly holstered his sidearm, then held a hand out to the barmaid to help her up.

Mattie couldn't believe what had just happened. One moment she was facing her worst nightmare, and the next her "general" had come out of nowhere to save her again. She didn't immediately take his hand but merely stared up at him, thinking him some wonderful, avenging guardian angel in blue. He was tall and strong and brave and handsome. And in that instant, Mattie fell in love.

"Are you all right?' Philip asked when she didn't immediately respond to his gesture of help.

"Oh-yes…" Mattie stammered nervously, summoned back to reality.

She put her hand in his, and a thrill coursed through her. His touch was strong yet gentle as he helped her to her feet. She almost didn't want to let go, but she knew she had to. She wasn't the clinging type—or at least she never had been until now. But somehow the thought of a little clinging with her general seemed suddenly quite wonderful.

"Thank you," she breathed, lifting her gaze to his.

The emotions stirring with her were confusing. One moment she'd been fighting for her very life, and the next she'd been rescued by her knight in shining armor. The fantasy was real, only instead of armor, her knight wore a blue cavalry uniform. She felt him drawing his hand away and abruptly released her grip on him. Certain she was blushing, she was grateful for the darkness to hide her disquiet.

"I'm glad I found you in time," Philip told her, peering at her, trying to determine if the drunk's blow had injured her. "Are you sure you're not hurt?"

Mattie lifted one hand nervously to her cheek. She winced at the tenderness there. "I'll be fine," she said.

Philip looked around the deserted area. He couldn't leave her out there to fend for herself. "May I escort you home?" he asked.

"Well, I…" She wasn't sure what to say. In all her eighteen years, she'd never had a man so politely offer to escort her anywhere.

Philip thought he understood the reason for her hesitation— that she believed he was just like the other men and would try to take advantage of her. He spoke up quickly, wanting to put her mind at ease. "Miss Mattie, I only want to see you home safely. I wouldn't feel right leaving you here to your own devices after what you've been through tonight." He crouched to pick up her derringer from the ground, then straightened and offered it back to her. "Would you really have shot him?"

She took the gun and stared down at it. When she looked up at her general again, she answered simply and honestly, "I don't know."

"You shouldn't carry a gun unless you're willing to use it," he told her. "Otherwise it could be used against you. Do you know how to fire it?"

"Yes."

Philip nodded his approval. "That's a start. If you ever find yourself in a situation like this again, don't hesitate to shoot to defend yourself."

"Don't worry. It's never going to happen again."

Given her profession he had no idea how she could be so sure, but he was glad to hear it. "May I see you home now?"

"Thank you."

Mattie started to walk from the alleyway but sound herself a bit unsteady from the trauma of all that had happened. Philip gallantly offered her his arm. For a moment, she stopped and stared at him, once again surprised by his courtly manner. Then, grateful for the offer; she accepted his help. Mattie told him where she lived, and they moved slowly but steadily toward the run-down boarding house.

Mattie didn't say much during the walk. She wasn't sure what she could say to him. Lord knows, she didn't have anything in common with her general—him being so important and all. She simply held on to his arm, feeling the power there, knowing he was a brave man. She was certain there would never be another moment in her life as special as this one. She almost didn't want the walk to end. If they could have kept going forever; she would have, for she felt safe and protected by his side. They reached the boarding house all too soon, and it was time for them to part.

"This is it," she said simply, sorry they were there.

"Oh." Philip looked up at the decrepit building and struggled to keep his dismay from showing. The place was hardly suitable for a young woman. "Do you have family here to take care of you?"

"No. I live alone."

"Shall I escort you in?"

"No," she answered quickly, not wanting him to see the squalor of her pitiful room. It wasn't much, but everything she owned was in that room—some clothes and the few family keepsakes she'd managed to save. Her general, being the gentleman he was, wouldn't understand her way of life. She was certain he came from a moneyed background, for he had that kind of self—assurance about him; he was calm, collected, and certain that everything was going to turn out the way he wanted it to. She wished she had his kind of confidence, but things seldom turned out well for her. Just look at what had happened tonight. "But thank you for bringing me home.'

"Do you need any help?" he offered.

"No." Mattie didn't dare look up at him again. She feared that too much of what she was feeling would show in her expression. *Do you need any help?* The thought almost made her hysterical. She needed help all right, but she would do what she always did. She would survive on her own. She'd been taking care of herself for the last ten months since her parents had died and left her alone and penniless, and she would keep on doing so. She had no alternative.

Mattie hurried toward the door, hating that the moment was over yet knowing there was no way to linger and make it last any longer. Her general was a stranger; and he would remain that way. She would never see him again after tonight. He was just passing through her life on his way to better things.

It suddenly occurred to her that she didn't even know his name. Stopping, she turned back, and found that he was still there, keeping watch.

"What's your name?" she called out softly, just a hint of longing in her voice.

Philip gave her a half smile. "My name is Philip. Philip Long."

"Good-bye, Philip Long," she said quietly as she stared at him, committing to memory the vision of him standing guard over her.

Something about her good-bye bothered Philip, but he wasn't sure why. "Go on inside. I'll wait here until I'm sure you're safe."

"Yes, General."

Only when Mattie had disappeared inside and shut the door did Philip walk away. He considered returning to the saloon for another drink, then thought better of it. He'd go straight to his hotel and bed down. He was due to head out of town tomorrow and needed to get a good night's rest. The stage ride would be rough on this last part of his return journey to the fort. He wasn't looking forward to the long days of travel, but he was anticipating getting back to his command at McDowell. The cavalry was his life.

As Philip strode through the night, thinking about returning to the fort, thoughts of his dilemma interfered. He suddenly wondered where in the world he was going to find a suitable wife on such short notice. There were few available women at McDowell. His commander did have a daughter of marriageable age, but Philip knew that nothing could ever come of a relationship with her. She was passably fair but incredibly dull. Any attempts he'd had at intelligent conversation with her when they'd danced together at various functions had fallen terribly short. One thing Philip knew for certain: he couldn't marry a dullard. He needed a woman who was smart and quick-witted. He needed someone like his friend Sheridan St. John, or her cousin Maureen. The trouble was, they were both already married—Sherri to a scout from the fort and Maureen to a newspaperman in town.

Thinking back, Philip understood now why his father had tried to force him to get serious about Dwylah. He'd been too restless to think about marriage then, but his father had thought her the perfect match for him. Young, pretty, smart, and the daughter of a congressman from their home state, she'd have done well as an officer's wife. But Philip knew there was no point in dwelling on Dwylah Carpenter. She had long since married someone else and had several children.

Philip had to find someone, though, and try to make a go of a marriage he didn't really want. Where he was going to find his bride in the middle of Arizona Territory, he had no idea, but he was going to be on the lookout from now on. According to the will, he had only a little over five months left.

3

Dawn found Mattie huddled on her bed, clutching her blanket to her breast, trying not to cry. She'd passed a miserable night.

Last night, Cal had fired her.

The realization that she was in serious trouble had haunted her through the long hours of darkness. It had been bad enough that she'd had to fight off Micah Johnson, but knowing that in just a few days she would be completely out of money and officially destitute scared her. She tried to comfort herself with the knowledge that she'd suffered through bad times before and survived. She told herself she could do it again. But, somehow, she knew it wouldn't be in this town.

After her parents' deaths, she had come here, believing an aunt and uncle still lived in the area. Once she'd arrived, though, she'd found that they had moved on. She'd been out of money and had no one to help her. She'd tried to find a job, but the only work she could get was at the Palace Saloon. She'd balked at being a barmaid, but desperation and hunger had forced to take what Cal had offered. Now, after months of working in the saloon, she was certain no one else would hire her. Despite her attempts at chaste behavior, her reputation was ruined. She had no family or friends, and certainly no marriage prospects. She was in dire straits, and she had to think of something fast.

The idea of packing up and leaving sounded wonderful, but she didn't have enough money to pay for a stage ticket anywhere and keep eating, too. Her choices were severely limited—unless she decided to put her morals aside in favor of survival and go back to

81

work at the Palace, doing the things that Cal and Micah both wanted her to do.

Mattie shuddered at the thought. If there was one thing she wouldn't do, it was sell herself to men.

She finally gave up and let her tears flow. Crying wouldn't solve anything, but she hoped it would make her feel better. Still, she had little time to feel sorry for herself. She had to figure out a way to survive.

An image of her general shone in her thoughts, and she smiled a watery smile. He had been wonderful. She sighed deeply. She would never see him again, but she would always remember his kindness.

Philip Long

She sighed again as tears streaked down her cheeks.

Morning couldn't come soon enough for Philip. He awoke just before dawn, as was his usual schedule, and lay in bed, enjoying the peace of the moment. But then thoughts of his father's demands returned with a vengeance and seemed all the more infuriating in the quiet of the predawn darkness.

Marriage.

To please his father.

Thinking that way irritated him. Why did he have to marry someone who would please his father? He should marry a woman he wanted, not one his father wanted.

A vision of Mattie floated before him. He grinned as he imagined what his father would have said if he'd ever taken Mattie home to meet him. His father would have judged her immediately and found her wanting. Philip had to admit that he'd judged her immediately, too, but he had been proven wrong. Mattie was no prostitute. Why she was working in the Palace Saloon, though, was a mystery to him.

As he lay there, thinking about the night before, he found he wanted to see Mattie one more time. He wanted to make sure she had suffered no lasting ill effects from Micah Johnson's attack. His stage wasn't due to leave until early that afternoon, so there was plenty of time to stop by the Palace. He would feel better knowing she was all right.

*

"Mattie Jackson ain't here," Cal said, looking disgusted. "She's been nothing but trouble for me from the first night I hired her; so I fired her last night after that scene she made with Micah."

"You fired her?" Philip repeated, frowning.

"What's it to you?"

His pointed question made Philip think. What was it to him? Why did he care? Mattie hadn't said a word about being fired when he'd walked her home. He wondered why. She could have taken him up on his offer of help. He would have given her some money. Certainly, judging from the boardinghouse where she lived, she didn't have much.

He realized then that Mattie was too proud to ask for help. She did carry a gun and seemed determined to be self-sufficient.

"It's nothing to me. I just wanted to make sure she was all right."

"Who cares?" Cal shrugged, then snarled, "Women are all alike, whether they sell it or give it away. Hell, when you think about it, even brides are selling it for a price. A man's got to vow to take care of them for the rest of their days just so they put out a little." He moved off to wait on another customer.

Philip suddenly felt the need to get out of there. He walked outside into the sunshine and strode down the street. Getting fired from the Palace was probably the best thing that had ever happened to Mattie Jackson, whether she realized it or not. But Philip knew she would need some way to support herself, since she'd mentioned that she didn't have anyone to help her. He found himself heading for her boarding house.

*

Mattie was surprised by the knock at her door. She'd gathered her wits and had been trying to come up with a plan for the future. Things looked bleak right now, but she would find a way-somehow. She went to the door and opened it expecting to find Mrs. Harper there. Her landlady was the only person who ever bothered to check on her.

"Oh!" The sight of her general standing there left Mattie momentarily speechless.

"Miss Mattie, I'm glad you're here. I wanted to talk to you. May I come in?" Philip asked, remaining just outside her door: He was staring down at her; amazed by the difference in her this morning. Last night, in her low-cut red dress she'd looked older and wiser and…somehow used—jaded, almost. Today, her face was washed clear of paint, and she was wearing a demure if slightly shabby day gown. Her hair was tied with a simple ribbon and tumbled about her shoulders in a dark, lustrous cascade, giving her an almost-well—wholesome look.

Mattie knew she should never let an unrelated man into her room, but this was her general, and he'd already proven himself a true gentleman. She opened the door wider to allow him to enter. "I'm surprised to see you again."

"I went by the Palace to talk to you. The bartender told me he'd fired you last night. Why didn't you tell me that when we were together?"

"What difference would it have made?"

"You had already suffered enough abuse last night without losing your job, too."

"Cal thought I should be more than just a barmaid. He told me I should keep men like Micah happy. I refused."

"You did the right thing," Philip stated firmly, proud of her determination.

She gestured for him to sit down in the one and only chair in the room while she sat on the side of her bed. "Maybe, but I won't be able to pay the bills for long."

"Surely, there are other jobs you could take."

Mattie laughed derisively. "Not in this town. I may not have done anything bad while I was working at the Palace, but the good townsfolk won't believe that. They'll think the worst about me, no matter what."

"What are you going to?"

"I don't know. I barely have enough money to buy a ticket on the stage, let alone feed myself for the next few weeks."

"It's that bad?" His desire to help her grew even stronger.

"Yes," she answered without hesitation. There was no point in lying to him. "So why are you here?"

"I wanted to see if I could help you," Philip began.

As he spoke, Cal's harsh, demeaning words echoed in his thoughts. *"Hell, even brides are selling it for a price."*

An idea came to Philip—one that would cause Mattie no

dishonor yet would solve both their problems. She was poor and in desperate need of a job. He was wealthy—or at least soon would be, once he claimed his inheritance—and in desperate need of a wife. He could *hire* Mattie to be his wife! He smiled at the brilliance of the idea. The marriage would be in name only, of course, and they could get an annulment as soon as his year was over. Such an arrangement would suit them both perfectly!

"You want to help me?" she said cautiously, wondering at his smile.

"Yes, and I think I just figured out how."

"You did?"

"Yes, I have the perfect solution-for both of us."

"Both of us? I didn't know you were in trouble."

"I'm not in trouble exactly," he began. "I'm going to be honest with you. I can offer you a position that will pay handsomely and get you out of town."

"Why would you?'

"Because, right now, I need your help as badly as you need mine."

"I don't understand." She was confused and growing a bit nervous. Why would a man like her general need her?

"It seems, Mattie, that I am in dire, immediate need of a wife." He met her gaze forthrightly as he spoke, and he would remember forever the change in her expression at his words. She was stunned and staring at him in total disbelief.

"You need a wife?" Mattie repeated, unable to believe what she was hearing. What female in her right mind wouldn't want to marry him? Her general was perfect. He could have any woman he wanted. Why did he feel the need to make a bargain with her?

Philip quickly explained the stipulation—and its deadline—in his father's will. As he talked he realized just how perfect his plan was. If he married Mattie, he would not be surrendering completely to his father's order. He would be marrying someone his father would think was totally unsuitable. The will didn't dictate whom he had to marry; it just said that he had to marry.

"So," he concluded, "I'm making you an offer I hope you will accept. Today. Right now. Before I have to leave. I would like you to marry me as soon as possible and come with me to Fort McDowell. We must make the relationship convincing, even to legal skeptics, and we must remain married for one year, but you and I will know it is a marriage in name only. When the year is over, we can get an annulment and go our separate ways. I will pay you handsomely for your time. You'll never have to work again."

Mattie wasn't sure whether to laugh or cry. It seemed like a fairy tale, a dream come true. The man she thought of as a true hero, her general, her Philip Long, had come to rescue her. He was going to save her from her terrible fate. He was going to marry her and take her away from all this. Her spirits soared.

But then, their marriage would be in name only, and they would part after a year.

The realization that her fantasies were just that-fantasies-hurt. This was no love match for Philip, and it never would be. He'd made it clear that it would be a business arrangement, nothing more. And she had to decide right now what she was going to do.

"Miss Mattie?" Philip said questioningly, for she hadn't responded to his offer, and he couldn't read her expression. "Will you accept my proposal?"

Mattie took a deep breath. "Yes, Philip Long, I accept your proposal. I'll marry you."

Philip smiled, "Good. This will work out well for both of us."

"Yes, it will," she answered, still stunned by what had transpired. She was going to marry her general!

Philip suddenly felt a bit awkward. He'd just asked this woman to marry him, and she'd said yes. What was he supposed to do next? He told himself to focus on one thing at a time. "Would you like to get married here?"

"No!" Her answer came quickly. "The sooner I get out of this town, the better."

"All right. I planned on leaving on the two-o'clock stage. Can you be ready by then?"

"Yes. I don't have much to pack." She glanced around the room at her paltry possessions.

"There's an overnight stop at a way station, and then we can be married in the next town."

"That'll be fine."

"I'll check out of my hotel and come back for you." He stood.

"I'll be waiting for you."

Mattie lifted her gaze to Philip's, and for an instant she was lost in the depths of his eyes. She saw kindness and gentleness there. She wondered what it would be like to kiss him, then realized how silly the thought was. Her general had offered her a job. Nothing more. Still, a glimmer of hope burned within her heat. Philip had said they'd have to stay married a year to claim his inheritance. That meant she would have twelve whole months to try to win his love.

4

Mattie stared out the stagecoach window but gave no thought to the passing scenery. She couldn't. Every fiber of her being was focused on Philip as he sat so close beside her. They had been traveling for several hours now, and with each bump of the stage, his thigh pressed against hers. Mattie found that simple physical contact most distracting, but Philip appeared completely unaffected. Several times she'd cast surreptitious glances his way to see if he'd even noticed, but his expression remained inscrutable.

Mattie realized she shouldn't have been surprised by Philip's lack of reaction to her nearness. He'd made it perfectly clear from the start that their relationship was a business arrangement. He would marry her, but that didn't mean he cared about her. What he cared about was his inheritance.

She told herself that the deal they'd made was a blessing for her. Philip had shown up just in time to save her from a terrible fate, and she would forever be grateful. She would repay him by doing exactly what he wanted her to do. She would play the role of his wife until such time as he was ready to part from her; then she would leave him and never look back. There would be no emotional scenes, no heartbreak, no despair in their parting. It was strictly business. They meant nothing to each other.

On a logical level, Mattie accepted that she had no real future with Philip. But in truth, her heart ached with the knowledge that for the next year they would act married, but they would never be anything more than strangers to each other.

That was the way Philip wanted it, and Mattie was certain she knew why. She was, after all, just a saloon girl.

Self-consciously, she smoothed the skirts of her simple day gown. She wanted to make Philip proud of her, and it bothered her that this was her best dress. It was old and far from stylish. Since Philip had paid for her ticket, though, she did have a few dollars left to her name, so she intended to buy a new dress for her wedding once they reached town. Even though theirs wasn't going to be a "real" wedding, she wanted to look her best for him.

Mattie closed her eyes and imagined herself standing at an altar in a beautiful white lace gown and veil. It was an image she'd cherished since she was a little girl. She'd always dreamed of walking down the aisle and marrying a handsome prince, and very soon she would be. Only her "prince" was actually her general.

Philip was having second thoughts about his situation. He rarely acted impulsively, but he had done it this time. Not that he'd been without motivation. He had to get married, and he was doing what needed to be done to accomplish that end.

At the time, proposing to Mattie had seemed a brilliant strategy. Now, though, he wondered if he'd done the right thing. Helping her out of a desperate situation was one thing; throwing her into an even more difficult one was another.

Mattie was about to enter a world completely foreign to her. As an officer's wife, much would be expected of her, and it was up to him to make sure she'd know what to do. He wanted everything to go smoothly for her. He wanted her to be happy.

He glanced over at her to find her staring out the stagecoach window, completely unaware of the challenges she would be facing shortly. Philip vowed to himself then and there that he would make sure everything went as easily as possible for her. After an obviously hard life, she would be his wife, even if in name only, and he wanted to take care of her.

Of course, if she was going to be Mrs. Philip Long, she would have to look the part. His gaze went over her critically, assessing. The first thing he was going to do was make sure she had a suitable wardrobe. Officers' wives could be gossipy and sometimes judgmental, and he wanted to protect Mattie as much as he could. When they reached town tomorrow, one of the first things he would do was look for a dress shop and provide Mattie with a new wardrobe with which to begin her life at Fort McDowell.

The stage hit a jarring bump, and Mattie was thrown hard

against him. Philip instinctively slipped an arm around her shoulders to steady her.

"That was a rough one," he told her with a smile.

"Yes, it was," she agreed.

As he looked down at her, he was lost for a moment in the depths of her green eyes. He suddenly became aware of how fragile she felt beneath his touch. Mattie had acted so strong and brave that he hadn't really thought of her as delicate. The realization surprised him. When she shifted away from him, he quickly withdrew his arm and let her go.

"This is one helluva trip," the grouchy-looking old man sitting across from them complained. He was the only other passenger, and he'd been sleeping most of the way. The last bump, however, had jarred him awake. He was scowling and looking irritated with the world. "I'll be damned glad when it's over. Oh, pardon me, ma'am. I forgot there was a lady on board."

After her long months at the Palace, Mattie was amazed that the man apologized for cursing in front of her, and even more amazed that he thought she was a lady. It pleased her so, she had to fight to keep from laughing aloud. "I understand," she told him. "These roads are rough."

"That's putting it politely. I'll be glad when we finally make our destination."

Mattie hid a smile at his complaining, considering that he'd been asleep for most of the trek so far. She had to admit, though, that she couldn't have agreed with him more. Sitting this close to Philip was proving to be both heaven and hell. She shifted her position to put a little more space between them. It wouldn't last long, but it was a bit of a reprieve for now. "How much farther is it to the way station?"

"Another hour or two," the codger answered. "By the way, I'm Gene Gibson."

"It's nice to meet you. I'm Mattie Jackson, and this is my fiancé, Philip Long," she said.

Philip nodded his greeting.

"It's nice to meet you both. Where are you heading?" Gibson asked.

"To Fort McDowell," Mattie told him. "I'm really excited. This is quite an adventure for me."

"I don't know if I'd call it an adventure. I hear there've been a lot of Indian raids going on thereabouts lately. I hope you have a safe trip out."

"Oh, we will," Mattie insisted. "No Indian would dare attack us with my general along."

Philip almost groaned.

Gibson snorted a laugh as he looked at Philip. "General? Pardon me, ma'am, but in case he ain't told you yet, he ain't a general. He's a captain."

"He's a general to me." She smiled brightly as she gazed up at Philip. "We'll be getting married once we reach Crawford's Gulch."

"Well, congratulations. You're a lucky man," he told Philip.

"Yes, I am," Philip responded.

"So where are you heading, Mr. Gibson?" Mattie asked engagingly.

Philip listened to their conversation, joining in only when asked a direct question. He was amazed at how easily Mattie had charmed the old man. He'd expected Gene Gibson to be surly for the rest of the trip, but Mattie had the man relaxed and smiling and telling her all about his family waiting for him in Crawford's Gulch.

The next several hours passed quickly, and when they pulled to a stop at the way station, Gibson looked surprised.

"I can't believe we're here already," he said to Mattie as the driver opened the door for them to climb down. "It was a pleasure having you to talk to. You certainly made the time go faster. If your officer there hadn't claimed you already, I'd be tempted to see about courting you myself."

Mattie actually found herself blushing at his kind words, while Philip merely smiled slightly.

Through the evening at the station Philip stayed attentively by Mattie's side, playing his role of fiancé perfectly. After they'd eaten the hot meal that was provided, everyone bedded down for the night. The men slept in a bunkhouse out back, while Mattie was given the small room in the main house that was reserved for female travelers.

She appreciated the privacy. She was exhausted and needed some rest. But as she started to undress, she realized that by this time the following night she would be Mrs. Philip Long! She would be beginning a whole new life. A life with Philip. Although, she acknowledged sadly, they would be sharing nothing meaningful, no matter how she looked at it, she knew things would never be the same again. And sleep was long in coming.

They were up at dawn and soon on the road again. They didn't reach their destination of Crawford's Gulch until late in the afternoon.

Philip climbed out of the stage first and put his hands at her waist to help Mattie descend. He thought her light as a feather as he set her before him, then went to retrieve their bags.

Gene Gibson started to climb out next, and it was then that excited shouts and squeals erupted.

"There's Grampa!"

Philip and Mattie both saw three young boys no older than ten running at full speed toward Gene, who was soon enveloped in enthusiastic embraces.

"It was nice to meet you two," he called out to Mattie and Philip as he was surrounded by loved ones and hustled away.

"You, too!' Mattie responded.

The driver climbed back up to his seat and drove the stage off to the stable area, leaving Mattie and Philip alone.

"Well, here we are," Philip announced as he looked around the town. Crawford's Gulch wasn't very big, but Philip was certain it had to have a justice of the peace somewhere, not to mention a shop where he could find Mattie at least one or two dresses. "Let's find the hotel and check in. The desk clerk should be able to tell us what we need to know about getting hitched in Crawford's Gulch."

Mattie accompanied him without a word, not quite sure what to say. In a very short time, they would be married. She was excited and a bit frightened too. She leashed both emotions and tried to appear calm.

When they entered the hotel, Philip registered and then asked the clerk for directions to the justice of the peace.

"His name is Russell Bailey, and his office is just down the street about three blocks."

"Thanks." Philip escorted Mattie upstairs to their chamber and held the door for her as she entered.

Mattie stepped inside and found herself staring at a large double bed. She knew a moment of nervousness as she realized that this very night she would be sharing this room with Philip.

"Do you want to freshen up a bit before we go to the justice of the peace?" Philip asked casually as he carried their bags in.

"Yes, please." She was amazed at how calm he seemed about the whole situation.

"I'll leave you alone then and be back in a little while."

"Thanks."

Once Philip had gone, Mattie took a look at herself in the mirror over the bureau, and she knew what she had to do. She had to go buy the new dress for her wedding. On the ride into town, she had noticed a small ladies' shop next to the general store. She would make a quick trip there to see if she could find something suitable.

Mattie knew she was romanticizing the ceremony—this wasn't a real love match—but she did want to look her best for Philip. She wanted him to be proud of her. After freshening up a bit, she got out her small purse and counted all the money she had in the world. It wasn't much, but she hoped she could find something she could afford. She did so want to please him.

Philip found a saloon down the street from the hotel and went in for a quick drink. He stood by himself at the end of the bar, thinking about the changes the next few hours would bring. He was about to marry Mattie Jackson. The prospect of marriage had never before excited him, but somehow he knew that this coming year with Mattie would not be dull. He hadn't told her yet that he wanted to take her shopping for new clothes. He wanted to surprise her when he went back to the room.

After stalling a reasonable amount of time, Philip quit the bar and headed back to claim his bride to be. He knocked at the hotel room door before opening it, for he didn't want to startle her. But when he received no answer, he stepped inside the room, and he was shocked to find it empty.

"Mattie?"

He searched for her, but the room was too small to offer any place to hide. It was then that he noticed her purse was gone, too, and the reality of what had happened hit him.

She had fled. She'd changed her mind about the marriage and had not had enough nerve to tell him to his face.

She was gone.

5

Philip pivoted and strode from the hotel room, swearing under his breath. He'd sensed that Mattie had been a bit uncomfortable when they'd entered the room together. That was why he'd excused himself; he'd wanted to give her some time to compose herself before they went to the justice of the peace. But now it seemed his attempt at being solicitous had failed. Mattie had walked away, and she hadn't even said good-bye.

Philip's expression was thunderous as he made his way to the lobby. Wherever Mattie had gone, she couldn't have gotten far. The town wasn't that big. He was going to find her. He couldn't let her just disappear this way.

"Did you notice my fiancée leaving the hotel?" Philip demanded of the desk clerk.

"Why, yes, sir. She left right after you did."

"Did she mention where she was going?"

"No, but I did noticed that she headed down the street toward the general store."

Still frowning, Philip started off in the direction the clerk had indicated. He kept careful watch as he made his way down the street. His confidence in his ability to find Mattie was rock solid. He'd been successfully tracking renegade Indians for years, so finding one woman in a town the size of Crawford's Gulch didn't seem too challenging.

Twenty minutes later, Philip was beginning to have his doubts. He'd covered most of the town, and had yet to catch sight of Mattie anywhere. Why would she feel the need to flee him this way? Had he completely misjudged her character? He didn't think he had.

She hadn't stolen anything out of their room. She had simply vanished without a word.

Philip was heading back toward the hotel when he walked by the ladies' shop he'd passed earlier. He took a quick glance inside and came to a halt. Mattie was there. She was standing on a riser wearing a pale blue gown while a seamstress was working on the hem. He entered the shop abruptly, standing just inside the door.

"Mattie?"

Mattie gasped, surprised that Philip had found her. She'd known the fitting was taking a little longer than she'd expected, but she hadn't thought she'd been gone so long that he would come looking for her. She had so wanted to surprise him. But it wasn't to be. Looking over her shoulder, she saw the dark look on his face and wondered what had angered him so. "Philip, I'm sorry this has taken so long. I didn't realize it would be so complicated."

"What would be so complicated?" he demanded, remaining where he was, standing stiffly, as if prepared for trouble.

"You must be Mattie's 'general'," the seamstress said, smiling at him as she stopped working and stood up to greet him.

"Yes, he is, Dora," Mattie affirmed. Stepping down from the riser, she went to him. "Philip I wanted to have a new dress for the wedding, so I came here to see what I could find." When she saw his expression grow even darker, she thought he was angry because she was spending money. She hastened to calm him. "I'm paying for it, so you don't have to worry. I've just enough money left of my savings to buy it."

If Philip hadn't been an officer and a gentleman, he would have sworn out loud right then. He forced himself to calm down a bit. "I'm not worried about the cost of a dress. I was worried about you. When I got back to the room, I didn't know where you'd gone, and I feared something had happened to you."

"Oh." Mattie was completely taken by surprise by his concern.

The seamstress sighed dreamily, clearing thinking her new client a very lucky woman to have such a handsome, caring man in love with her.

"In fact," Philip continued, "I'd planned to see about getting you a few new dresses myself."

"You did?" Mattie was shocked.

"I was going to surprise you."

"But that wouldn't be right for-"

"It would be very right," he cut her off. "You're going to be my wife." Then, looking at the seamstress, he asked, "Do you have any other gowns already made up that will fit my fiancée?"

"I have two more that might do," she offered.

"We leave tomorrow at noon. Could you have any alterations that are needed done by then?"

"Absolutely."

"Fine. We'll take all three gowns. Do whatever needs to be done. We'll pick them up tomorrow before we leave."

"Philip, are you sure?" Mattie asked as Dora hurried to get the other two garments to show them. She knew the gowns would be expensive.

"I'm very sure," he told her, finally relaxing enough to really look at her for the first time.

The pale blue dress highlighted her flawless complexion and brought out the beauty of her dark hair. The neckline of the gown wasn't low cut but slightly scooped, and he knew exactly what it needed.

When the seamstress returned, Philip asked, "Will it be much longer to finish hemming the blue gown?"

"About twenty minutes," Dora answered.

"I'll be back for you then, Mattie. There's one thing I forgot to do."

The two women watched him leave the shop and disappear down the street.

"Your fiancé is one handsome officer. You're a very lucky woman," Dora told her as she worked on the hem.

"I know. I'm very lucky," Mattie answered.

Dora had just helped Mattie down from the riser when Philip returned and paid Dora for all three gowns. The price didn't seem to bother him at all. When he'd finished taking care of business, he turned to Mattie.

"Are you ready?" he asked, his gaze meeting hers.

"If you are." She was suddenly feeling a bit timid.

"You look lovely," Dora told her.

Philip took a small box out of his pocket. "I thought the gown was missing something," he said softly. He lifted the lid of the box and took out a golden heart-shaped locket. "And I thought this just might be it."

"Oh!" Mattie said softly. She had never seen anything so pretty. "This is for me?"

"It's my wedding present," Philip said as he came to stand behind her and fasten the necklace at her throat.

Mattie closed her eyes at the warmth of his touch, then lifted one hand to caress the necklace reverently after he'd stepped away. She'd never owned any jewelry before. She stared in the mirror in awe. "It's beautiful."

"You're beautiful," Philip said on impulse, surprising himself.

"Yes, you are," Dora agreed.

Mattie gazed at her reflection, finding a sophisticated young woman staring back at her. She could see no trace of the Mattie Jackson who'd worked at the Palace Saloon and had to wear gaudy red dresses and face paint. The woman in the pale blue gown appeared genteel, ladylike, someone who might be accepted by polite society. Mattie smiled, amazed at her own transformation.

"Are you ready?" Philip asked.

His question broke through her reverie, and she turned to face the man who would soon be her husband.

"I'm as ready as I'll ever be," she said in a soft voice.

"Shall we go?"

Philip offered her his arm in a courtly manner. Mattie accepted it, and they left the store.

*

"Do you, Philip Long, take this woman, Matilda Jackson, to be your lawfully wedded wife, for better or worse, for richer or poorer, in sickness and in health, until death do you part?" Ben Strickland, the justice of the peace, asked.

"I do," Philip responded.

"Do you, Matilda Jackson, take this man, Philip Long, to be your lawfully wedded husband, for better or worse, for richer or poorer, in sickness and in health, until death do you part?"

"I do," Mattie answered breathlessly. She looked up at Philip and managed to smile. A part of her yearned for this to be a real ceremony, one that meant something to Philip, but in her heart she knew better. She fought down her own betraying thoughts and emotions. There was no love between them, and she had to remember that.

Philip took Mattie's left hand and slipped a simple gold bank onto her ring finger, marking her as his wife.

"By the power invested in me, I now pronounce you man and wife. Captain Long, you may kiss your bride," the justice told Philip with a grin.

Philip turned to take Mattie into his arms. He felt her tense at the contact, and with utmost care, he bent and captured her lips in a simple kiss. He'd meant it to be a chaste, innocent exchange, and it was. Yet something in it stirred him, and suddenly he needed more. He deepened the kiss, tasting of her sweetness. He was shocked to find he wanted even more, and he forced himself to draw back from her, keeping himself in check. He saw Mattie's wide-eyed look and realized she'd been just as surprised as he had by the power of their kiss. He turned to the justice of the peace.

"Thank you, Mr. Strickland," he said, keeping a possessive arm around Mattie's waist.

"My pleasure. I always enjoy weddings. You two be happy together, now."

"We appreciate your help," Philip said cordially as he paid him for performing the ceremony.

They left the justice of the peace's office and didn't speak until they were almost back to the hotel.

"I guess this means we're married," Mattie said quietly.

"Yes, we are," Philip said. "I thought we should have dinner and celebrate a little before we call it a night. What do you say?"

"All right," she agreed, still stunned by all that had happened in the past few days. She was now married.

She was Mrs. Philip Long.

They made small talk as they dined at a small restaurant near the hotel.

Mattie found herself growing more and more nervous with each passing moment. Soon they would finish eating and return to the hotel. Soon she would be alone with him in their room. Though she had worked at the Palace, she was still an innocent in many ways. She'd had no brothers and no gentlemen callers to speak of. She wasn't quite sure how to behave alone with a man.

Reminding herself that this was a marriage in name only, Mattie told herself she had nothing to worry about. Philip had made it plain he had no intention of making love to her, so she was getting nervous for no good reason. Besides, she concluded logically, what did it matter if they shared a hotel room? They *were* married.

But Mattie's mood was still unsettled when they started back to the hotel. She walked in silence by Philip's side, trying to anticipate what the night would bring.

As Philip escorted Mattie back to their hotel room, he was feeling quite pleased with the way everything had gone. Their marriage had taken place without any difficulties. Now all he had to do was send notice and proof to his father's lawyer that the ceremony had taken place and then stay married to Mattie for one year to claim his inheritance.

Philip still resented his father for forcing him to wed, but he was satisfied with his own choice for a wife. In fact, he was finding himself drawn to Mattie in ways he'd never thought possible. There was a refreshing air of innocence about her-surprising, since she'd worked at the saloon, but nevertheless real. He found, too, that he quite liked her. She was bright and witty and open with her opinions. She said what she was thinking, and in his experience he'd found that a true rarity among females.

"Tired?" he asked her as they neared the hotel.

"A little," she answered, looking up at him. "What about you?"

"Very. I'm looking forward to getting into bed."

His statement sounded innocent enough, but Mattie swallowed nervously. He was looking forward to getting into bed. If he planned on using the bed, she wondered where she was going to sleep.

Mattie pictured herself trying to sleep in the small chair in their room. That would likely be torture. Probably she'd end up on a pallet on the floor. She convinced herself it wouldn't be that bad. She'd certainly slept in worse placed since her parents died.

When they reached their room, Philip unlocked the door and held it open for her to enter ahead of him. "You might as well go ahead and get comfortable," he said as he closed and locked the door behind them.

The sound made her all the more jittery. "Well, I didn't...I mean, I was wondering..."

He turned to look at her and frowned when he saw how

stiffly she was holding herself, staring at the bed. "Mattie? What's wrong?"

Girding herself, she turned to face him. "I'll need an extra blanket."

"Why? It's not that cold."

"For a pallet," she said simply.

6

Mattie was surprised by the sudden change in Philip's expression. She was certain that the look he gave her could cow even the bravest of his enlisted men. But she wasn't a soldier under his command. She refused to flinch.

"What are you talking about?" he demanded.

"I'm talking about where I'm to sleep tonight. We had an agreement about this 'marriage' of ours. Should we be sharing the same bed, do you think?"

For a moment, Philip was silent. He had to admit to himself that he had enjoyed their wedding kiss, but he had not thought much beyond that point. His ego, however, was a bit bruised by Mattie's brusque treatment of the subject.

"You're right," he agreed. "We shouldn't be sharing a bed. But you won't be the one sleeping on a pallet. I will." Philip eyed the chair, wondering if he could find any rest there. The floor certainly didn't seem any more inviting, but he had made a deal with Mattie, and he had to uphold his end of it.

"Are you sure?" Mattie couldn't believe that he would give up his comfort for her. No one had ever put her needs first.

"I'm sure. Let me give you some privacy to undress. We won't be able to avoid close quarters for an entire year, especially after we're at McDowell, but I can leave now for a while," he offered.

"No, it's not necessary," Mattie answered, not wanting to put him out even further. "But would you mind turning your back for a few minutes while I change?"

He smiled at her. "Not at all, ma'am."

"You won't look?"

"I give you my word as an officer and a gentleman."

"Thank you," she said, smiling back.

Philip walked to the window and looked out, keeping his back to Mattie. "Would you like me to speak to the clerk and see if it's possible to get a bath brought up for you in the morning? Our stage doesn't leave until noon."

"That would be wonderful!" She was delighted at the prospect. Certainly she'd washed up before the wedding, but getting the chance to soak in a real bath would be heavenly.

Philip smiled to himself. He remembered how much his mother had enjoyed her baths and was glad that he'd pleased Mattie. He heard the rustle of her clothing as she started to undress, but he kept his gaze directed at the street below.

"Philip?" Mattie finally gave up trying to unfasten her gown by herself. "I need your help."

He turned, and she presented him with her back, lifting the thick mane of her hair out of his way.

"I thought I could do it myself, but I can't." Mattie stood perfectly still before him.

Philip stared down at the tantalizing line of her neck and shoulders and found he wanted to press a kiss there. Or maybe several kisses, right along the line of the locket's fine gold chain. Jerking his wayward thoughts away from the dangerous direction they were taking, he quickly unhooked Mattie's gown. It gaped open, but she was holding the bodice-close, so he was treated to only a glimpse of her back as she moved away from him.

"Thank you," she said a bit nervously. The warmth of Philip's nearness and the touch of his hands had aroused new feelings deep within her, and she knew she had to get into her nightclothes and under the covers before she'd feel safe. Though what it was she needed to feel safe from, she wasn't quite sure.

"Do you want me to unfasten the locket, too?'

"No. No, I'd like to keep it on." She lifted one hand to her throat to touch the necklace. She never wanted to take it off again.

Philip returned to his vigil at the window. He was tempted to lift his gaze just a little to watch Mattie's reflection in the glass as she finished undressing, but he didn't. He'd given her his word, and he stood by it.

"You can turn around now," Mattie told him as she lay down

and pulled the covers up to her chin.

Philip turned toward her but stopped at the sight of her in bed. Her eyes were wide, and her expression was wary and a little frightened. It troubled him that she might be afraid of him. He knew this was the first time they were alone together in such intimate confines, but he wanted her to trust him and to be able to be comfortable in his presence.

"Mattie," he began seriously, "I want to make you a promise tonight."

"About what?"

"I want you to know that I will never do anything to hurt you and that I will never try to take advantage of you in any way."

Relief rushed through her, and she nodded, only a bit embarrassed that Philip had seemed able to read her thoughts so easily.

"I'll just get undressed myself. You go ahead to sleep."

Philip moved to the dresser, and, after turning the lamp down low, looked through the drawers and found an extra blanket he could use. He tossed it onto the chair and started to get ready for bed. He shed his jacket, then unbuttoned his shirt and stripped it off.

Mattie had closed her eyes and curled up, trying to sleep. But then for some reason she had to open her eyes to take a look. She saw Philip standing near the dresser, naked to the waist and getting ready to shed his pants. He looked so handsome, all she could do was stare. His shoulders were broad, and his chest was heavily muscled and powerful. A hot blush stained her cheeks at the sight, and she quickly shut her eyes lest she see even more of him than she had intended to.

Philip was unaware of Mattie's gaze upon him. He took off his boots, then started to doff his pants. But he thought the better of it. Mattie was uncomfortable with their current situation, so he would bow to her delicate sensibilities.

Gathering up his blanket, he turned the lamp all the way down and sought what ease he could find in the room's one chair. He discovered quickly that there was little rest to be had there. The chair was definitely not meant for someone his size to relax in. Even so, he was determined to get some sleep.

Mattie had thought, as tired as she was, that she would immediately fall asleep once her head hit the pillow. But it didn't happen. The knowledge that Philip was so close at hand disturbed her—though not necessarily in a bad way. She was just very, very aware of his nearness. Long minutes passed as she lay, unmoving, seeking the peace and forgetfulness of slumber. But still it didn't come.

Philip was miserable. It was bad enough that he couldn't forget how beautiful Mattie had looked tonight, but he could not find any rest at all in the cramped chair. After almost an hour of suffering, he finally gave it up. He stood and spread the blanket out on the floor. He'd been out on patrol and had slept by campfires many a time. He was certain the hotel floor had to be more welcoming than some of the terrain he'd slept on in the wilds.

He lay down. The floor was hard, and thoughts of Mattie and how she'd looked when she swept her hair up out of his way to bare her back to him haunted him. It had been a purely innocent gesture on her part, but he had found it a very sensual one. He rolled over with a disgusted growl, telling himself he was the lowest of the low to even be thinking about her that way.

"Philip? Are you all right?" Mattie had heard him make a strange sound and realized that he'd moved from the chair to the floor.

"I'm fine," he ground out.

He did not sound "fine".

"Are you sure? Was the chair that bad?"

"The floor will be all right. Go to sleep."

Mattie was quiet for a second, then offered, "Do you want to share the bed? I promise I'll stay on my half. I won't touch you or move around too much and disturb you or anything."

Philip almost groaned out loud at her offer. Trying to be logical, he asked himself why he was so miserable but couldn't really find an answer.

"You don't want to?" Mattie asked when he didn't respond.

Philip got up slowly. The softness of the mattress was inviting, and with Mattie lying there, it was even more so. "I'll take you up on your offer, but I'll sleep on top of the covers."

"Oh."

He grabbed up his blanket and stretched out next to her. He took care to stay as far from her as he possibly could, and he lay very still.

"Good night." She was smiling in the darkness, glad he would be more comfortable now.

"Good night," he responded.

But for some reason, he didn't really think it was.

Mattie had thought she might have trouble sleeping with Philip lying so close to her. She quickly fell asleep, though, and slept soundly through the rest of the night.

Philip lay on his marriage bed, pondering the irony of his situation. If anyone had ever told him that when he finally got married he would spend his wedding night like this, he would have laughed. But he wasn't laughing now.

When the quiet, even sound of Mattie's breathing came to him, he realized she'd fallen asleep. He shifted his position slightly so he could look at her as she slumbered beside him. In the semidarkness, he took the time to study her, and he realized she was quite lovely. He realized, too, that she was his wife.

Philip did not sleep well all night.

In the morning, when he awoke, Philip slipped carefully from the bed, taking care not to disturb Mattie. He wanted to wash up and dress before she awoke so he wouldn't embarrass her. It surprised him that she still wasn't stirring when he'd finished, but he realized how very tired she must be. He quietly let himself out of the room.

He returned some time later, quite pleased with himself. "Mattie?" he called to her once he'd let himself back into their room.

She awoke quickly but was still groggy from the depth of her slumber. "Is something wrong?"

"No, but your bath will be up here in a few minutes, and I wanted to give you time to get ready."

"My bath? Oh, thank you!" It took her a moment to remember, and she was thrilled with what he had accomplished for her.

"Will you need any help?"

"No, I'll be fine," she told him quickly.

"Then I'll go on to the dress shop and pick up your other gowns. That should give you enough time to bathe."

Before he could leave, a knock came at the door, and he opened it to admit the maids with the bath. Mattie pulled the covers up high as they hurried into the room to set up the tub.

"My wife is most appreciative of your help," Philip told them when they were leaving. He looked back at Mattie. "I'll leave you to your privacy now. I'll be back in about half an hour."

Mattie nodded, and he quit the room. When he'd gone, she got up and undressed quickly. She couldn't wait to take full advantage of the hot water.

Philip made his way to the dress shop and was pleased to find it was just opening as he got there. The dresses were ready. He headed back to the hotel, trying to strike the vision of Mattie bathing from his thoughts. It wasn't easy. He was half relieved when she was already dressed and ready to go to breakfast when he returned.

"So, what is it going to be like when we get to your fort?" she asked once they were in the restaurant.

Philip's expression turned serious as he looked at her. He had been anticipating this conversation but was not looking forward to it. "I'm afraid it's going to be different from anything you've likely experienced before," he told her.

"It is? Why?"

"Being an officer's wife may not prove easy for you. Much will be expected of you, and the other women..." He hesitated.

"What are they like?" she asked cautiously.

"It's been my experience that the other officers' wives can make life difficult for a newcomer if they choose to. Don't be surprised if they seem a bit close-minded or judgmental at first."

"They sound like a warm, wonderful bunch," she said drolly to cover her nerves. Would she end up embarrassing Philip instead of doing him proud?

"Sometimes they can be quite nice. I've seen them at their best and at their worst. I'd be lying to you if I said they were going to immediately accept you into their midst."

"What do I need to do to make them like me?" she asked, determined to do her best by her new husband.

"First, just be yourself," he began.

Mattie smiled at him. He almost sounded as if he liked her himself and wasn't the least ashamed of her less than glamorous circumstances.

Then he went on. "There are a few things, though, that are important to remember." His gaze held hers as he spoke. "You'll have to watch your language and your appearance. Don't ever cuss in front of them, and don't wear any kind of face paint or...gaudy attire."

"You don't think they'd approve of my red dress from the Palace?" Mattie asked. When she saw his stricken expression, she grinned at him. "Don't worry, General. I was only teasing. I didn't even bring that red dress with me."

"Good," Philip said. "Probably most important, though, is that you'd better not call me 'General' in front of them—especially not in front of the general's wife." He could just imagine the outrage that would ensue. "When you're with them, always be on your best manners. They will be judging both of us, you and me, by your behavior, so you have a standard to uphold. An officer's wife is to be an asset to his career."

"I am?" She suddenly felt a bit alarmed by all that he'd told her. "I thought we were just doing this so you could claim your inheritance at the end of the year. I didn't know I was going to affect your career when I agreed to marry you."

"Don't be afraid," he tried to reassure her. "It won't be that difficult. You'll do fine."

"But I really won't know anybody to seek guidance from but you, and I'm sure you'll be very busy most of the time."

"You'll have one ready-made female friend—I can guarantee that."

"Who?"

"Sheri," he answered, smiling as he thought of his novelist friend. He had once been rather smitten with Sheridan; she'd been the first real writer he'd ever met. He had hoped she might feature him in one of her dime novels she was writing, but she'd fallen in love with Brand, a scout at the fort, and had used him instead as the hero in a series of books. The books featuring Brand had sold well, the couple had married, and they were now ranching in the area. Philip was proud to call both her and Brand his friends.

"Who's Sheri?" Mattie asked suspiciously, suddenly wondering, judging by his expression, if there was another woman Philip truly loved.

"Sheridan is married to my friend Brand. He was a scout for McDowell. She's a writer."

Finding out that the other woman was married eased Mattie's fears. Hearing that she was a writer amazed her. "You know a real writer? I love to read."

"You can read?" Every day it seemed he was learning something new about Mattie that pleased him.

"Oh, yes. My mother insisted that I learn how when I was young. What does Sheri write?"

"Dime novels. I've got one with me, if you'd like to read it."

"I'd love to."

"Once Sheri learns you've read her books, you'll have a friend for life."

Mattie couldn't wait to get back to the room to start reading. "Will she be at the fort often?"

"She and Brand visit regularly. I think you'll like them both."

"From what you're telling me, I'm not sure how comfortable I'm going to be living at the fort, but I am going to enjoy meeting this Sheri."

"I'm sure she'll be glad to help you if you have any trouble with the other officers' wives."

"I've got the feeling I'm going to need all the help I can get."

"Well, let me tell you about the people you're going to be meeting." Philip took the time to describe all the women, their husbands, and their places in the hierarchy at the fort.

"I hope I can remember everybody," Mattie said when he finally finished.

"It may take you a few days, but I'm sure you will."

"I hope I can do you proud," she said, wanting to please him.

Philip's gaze met hers across the table. He saw the earnestness in her expression, and something tugged at his heart. "You will," he told her.

7

"We're here," Philip said as the coach slowed to a stop in front of the stage office in Phoenix.

"Already?" Mattie glanced up, surprised. The last few days of travel had passed quickly because Philip had given her one of Sheridan St. John's books to read. The hours and the miles had flown by while she'd been absorbed in the exciting tale. She was delighted, though, to learn that they were finally nearing the end of their long trip.

Closing the book, she prepared to descend from the stage.

Philip climbed out first and reached up to help her down. "I'll see about transportation out to McDowell," he told her as he stacked their baggage near the stage-office door.

"What should I...?"

"Philip?"

When they heard a man call his name, they looked up.

Philip broke into a smile at the sight of the tall, dark, broad-shouldered man coming toward them. "Brand! I can't believe you're in town!'

The two men shook hands.

"How did it go back East? I'm sorry about your father. Sheri and I didn't hear about his death until after you'd gone."

"It wasn't easy, but I've taken care of everything," he said, sadness in his tone. Then he brightened. "I have someone I'd like you to meet."

Brand looked to Mattie.

"This is my wife, Mattie. Mattie, this is Brand. I was telling you about him and his wife, Sheri."

"You got married?" Brand glanced at Philip in surprise. "You, the career officer, always too caught up in the military life to even think about starting a family?" Then he smiled warmly at Mattie. "I can see why it finally happened." He shot Philip an approving look. "Mattie, it's a pleasure to meet you."

Mattie looked up at the dark-haired man and smiled, realizing this was the real "Brand, the Half-Breed Scout" she'd been reading about in the book Philip had given her. "It's good to meet you, too. I've heard wonderful things about you and your wife from Philip, and I'm really enjoying your wife's writing." She showed him the dime novel she was holding.

"Sheri is going to love you, I'm sure," Brand laughed.

"Is she here in town, too?" Philip asked.

"Yes, and she'll want to meet Mattie and see you before you head back out. I'll go see if I can find her."

"I'm going to arrange our transportation to McDowell; then we'd like to get something to eat."

"Why don't we meet you at the hotel restaurant?"

Brand left to find his wife, while Philip took care of their business. A short time later they were seated in the restaurant, and Sheri came in with Brand.

"Philip, I am so sorry about your father," Sheri said as she approached him.

"Thank you." He stood to greet the pair. "Where's the baby?"

"With Maureen right now. But what's this Brand just told me about your getting married?" She smiled at Mattie.

Philip quickly introduced them.

"I love your writing," Mattie told Sheri without hesitation as the couple joined them at their table.

The two women launched into a discussion of the book Mattie had been reading, while Philip and Brand looked on in good humor. The meal was served, and the conversation never lagged. When it was time for Philip and Mattie to leave for the fort, Sheri and Brand walked out with them to see them off.

"I'll come to the fort with Brand the next time he makes the trip," Sheri promised.

"I'll be looking forward to it," Mattie told her, and she meant it. "I'm a little intimidated by everything Philip's told me about the officers' wives."

"Don't be. You'll do just fine."

Sheri's words bolstered her confidence, and Mattie was feeling much better as they began the last leg of their journey to the fort.

Mattie had never been at a military fort before, and she was impressed by what she saw when they arrived at McDowell. The parade grounds were spacious, and the buildings looked clean and well kept. Philip ushered her toward his quarters, and she noticed as they made their way that she was given many curious looks by the soldiers they passed.

"Welcome home," Philip said as he held open the door for her.

Mattie stepped inside. *Home.* She wondered if she would ever come to think of this place that way and immediately told herself it would be better if she didn't. Theirs was a temporary arrangement. It wouldn't do for her to get too attached.

"This is lovely, Philip," she told him.

"It's not very big, but I never needed much room before."

"This will be fine," Mattie assured him. The three rooms were larger than anything she'd lived in lately.

She roamed around, peeking into the bedroom and exploring the small kitchen.

"While you're unpacking, I'm going to report in to General Mason and let him know I'm back, although word had probably reached him already," he told her with a grin.

"Talk travels fast here?'"

"Very, and I'm sure there's a lot of speculation about who you are." He started for the door.

"Philip?"

He looked back.

"There is one thing. The bedroom-there's only the single bed in there."

"I'll check and see about a double."

With that he was gone, and Mattie was left staring after him. She had thought he might reassure her that he would be sleeping elsewhere. Or at least that he would get a second mattress. But it didn't look that way. Then again, she supposed, how would it look for newlyweds to be sleeping apart?

*

111

"How did everything go? Did you get your father's estate settled?" General Mason asked as Philip sat across his desk from him.

"Yes, sir. Everything's been taken care of."

"And what's this I hear that you've brought a young woman back with you?" he questioned in his usual blunt style.

Philip smiled. "I warned Mattie that news traveled fast here."

"This is my command. It's my job to know everything that happens here."

"Well, sir, I got married while I was away. My wife's name is Mattie."

The general rarely showed surprise, but Philip's statement did evoke a raised eyebrow. The general's daughter, Caroline, had hoped of winning Captain Long's affections. She would likely be distressed by the news that he'd wed. "Married? This is quite a surprise."

"I know, sir. I met Mattie, and, well, it seemed we were meant to be together."

"Congratulations, Captain."

"Thank you, sir."

"We'll arrange a celebration of sorts to welcome your bride to the fort."

"Thank you again, sir."

"But there is something serious going on, so I am glad you're back. There have been numerous Apache raids to the north and east of us. I need you to take a patrol and ride out at first light. Make a sweep of the entire area."

"Tomorrow, sir?" Philip had hoped to have some time with Mattie to help her get oriented.

"First light. That's an order, Captain." He was unyielding.

Philip saluted. "Yes, sir." He was a military man.

General Mason watched him go. In her pique, his daughter might just be glad that he'd sent Philip on such a dangerous mission.

*

"You have to leave tomorrow?" Mattie was staring at him, shocked. "Why?"

"Orders, Mattie," he answered.

Usually Philip accepted such orders willingly, he'd always

enjoyed the adventure. But the prospect of leaving Mattie alone, in a place where she knew absolutely no one, didn't sit well with him.

"I knew you'd have to perform your duties, but I didn't think you would be leaving so soon."

"Neither did I."

"How long will you be gone?"

"It's hard to say. Likely several weeks."

"What will you be doing?" she asked, curious.

"Tracking some Apache renegades."

Her eyes grew round. "Won't that be dangerous?"

He saw her concern and hastened to ease her fears. "We'll be fine. My men are the best. We'll find the raiders doing the killing and get back here as fast as we can."

"But you could be attacked yourselves," she said worriedly, considering his dangerous profession.

"We're always careful, Mattie."

"Couldn't someone else go in your place?"

"No. It's what I do. I'm a cavalry officer, and I'm very good at my job," he told her without false modesty. "Now, since I'm leaving so soon, there's a lot we have to do before tomorrow. I'll show you around the fort, so you'll know where everything is."

"This is where it's important we make sure everyone believes we're really married, right?"

"Right."

They left his quarters, and he introduced her to everyone they met as they walked the grounds. Philip watched Mattie with the others and was impressed by how well she handled herself. They stopped at the store and purchased the supplies she would need while he was away.

"Why, Philip, I didn't know you were back!"

Caroline Mason's call stopped Philip in his tracks, and gentleman that he was, he was forced to greet her with Mattie on his arm. Caroline was a pretty enough girl, with her blond hair and blue eyes, but Philip had never been attracted to her. Especially not after he'd found out how dull she was.

"Hello, Caroline. It's good to see you."

"It's good to see you, too," she said, flirtatiously, then turned a curious but slightly cold, assessing look on Mattie. "Who's this?"

"Caroline, may I present my wife, Mattie. Mattie, this is

Caroline Mason, the general's daughter."

"It's a pleasure to meet you," Mattie said smiling. Her smile faded, though, as she watched the other woman's expression turn even colder.

"Your wife?" Caroline bit out. Then she quickly recovered her composure. "Welcome to Fort McDowell. Well, I must be on my way."

Philip immediately steered Mattie toward the items they were after. Mattie glanced back to see the other woman striding from the shop, her back straight, her manner tense. She wondered at her response to Philip's announcement.

"Does Caroline care for you?' Mattie asked once they'd returned to his quarters.

"We've danced a few times at various social functions, but she never meant anything to me."

Mattie nodded, believing him. Certainly Philip could easily have married Caroline if he'd wanted to. It lifted her spirits a bit to know that he'd chosen her, when he could have had someone like Caroline Mason-a general's daughter and clearly a lady born and bred.

"I didn't have time to find out about getting another bed for us, but since I'm leaving first thing in the morning, I'll just sleep on the sofa tonight," he told her.

"I can take the sofa, if you'd like the bed. I don't want you to lose any sleep."

He gazed at her, knowing she meant it and wondering if she had any idea just how much sleep he had lost since their marriage. It would probably be a relief to lie alone on the sofa. At least he wouldn't have the temptation of her curled up so closely and so trustingly beside him.

"The sofa will be fine."

*

Later that night, as Mattie lay alone in bed, she found she was actually missing Philip. Though they'd shared only a few nights together on the trip, she'd become accustomed to his nearness, to the warmth of him and the clean, manly scent of him.

Mattie sighed and plumped up her pillow, seeking a comfort that was proving elusive. The painful reality that Philip would be riding out into danger in the morning haunted her. Through the long, dark hours of the night she worried about his safety and silently prayed that he would be safe while he was away from her.

The depth of her concern for Philip proved to Mattie all the more that she loved him. She had never let on, for she hadn't wanted to complicate things for him, but there could be on denying the truth of her feelings. She had never known a man like Philip, and she wanted him to come back home to her—even if their marriage was a sham.

The night passed, but Mattie got little rest. When she heard Philip moving around, she got up, donned her wrapper, and sought him out. She was surprised to find him already up and dressed. She thought he had never looked more handsome, so tall and proud in his blue uniform. He was a fine commander, she could tell. He had an air of authority and control about him.

"Philip?"

He looked up from where he stood buckling on his gun belt. "I'm sorry, Mattie. I didn't mean to wake you."

"Do you have to leave already?"

He nodded. "We have to head out at dawn. We can say goodbye now, and you can go on back to bed if you want."

"Would it be all right if I got dressed and went with you to watch you leave?" she asked, not ready to say goodbye to him just yet.

"If you'd like to, you can, but you'll have to hurry." He was strangely touched by her sentiment.

"I won't be but a minute," she promised, and she hurried back into the bedroom to dress.

Philip had just gathered his saddlebags when she appeared in the doorway.

"I'm ready whenever you are," Mattie told him, smiling to hide the truth of what she was feeling. She wanted to grab him and hold on to him and never let him leave, but instead she acted the demure young lady.

"We'd better go," Philip said, thinking she looked quite pretty and realizing for the first time that the just might miss her while he was away. "Will you be all right here alone?"

"I'll be fine. Don't worry about me. You just be careful."

"We will be," he assured her confidently. As deadly as the

renegades could prove to be, the scouts who rode with the troops were very good. He believed all would go well.

They left the house and made their way to the staging area. Most of his men were already there, waiting for the order to move out. Philip left Mattie alone for a moment as he spoke to Sergeant O'Toole, then he returned to say his final good-bye.

"I hope everything will be all right for you here while I'm gone," he told her, feeling a bit awkward. He'd never had to say goodbye to his wife before, and certainly not with an audience watching.

"I'll be waiting for you," Mattie said, gazing up at him in the first glow of the morning light.

Philip wondered whether he should make a show of kissing her or not. It was the perfect opportunity, so he decided to take full advantage of it. It wasn't often that he got the chance. "I'll see you when I get back."

With that, he drew her to him and pressed a tender kiss to her lips. He wanted to do more-so much more—but he couldn't. Not now. Not ever.

Mattie's heartbeat quickened as Philip's lips moved over hers. It felt so right to be in his arms, so right to be kissing him this way. But all too soon the kiss was over.

"Good-bye, Mattie," Philip said. He ended the kiss yet seemed almost reluctant to let her go. He stood staring down at her for a long moment.

"Captain? We're ready to ride, sir!" came the call.

Mattie noticed for the first time that the soldiers had all mounted up and were watching them with bemused expressions. She'd been so caught up in Philip's kiss that she hadn't even noticed that they were the center of attention. His kiss had touched her very heart and soul.

"I have to go," Philip said almost regretfully as he let his arms fall away from her. He stepped back and started off.

Mattie didn't know what made her do it, but, impulsively, she ran after him. "Philip!"

He stopped, frowning, and turned back to her. In a bold move, she wrapped her arms around him and kissed him soundly. A fire of desire ignited within Philip, and he crushed her against him, returning the kiss full measure.

A cheer went up from Philip's men. They knew their captain and his wife were newlywed, and they were pleased to see the display of affection.

Philip realized what he was doing then, and with iron-willed self-control, he broke off the kiss and set Mattie from him. "Take care."

"You, too," she whispered, blushing at the men's cheers.

Mattie watched as Philip mounted his impressive black stallion. When he reined the powerful horse in so he could glance her way one last time, Mattie saluted him smartly and called out, "I'll miss you, my general."

Philip smiled in spite of himself as he led the troops from the fort.

8

Mattie was crying as she sat alone and miserable in the parlor of Philip's quarters. She wondered, as feelings of unworthiness overwhelmed her, why she had ever agreed to be a part of Philip's deception. She should have known that she wouldn't fit in here. She should have known she wouldn't fool anybody with her act of being a lady.

Forlorn tears trailed down her cheeks as she thought about what she's just overheard at the Sutler's store. She'd wanted to get out of the house for a while, so she had gone to the store to look around. While she'd been wandering up and down the aisles, Caroline Mason had come in with her mother, Gloria. It was obvious they hadn't known she was there, for they had been talking about her.

"I don't know why Philip married that Mattie, Mother. She's nothing but a slut!" Caroline had said.

"Maybe that was exactly why," her mother had commented cattily.

"Do you mean you think she forced him to marry her?'

"Who knows? She certainly acts like a loose woman. Just yesterday, I saw her walking across the parade ground with Lieutenant Roberts. I wonder what they've been up to while her husband's away?"

Their conversation had continued, but Mattie had been so aghast at their cruel insinuations that she'd fled the store. Lieutenant Roberts had been helping her carry the groceries she'd bought. He had seen her struggling with them and had come to her aid. He had left her at her door, never venturing inside. He'd been a perfect gentleman, but Gloria had made the innocent encounter sound so dirty, so vulgar.

Her confidence had been shattered by the two women's remarks, and she wished with all her heart that Philip would hurry back. She wanted him there. She missed him.

A knock came at the door, surprising her. Now that she realized how the women at the fort felt about her, she really didn't want to talk to anyone or see anyone. Reluctantly, she wiped her eyes and went to answer the door. She was surprised to find Sheri standing there, holding her baby.

"Would you like some company? Brand had to come to the fort today, so Becky and I came with him." She had been smiling when she started to talk, but her gaiety faded when she realized Mattie had been crying. "Mattie? What's wrong? Are you all right? Has something happened to Philip?"

Sheri didn't wait any longer for an invitation. She stepped inside and closed the door. Mattie still hadn't spoken, so Sheri went on. "What's the matter? Can I do anything to help?"

Mattie sniffed loudly as she tried to pull herself together. "I'm fine, and so is Philip, as far as I know."

"As far as you know?"

"He had to ride out on patrol the first morning after we arrived here."

"If he's safe, then why are you crying?"

"It's nothing really." Mattie had a great desire to confide in someone, but she had to keep their secret.

"I don't believe that for a moment. You wouldn't be this upset if it was nothing." The baby began to get restless and fuss. "Can we sit down and talk for a while?"

"Oh, yes. I'm sorry."

They went to sit in the parlor, and Becky quieted immediately, content to play near her mother's side.

"She's a beautiful baby," Mattie managed.

"Thank you. She's our pride and joy. She already has her father wrapped around her little finger," Sheri told her with a grin.

They made small talk for a few moments, and Sheri spied the book Mattie had been reading.

"You really were serious about liking my writing."

"Very much," Mattie responded, glad to direct the conversation away from her tears. "Your books are fun. They keep me from being too lonely while Philip's away."

"It must be difficult for you, left here all alone like this. It's terrible that he had to ride out so soon. After all, you're newlyweds!"

"He had to go. He said some renegade Apaches had been raiding, and he had to go after them."

Sheri nodded, knowing how dangerous the Apaches could be. "We'll just pray that everything goes well for him and that he gets back to you real soon. Did he know how long he'd be gone?"

"He thought at least a few weeks. It's only been one week now, and I'm already missing him." She paused and smiled a teary smile. "Actually, I was missing my general as soon as he rode away."

"Your general?" Sheri laughed.

"That's my nickname for him. Philip can be quite impressive, you know."

Sheri thought back to their first encounter with him. "Yes, he can be. When I first met him, he was a lieutenant. He's proven himself to be a strong leader and an excellent cavalryman. Maybe one day soon he really will be a general."

Both women laughed.

"You're laughing now. That's good," Sheri told her.

Mattie smiled. "I'm glad you came by. It's been a rough morning."

"Do you want to talk about it?"

Mattie supposed it wouldn't hurt to confide a little, so she told Sheri about overhearing the general's wife and daughter talking about her at the Sutler's store.

"Oh, Mattie." Sheri sounded stricken. "That's terrible. I am so sorry."

"Lieutenant Roberts was just being a gentleman yesterday," Mattie said, her eyes welling up with tears again. "He carried some groceries for me, and he left me at the door. He didn't even come inside."

"Don't worry. I'm sure that even if Philip heard any such gossip, he wouldn't believe a word."

"I hope you're right. It's just that…" Mattie stopped when she realized how close she'd come to blurting out the whole truth.

"Philip loves you, Mattie. He wouldn't have married you if he didn't," Sheri said in reassurance.

A great sorrow filled Mattie. "If you only knew," she said

with a sad laugh.

"I know about love. Don't forget I do a lot of research for my books, and I know a love story when I see one. That man loves you, Mattie."

"This time I'm afraid you're wrong, Sheri," she said in a choked voice.

"Mattie, what are you talking about?"

"Can I trust you, Sheri?" Mattie felt in her heart that she could, but she needed her word on it.

"Oh course you can," Sheri said sympathetically, clearly eager to help in any way she could.

Mattie drew a ragged breath and started at the beginning. She told Sheri of her parents' death, of her desperation to get a job to support herself, and of ending up at the Palace Saloon. She'd expected disapproval when she told Sheri she'd been a barmaid and was amazed when she found the other woman smiling at her.

"I'm proud of you, Mattie. You're a survivor. Not many women could do what you did."

"I wish there had been some other way. But then again, if I had been working somewhere else, I never would have met Philip."

"How exactly did you meet?" Sheri asked, urging her on.

Mattie told her about that night at the saloon, how a drunken Micah Johnson had harassed her and how Philip had come to her defense.

"He is a gentleman," Sheri agreed.

She went on to explain how Cal had fired her.

"He fired you because you wouldn't prostitute yourself?" Sheri was shocked.

Mattie nodded. "It was terrible, and then, when I left, Micah and his friends were waiting for me. They grabbed me and—"

"They didn't…" Sheri looked horrified.

"They tried, but Philip saved me—again. I think it was in that moment that I knew I loved him," she said simply.

"And he swept you off your feet and you were married?" Sheri guessed romantically.

"In one of your books, it would have worked out that way, but not in real life."

Sheri gave her a questioning look. "What happened?"

Mattie drew another ragged breath, meeting Sheri's gaze. "I

didn't think I was ever going to see him again. But when he found out from the bartender the next morning that I'd been fired, he came to my room at the boardinghouse and made me an offer I couldn't refuse."

"An offer?" She sounded confused.

Mattie explained. "Philip's father's will stated that Philip had to marry within six months of the execution of the will, and stay married for twelve months, or he would forfeit his entire inheritance."

"No! What parent would do that to his child?"

Mattie shrugged. "So you see, Philip asked me to marry him, and stay married to him for a year, so he could claim his inheritance. It's to be a marriage in name only, and at the end of the year he'll pay me a generous amount and give me an annulment. The only trouble is, Sheri, I love him. I fell in love with him that night he saved me from those men. He's wonderful and..."

"And he doesn't realize what a treasure he has in you," Sheri finished with a conspiratorial grin. "How would you like to make this marriage a real one?"

"Oh, Sheri." Mattie looked at her hopefully for the first time. "Is there any way I can make Philip fall in love with me?"

"I think he's already well on his way."

"You do?"

"Yes. We just have to make him realize it."

"'We'? You'd help me?"

"Absolutely," Sheri said with conviction. "I like Philip, and I think he'd be making the biggest mistake of his life if he let you go."

"Thank you," Mattie's words were heartfelt. "But..."

"But what?"

"I'm just afraid that everyone is going to think like Caroline and her mother. I'm not a slut, but I may not be good enough for Philip. He deserves someone who is..."

"Exactly like you," Sheri finished. "You are lovely and smart and kind and thoughtful."

"But Philip is an officer, and he deserves a real lady for his wife. I don't know how to be a real lady."

"You *are* a real lady. The general's wife and daughter may pretend to be ladies, but on the inside, they're mean and vicious. How dare they say those things about you?"

Mattie shrugged, feeling helpless.

"All we have to do is work on your self-confidence and polish you up a bit."

"And we can do that?"

"Yes, we can—starting right now," Sheri said. "When Philip gets back, he's going to be thrilled to see you."

Sheri gave Mattie a confident smile as she began to plot.

*

Philip and his men were tired as they made camp for the night. He ordered guards posted but allowed no fire to be built. They were closing in on the renegades, and he didn't want to reveal their own location. After making sure everything was secure, Philip bedded down himself. He kept his rifle and sidearm close at hand. The renegades were ruthless, and he had to be ready for trouble at any moment.

They'd been trailing the Apaches for endless miles and days, and he believed they were close now. His scouts had told him that the band was hiding out at a canyon just up ahead, and he intended to attack with full force at first light. With any luck at all, they would trap the murderous Apaches there and end the reign of terror they'd been inflicting on the area.

Philip needed rest, but a vision of Mattie slipped into his thoughts: the image of her with her hair swept aside for him as he'd unfastened her gown. She was lovely. There was no denying it. And he missed her.

The realization shocked Philip. *Missed her?* Supposedly his "wife" meant nothing to him. They were friends, he supposed, but nothing more. True, they were married, but not really. Then the memory of the kiss she'd given him as he was leaving returned with a vengeance. It had been surprisingly sensual and definitely heavenly. He'd found that he'd hated to ride away from her that day. And then she'd jauntily saluted him!

Philip smiled in the darkness. Mattie had grit *and* wit. And he admitted to himself that he certainly would enjoy kissing her a whole lot more. No other woman had ever intrigued him the way she did. She'd faced rough times and places and people in her life, yet there was still an air of innocence about her that drew him to her. He wondered how she was doing back at the fort. He'd regretted leaving her alone there so abruptly, and he was eager to get back to her. He missed her.

Again Philip's smile turned to a puzzled frown.

He missed her? He questioned once more.

Damned right he did, he finally admitted to himself as he accepted the reality of what he was feeling. He loved her.

The thought left him stunned.

He loved her?

Was that why she seemed to be constantly in his thoughts? Was that why he found himself worrying so about her comfort and welfare? He had never been in love before. Was that why it had taken him so long to understand what it was he was feeling?

Mattie certainly was different from any other woman he'd ever known. She was brave and smart, thoughtful and kind. What more could he have been looking for in a wife? Mattie was perfect.

He grinned. The good news was, she was already his wife.

He scowled. The bad news was, she didn't want to be. Theirs was a business arrangement, nothing more. Money was the only reason she'd agreed to marry him. She didn't love him.

Then a flicker of hope shone in his dark thoughts. Just because she didn't love him now didn't mean she couldn't fall in love with him. He hadn't exactly courted her or tried to charm her in any way. They'd been married less than a month. He still had eleven more to go. Surely he could find a way to win her heart before the year was up.

As he lay there in the night, Philip made a battle plan. He would track down and defeat the renegade Apaches. Then he would lay siege to Mattie's heart. This was a war, and he intended to win it.

It might not be easy to win Mattie's love, considering how he'd treated her so far, but he wouldn't give up.

And after he'd won—Philip wouldn't even allow himself to consider the alternative-he was going to spend the rest of his life proving to her just how much he really cared.

9

Early in the morning Mattie heard shouts coming from the parade ground. She hurried from the house to see what all the excitement was about. Her heart skipped a beat as she saw a column of soldiers riding in, and she hoped against hope that it was Philip and his men returning. They looked hot, dirty, and exhausted, yet their expressions were proud.

"Did you find them?" someone called out.

"We got 'em!" one of the cavalrymen replied as he rode by.

Mattie searched each man's face, looking for Philip. *Where was he?* When she finally saw him, she broke into a broad smile. He was riding tall and proud in the saddle and looked every bit the commander he was.

Mattie ran toward him without a moment's delay. She didn't care what the other wives were doing. She knew only a desire to go to her husband and assure herself that he was all right.

"Philip!" she called out to him.

Even with all the noise and clamor at their return, Philip heard Mattie's call. He looked her way, and across the distance his gaze locked with hers.

Philip had never known an emotion as fierce as the need he had right then to hold her. He wheeled his mount around and rode toward her. Sawing back on the reins, he all but threw himself from his horse's back and swept Mattie into his arms.

They stood in the middle of the parade ground, completely immersed in each other, unaware of the activity around them, as if they were the only two people in the world.

Philip looked down at Mattie. He wanted to tell her that he'd missed her and that he loved her and that he never wanted to leave her again, but "I'm back," was all he could manage.

"I'm glad," Mattie said in a soft voice.

Boldly she looped her arms around his neck and urged him down to kiss her. She felt him tense as their lip touched, and she hoped that as a good sign. Sheri had counseled her on ways to be enticing to a man, and she fully intended to use all her friend's advice on her husband. Mattie made sure her kiss was warm and welcoming, and when they broke apart, she smiled up at him sweetly.

"I missed you, my general," she whispered.

"I missed you, too," he admitted in a gruff voice.

"Captain Long!"

General Mason's shout interrupted the intimacy of the moment, and Philip stepped away from his bride. "I have to report in."

"Will you hurry back to me?"

"As quickly as I can," he promised. As a man who prided himself on his career above all else, it amazed him that he meant every word he'd just said to her.

An hour later Philip returned to his quarters. It was the first time he'd ever come home to anyone, and he found he liked the feeling as he let himself in to find Mattie waiting for him. He had, however, gotten his rampant desire for her back under some semblance of control. He'd realized as he'd listened to the general drone on about what had happened at the fort in Philip's absence that he had come very close to picking Mattie up in his arms and carrying her into the house and making love to her. The urgent need had been real, but logic now dictated that he woo her and win her love first. He had promised he wouldn't hurt her or take advantage, and he was going to keep that promise.

Mattie had been wondering what was taking Philip so long, and she was delighted when he returned. But he seemed a bit remote to her, so she kept her distance from him. She reminded herself that the kiss they'd shared on the parade ground had been merely an act for those watching them, nothing more.

"How did you meeting with General Mason go?" she asked.

"Fine. Routine. But he did announce one interesting thing," he answered as he started to strip off his shirt so he could get cleaned up. "There's going to be a reception for us tonight at seven o'clock."

"There is?" She couldn't believe it. "Why?"

"To officially welcome you," he told her. "If I hadn't had to ride out so quickly, it probably would have been held that first weekend we arrived."

"Oh." Mattie was not looking forward to the party. She didn't trust the general's wife or daughter and could just imagine what they might do or say tonight.

"You don't sound very excited about it," he said as he tossed his shirt aside and glanced at her.

"I'm not."

"Why? It'll be a good opportunity to meet everyone."

"I think I've met all the people I want to meet here," she said quietly.

"Did something happen while I was gone?"

"You said you wanted us to always be honest, right?"

"Yes." Philip turned serious.

"Then you need to hear this from me before you hear it from someone else," she began. And she went on to tell him about Gloria and Caroline Mason's remarks at the store. "Lieutenant Roberts did help me carry groceries, but he was a perfect gentleman."

Philip grinned at her. "That's good to know."

She frowned, wondering why he was smiling. "It is?"

"Yes," he told her. "I asked Roberts to keep an eye on you for me. I'm glad he did."

Mattie stared at him as tears burned in her eyes. He had cared enough to ask someone to watch over her. It was one more reason to love him. "But what about what the women were saying?"

"Mattie," he said patiently, coming to stand before her.

Mattie found herself gazing at the broad, powerful expanse of his chest. She wanted to reach out and touch him, to caress the hard-muscled ridges of his chest and shoulders, but that kind of familiarity was forbidden to her. She clasped her hands before her and lifted her gaze to his.

"I warned you on the way here that you might have trouble with some of the women. Just ignore them. I know how they are, and I also know that Caroline is probably more than a bit jealous of you."

"So she did love you then."

"No. There was no love between us. I might have seemed a good match for her, but I wasn't interested. You're the woman I married, Mattie." He made the statement firmly, wanting to put her fears to rest about any relationship he might have had with Caroline.

Mattie ached to believe that he'd said that to impress her with his devotion, but she knew better. She moved away, needing to distance herself from him, and busied herself laying out clean clothes for him while he bathed.

The day passed quickly. Philip had duties to attend to around the fort, so she was left to her own devices. She started getting ready for the party early, wanting to make sure she looked her best for Philip. She decided to wear the dress she'd gotten married in, for it was her most fashionable gown. Sheri had shown her how to style her hair up, and she worked on it for quite a while, artfully arranging it so she would look more sophisticated. She hoped Philip would approve. She had just put the finishing touches to her coiffure when she heard him return.

"Mattie?"

"I'm in here," she called out.

Philip was not looking forward to the reception tonight, but he knew there was no way out of it. He would do what was expected of him, but he would rather have had an evening alone with Mattie. He strode toward the bedroom door and stopped short at the sight of her. He blinked, finding it hard to believe that this was the same girl who'd served him drinks at the Palace Saloon. Any and all traces of that Mattie were gone. In her place was a sleek, gorgeous woman who took his breath away.

"You are beautiful," he said tightly. He forced himself to remain where he was, when all he wanted to do was sweep her up in his embrace and carry her to the bed that was oh, so nearby.

"You like my hair this way?" she asked nervously. She wanted to look her best so he would be proud of her, but she was having trouble reading his expression.

"Very much. I guess I'd better get ready, too, if we're going to be on time for this reception."

Mattie quickly left the room so he would have privacy while he was changing. Philip watched her go, admiring the view.

A short time later, as Philip and Mattie drew near the general's home, they could hear music coming from inside. He glanced down at her, thinking she might be a bit nervous going into this reception. He was surprised and pleased to see that she seemed calm and sure of herself.

"Good evening, General Mason, Mrs. Mason, Caroline," Philip greeted them as he and Mattie entered the house.

"Good evening, Captain Long, Mrs. Long," the general and his wife replied.

Caroline stood with her parents in the receiving line but managed only a tight smile. The look she turned on Mattie was cold.

Mattie saw it and chose to ignore it. She smiled serenely at the other woman and held on to Philip's arm. She would do him proud tonight. After tonight, no one would ever say she wasn't a lady again.

There were many people at the reception when they arrived, and Philip drew Mattie around the room, making sure that she met all his friends. When the dancing began, he turned to her and asked, "Would you like to dance?"

She was so glad Sheri had drilled her on dancing, which she'd never done before. "I'd love to, my general," she told him, lightly resting her hand on his shoulder as he led her onto the dance floor.

"Keep it to a whisper tonight if you're going to call me general," he teased.

"Yes, sir."

Her expression was innocent enough, but there was a hit of devilishness in the curve of her lips. Philip was staring down at her, very, very tempted to kiss her. Instead, he concentrated on dancing, sweeping her around the floor. She moved gracefully with him, and he was delighted that she was so good at the steps.

"The locket looks wonderful with that dress," he told her. "My mother would be most pleased."

"Your mother?" The knowledge touched her heart.

"It was hers," he admitted. "The wedding ring was, too."

Mattie looked down at the simple gold band that marked her as his. "I'm proud to wear them. She must have been a wonderful lady."

"She was," he confirmed.

The song ended, and Philip seemed sorry to let Mattie go.

The musicians almost immediately started up again, but before Philip could prevent it, Mattie was claimed for the dance by one of the single young officers. Philip smiled and bowed slightly to her as the man led her away.

Philip got himself a cup of punch and went to stand at the

side of the dance floor. He noticed that Caroline was not dancing, but he made no move to go to her and invite her to dance. He wanted nothing to do with her, knowing what Mattie had told him. He remained where he was, watching his wife. When that dance ended and another started, Mattie was claimed by Lieutenant Roberts before Philip could get to her. She gave him an apologetic look, but he only smiled in approval. It wasn't often that a new woman came to the fort, and he understood how much the single men enjoyed dancing with a lady. He'd felt the same way—before Mattie.

"Your wife is most popular tonight, isn't she?" Caroline said as she came to stand at his side.

"Yes, she is," Philip agreed. He was certain that Caroline wanted to dance with him, but he was not going to ask her. He turned his attention back to Mattie's dancing.

Caroline was stung by the way he ignored her. "There are things you don't know about that precious wife of yours." Her tone was hateful.

"Really?" He did not even glance at her but kept his gaze warmly on his wife.

"Yes, really!" she said, growing angry. "While you were gone, she was acting like a slut. Why, she was flirting with the very man she's dancing with!"

Philip stiffened at her words. He turned on Caroline, his temper barely under control. "I would be careful whom you say such things to, Caroline," he ground out.

"That's why I'm telling you," she said, trying to sound sympathetic. "I thought it was important that you know your wife's a…"

"Don't say it," he snarled.

Caroline saw that his anger was real, and she realized, too late, that perhaps she'd handled this the wrong way. But it was too late to change course now. "Well, it's just that I saw them together, and I thought you should know when your wife is whoring around."

"For your information, Miss Mason, Lieutenant Roberts is my friend. Since Mattie didn't know anyone here at McDowell, I asked him to keep an eye on her. I had a feeling that you 'ladies' wouldn't be all that welcoming, and it looks as if I was right."

"But…" Her eyes were wide as she looked up at him, frightened by the anger she saw in his expression.

"I think you've said enough for one evening, Miss Mason. If you'll excuse me?" He turned his back and walked away from her.

Caroline watched him go, her expression pale and stricken.

The music ended, and Philip went straight to Mattie and took her in his arms as the next song began.

"You look angry," she said. "Is something wrong?"

Philip looked down at her and saw the openness and beauty that he loved. "No, nothing's wrong. In fact, everything is very right, Mrs. Long."

He had never called her that before. "I'm glad."

"So am I." He tightened his arms about her just a little to bring her even closer to him.

Mattie loved the feel of his arms around her. The other two men had been nice to dance with, but only Philip's touch sent shivers of awareness through her. The power of him, the scent of him, the warmth of him, all touched her. She loved him and never wanted to be away from him again. She wanted to tell him of her love, but she held back, fearful of his reaction.

And then their gazes met.

In that moment, somehow, they both knew the truth. Passion flared in the depths of Philip's eyes. Mattie instinctively responded, her pulse quickened, and she trembled before the power of his desire.

"I'm new at this military—wife thing. I don't know protocol, but would it be rude if we left now?"

"You just read my mind, wife," Philip said in a husky voice. "Let's go."

He swung her around and maneuvered them closer to the door. Without speaking to anyone or saying any goodbyes, they slipped away into the cool, dark night.

10

Outside, Philip took Mattie's hand and led her quickly away, seeking someplace where it would be just the two of them, alone and uninterrupted. As they passed a deserted walkway, he drew her into its shadowed privacy.

The stood together; neither speaking, just looking at each other. Then, ever so slowly, Philip drew Mattie to him and kissed her. His mouth claimed hers hungrily, telling her without words just how much he wanted her, how much he needed her. She responded without reserve, wrapping her arms around him and glorying in her nearness.

Philip gave a low growl as he ended the kiss. He knew that if he continued it there, they might not make it back to his quarters. Mattie looked up at him, a bit confused by his abrupt ending to a wonderful embrace.

"Let's go home, Mattie," he said softly, and he took her hand as he started toward their house.

Neither spoke, as if each were fearful of breaking the magical spell of the moment.

Overhead, the moon was a silver sliver surrounded by twinkling stars. Mattie made a wish on the first one she saw.

Philip was tormented. He loved Mattie. He wanted to make love to her. He wanted to hold her and never let her go. But he still wasn't quite sure how she felt. True, her kiss was heavenly, and she seemed to be willing, but what is she wasn't? When they reached their quarters, he opened the door for her. He followed her inside and locked the door behind them.

Mattie went to light the lamp, but Philip stopped her. He

took her in his arms again and held her close. She melted against him, reveling in the intimacy of the moment. She wondered, though, why he wanted to hold her. There was no one around now.

"Philip," she ventured, needing to know what he was thinking, "we're home. We don't have to pretend anymore."

"I'm not pretending," he finally admitted.

"You're not?" Mattie pulled away to look up at her general.

"No, Mattie. I love you," he said simply. He kissed her again, tenderly, softly. "I want you to be my wife in all ways."

She was stunned and tears filled her eyes. She'd never dreamed he would fall in love with her, despite her planning with Sheri. Deep in her heart, she'd doubted he would ever love her. She was Mattie Jackson, barmaid from the Palace Saloon.

"Sweetheart, what's wrong?" he asked at her silence.

"You're my general, Philip. You deserve better than someone like me. You deserve a real lady," she told him, her voice choked with emotion.

"Ah, Mattie, how many times do I have to tell you? You're more of a lady than anyone I know."

He kissed her passionately this time, wanting to feel her response, wanting to know that she wanted him as much as he wanted her. Mattie needed no further encouragement. She surrendered to him, conquered by the power of his love.

Philip's lips left hers to trace a pattern of fire down her throat. She arched against him, wanting to know more. He lifted his hands to pull the pins from her hair, and the dark, glorious mane tumbled about her shoulders in a cascade of curls. He raked his fingers through the silken tresses, then sought the back of her gown and unfastened it. The dress slipped from her shoulders, but this time Mattie didn't try to stop it. She stood before him clad only in her petticoats and chemise.

"You're beautiful, Mattie," Philip said, reaching out to caress her.

She swayed weakly against him, overwhelmed by the emotions that filled her. He swept her up into his arms and carried her into the bedroom, laying her gently upon the single bed. After shedding all his clothing but his pants, for he didn't want to frighten her, he followed her down upon the bed, covering her body with his. He began to caress her, taking infinite care to arouse her and please her. He loosened her chemise and freed her breasts to his caresses and kisses.

Mattie gasped in shock at the exciting sensations this touch aroused but soon gave herself over completely to his ministrations. She had never been intimate with a man before, but this was Philip. This was her husband. This was the moment she'd been waiting for, longing for. He had told her that he loved her. But with the one last shred of sanity she had left, she knew she had to make sure he really wanted this-really wanted her.

"Philip?"

He lifted his head to gaze down at her, all the love he felt for her shining in his eyes.

"You know that if we make love…" she blushed before she finished. "We won't be able to get an annulment."

He smiled at her and chuckled. "Good."

"But…"

"Mattie, remember when you told me I was your general and you'd follow any order I gave you?"

"Yes," she answered hesitantly.

"Then love me, Mattie," he told her softly, "and that's an order that stands for a lifetime."

"Yes, sir," she answered.

And she did.

They lived happily ever after.

LOTTERY OF LOVE

1

Strains of the Beach Boys' "Little Deuce Coupe" played in the background as Zach Thomas made an adjustment to the engine of the '65 Mustang he was restoring.

"That should do it…" he said to himself, satisfied that he'd finally found the problem and fixed it.

This red, 2+2 Fastback was the car of his dreams. He'd been working on it in his spare time for over a year now and had been enjoying every minute of the challenge.

Ducking out from under the hood, Zach wiped the grease from his hands on a rag and slid behind the wheel of the car. He turned the key, and, as the engine roared to life, a smile of pure masculine satisfaction lit up his face. His hard work had paid off. Life was good.

"Hey, Zach! You working late again?'

Zach looked up to see Rod Matthews coming through the garage's side door. He turned off the engine and climbed out to talk to the nineteen year old college student who worked for him part-time. "What are you doing here this time of night?"

"I was driving by and saw the lights on. I thought you might be working on your baby." Rod gazed at the classic car with admiration. "Sounds like you finally got it right."

Zach threw the greasy rag at him in good humor, and Rod agilely dodged it. Zach turned to back to the engine to make one more final adjustment.

"There. Now, turn it on for me. I want to listen and see if—"

Rod didn't need to be asked twice. He loved the old Mustang and hurried to climb in. He gloried in the fantasy of sitting at the wheel. This '65 was one cherry machine. The engine roared to life like a finely-tuned instrument.

Zach frowned in concentration as he listened. Finally, he nodded to himself and waved to Rod to shut it down.

"All it takes is a gentle touch, the right tools, and perseverance," he said with satisfaction, slamming the hood and wiping any imaginary fingerprints off the paint job.

"Wouldn't those rules work for women, too?" Rod asked with a laugh as he came to stand beside his boss. He'd known Zach for years. Zach had been part of a group of friends his older sister, Elise, had hung out with during high school. Rod had always admired him and was glad to be working for him. Zach's Collision Plus, his garage and auto body shop, was the best in town. Zach had worked hard to build and maintain a sterling reputation, and Rod knew it was well-earned. No one was more honest or did better work than Zach.

"Who has time for women?" Zach quipped in return. "This little beauty takes up all my spare time."

"What are you going to do with it, now that it's finished?"

"I haven't decided yet," he said evasively, but in his heart he knew exactly what he wanted to do with it. He wasn't about to share that with Rod or with anyone else for that matter.

"Well, it's worth a pretty penny. You ought to sell it and start on another one. What was it worth in '65?"

"Retail ran about thirty-two hundred dollars."

Rod laughed. "You could get twenty grand for this one, easy, if you ever decide to sell."

"We'll see." He turned away from the car and started back toward his office at the rear of the garage with Rod following. "So, you were out just driving around bored?"

"No, I was studying at the library."

"What's your sister up to tonight?" Zach asked casually.

Rod glanced at his watch. "Right about now, she's making a sales pitch to Aaron Benedict."

"Aaron Benedict—the new owner of the Tigers?"

"The same. She's trying to land a contract with him to handle all of his catered affairs for the football team."

"That's exciting."

"I'll say. She sent him a proposal a week or so ago, and his office contacted her earlier this week to set up the appointment. This morning she was really nervous about making the presentation.

"She'll do great. She's a class act. This catering business of hers is sure to succeed."

"I hope so. It would really mean a lot to her. The contacts she'd make through the pro football team alone would be fantastic."

"If anyone deserves a break, it's Elise." Zach's words were heartfelt.

Elise had taken over raising Rod all by herself after their parents had died three years before. Her catering business had been brand new then and struggling, yet she'd assumed full responsibility for her younger brother. She was putting him through college now, even though their money was tight and they were scrimping on just about everything.

"It would be wonderful if she got this contract. Just think, I might get to meet all the pro football players."

"Let's hope she does."

"You like Elise, don't you?" he asked.

"Of course. I've known her since we were in high school."

"How come you two never hit it off? I think you'd probably get along great."

Zach shrugged. "I don't know. We've both been busy and just never got around to it."

"She was pretty heavy with that guy, Brad, for a while."

"And I was going out with Diana."

"Your timing's just off, I guess."

"I guess." Zach refused to be drawn into any speculation with Rod. Any feelings he had for Elise were private. He'd always thought she was beautiful and he had been attracted to her, but somehow, things had never worked out. That's why they'd remained just friends through the years.

"You ought to ask her out sometime."

"You playing Cupid? It's not even Valentine's Day."

Rod grinned and trailed after him into his small office.
page break?

Elise could barely contain her excitement as she held out her hand in a very professional manner to Aaron Benedict. "Thank you, Mr. Benedict. You won't be sorry you hired me."

"I'm sure I won't. Your company has a wonderful reputation for innovation and excellence. I'm looking forward to our association and hope it will be a long and prosperous one." The tall, fair-haired, sophisticated millionaire took her hand in a warm, firm handshake.

Elise smiled up at him. "Me, too. I'll get started on the plans for your kick-off media party right away. I'll have the details to you within a week. That way you'll have plenty of time to decide exactly what you want."

"I'm counting on having your undivided attention during these projects. That will be possible, won't it?" He met her regard squarely as he held on to her hand just a moment longer to emphasize his words.

"Of course. I always work very closely with my clients."

"Good. Then we understand each other." He smiled and moved away from her. He'd first seen Elise Matthews, owner of Catering Elegance, the year before at a social event he'd attended. He'd found her to be a bright, attractive young woman, and he'd been impressed with her work. Now that he'd bought the football team, he had the perfect opportunity to get to know her better on both a business and personal level. It would not present a hardship to him to have to work side-by-side with her on future projects. "I'll look forward to hearing from you."

"Yes, sir."

"My name's Aaron, Elise. We're going to be working together over the coming months, so there's no need to stand on formality."

"Fine, Aaron," she said his name softly, testing it, liking the sound.

"I look forward to hearing from you next week."

His phone was ringing, and he turned away to answer it. Elise knew she'd been dismissed and gathered up her briefcase and portfolio. She all but floated from his office. She managed to maintain her outward, controlled, businesswoman demeanor until she'd climbed into her car and shut the door. Only then did she let out the scream of excitement she'd been biting back since Aaron had told her she'd decided to go with Catering Elegance.

"Yes!" she shouted, victorious. At last, her life was changing…and this time for the better.

She headed home, eager to find her little brother Rod and celebrate. They could make it now! She'd just signed a six-figure contract with the millionaire owner of the Tigers. Catering Elegance was going places!

Elise was feeling on top of the world as she drove home. Up

ahead, she spied a gas station, and, feeling very lucky right then, she pulled in to buy some lottery tickets. It had been a long-standing family joke started by her father years before that one day someone in their family was going to be rich. He'd bought his lotto tickets twice a week, and after his death, Elise had continued his tradition. The last she'd heard, the pot was up to around ten million. She could be happy on ten million, and if she didn't play, she couldn't win. In a fit of extravagance, she bought five tickets and hurried off again in search of Rod.

It was by pure coincidence that Elise found herself driving past Zach's garage and caught sight of Rod's car parked out front. She pulled in near the side door.

"Rod? Zach? Are you in here?" she called out as she found the door unlocked and let herself in.

"We're back here!"

At the sound of their answering call, Elise rushed to tell them the good news.

"This is so exciting!!" she exclaimed when she reached them.

"You got it?" Rod asked, trying to contain his excitement.

"I got it!"

Shouts of happiness erupted from all three of them. Rod and Elise embraced. Zach, caught up in the celebration, gave Elise a big hug too.

"Congratulations!"

Elise was laughing as he set her away from hm. "Thanks, Zach. I guess Rod told you all about it?"

"He was just filling me in. It's about time something went right for you."

"You've always been my biggest cheerleader." Her dark eyes were sparkling with delight as she looked up at him. She couldn't remember a time when Zach hadn't been there for her. He was one of her best friends. "I think this calls for a celebration. What about you two?" Elise asked.

"Absolutely," Rod agreed. "Where can we go?"

"I'm not exactly dressed for a night on the town," Zach looked down at his grease-stained work clothes. They were hardly suited to dining in a good restaurant, and, as late as it was, it would take him too long to get cleaned up.

"We could order a pizza and eat here," Rod suggested.

"That sounds fine."

"Are you sure?" Zach asked Elise, who looked slim and elegant in her business suit and heels. "I don't want to ruin your big moment. You deserve to have a night out."

"A night out would be great, but pizza's all my budget can afford. I may have gotten the contract, but I haven't seen any money from Aaron yet."

"Aaron?" Rod said, surprised and awed. "You're calling him Aaron?"

"That's his name." Elise's color heightened a little. "He asked me to call him that since we'll be working so closely together."

"Cool." Rod grinned. His sister was calling the owner of the Tigers by his first name. With any luck, he could end up sitting on the sidelines with the football players during a game.

"Are you two game for pizza, or do I have to find myself two new dates?" Elise's question jerked Rod back to reality from his teenage fantasy.

"I'll eat pizza anywhere," he quickly answered her. "Wow! My sister and Aaron Benedict!"

"Don't get too excited there, big boy," she cautioned. "This is business."

"Yeah, yeah."

"What about you, Zach?"

"Sure," Zach agreed, glad to be celebrating her good fortune with her. He knew how much it meant to her to be successful. Several times in the past few years, when he'd known they'd been strapped for cash, he'd found ways to give Rod a bonus to help out. He'd known better than to offer the money directly to her. As proud as she was, she would have refused it and struggled on her own. "But I'm buying."

"It's my celebration," she argued. "Let me."

"No, not this time. You can buy next time."

"Are you sure?"

"Positive."

The pizza was ordered and quickly delivered. As they settled in to enjoy the fare, Rod lifted his soda in toast to Elise.

"You done good, Sis."

"Here, here," Zach seconded, taking a deep drink of his own soft drink.

"Thank you, sirs. Now, all I have to do is the best work I've ever done." The thought was a bit unnerving, but she knew this was her big break. She couldn't let any doubts or fears affect her performance.

"You will," Zach told her.

"I'm glad you have faith in me."

"There's never any doubt about that. What do you have to plan first?"

"A big kick-off party for the media at the end of the month."

"So, we're going to be hobnobbing with the rich and famous that soon?" Rod asked.

"You got it."

A silly grin spread across his face as he drifted off into his fantasy world again. "And to think, I used to resent dressing up and helping you with the catering."

"How times do change," she said with a shake of her head. "Well, I guess I'd better call it a night. I've got to get started bright and early in the morning. You ready to head out?" She looked at her brother.

"I'm all set." He rose and grabbed a piece of pizza to take with him. "Race you home."

"No way. The last thing you need is a speeding ticket."

"Aw, Elise... You're no fun."

"Good night, Zach." She dug in her purse for her keys and accidentally dropped her lottery tickets.

"You're still buying lottery tickets?" Zach asked.

"You'd better believe it, especially tonight. I was really feeling lucky after I left Aaron."

"Didn't your dad always buy them?"

"You remember that?"

"Oh, yeah. He always swore he was going to be a big winner one day."

"Well, I'm carrying on his tradition." She picked up her tickets and safely towed them away again. "The pot's up to over ten million dollars. If I win... no, when I win, it'll be only the Ritz, limousines, and Dom Perignon for me—no more pizza in a garage at midnight."

"You ready, Elise?" Rod opened the door for her.

"Yes. Good night, Zach, and thanks for the party."

With that, she and Rod were gone.

Zach stood in the doorway of the garage staring after them until their tail lights had disappeared from view. He turned then and looked around him. The heavily shadowed workshop looked abandoned. It was certainly a far cry from the Ritz. The cars parked inside or repairs looked dead and abandoned. To the untrained eye, the walls where the myriad of tool of his trade hung looked like a scene from a nightmare. It wasn't pretty, artistic, or sophisticated. It was just his life. And he loved it.

"The Ritz, limousines, and Dom Perignon…" he muttered to himself as he returned to his office to finish off the daily paperwork.

Zach sat at his desk and picked up the last piece of pizza, intending to finish it off. As he stared at the cold pizza in his work-scarred hand, he realized he was not Ritz or Dom Perignon material. He was just Zach Thomas, who loved to work on cars.

In irritation, Zach tossed the slice aside. Scowling, he went back to work.

2

Elise stood proudly in the banquet hall as all around her the entire press corps, along with reporters from all the major TV and radio stations, and the elite of the city's society celebrated the beginning of the professional football season. Players and coaches mixed with socialites, newsmen, and bankers. All were partaking of her fancy canapés and commenting on the wonderful decorations and theme for the evening's event.

"Magnificent, my dear," Aaron breathed in her ear as he came to stand next to her.

Elise glanced up at him and her breath caught in her throat. In a tux, she found him to be even more handsome and sophisticated than usual, and that was hard to believe. "You like the party?"

"I love it. The jungle theme…the waterfall…tropical flowers… How did you manage all this?"

"Secrets of the trade," she answered easily, with a smile. She wanted him to think that all had gone smoothly, but the truth be told, she'd had one heck of a time convincing the zoo officials to allow her to use of their tropical birds in the setting.

"It was a stroke of genius. I especially love the tiger sounds in the background. It adds just the right touch of danger and excitement."

"This *is* football."

"Do you like sports?"

"I love sports, and I've been a big fan of the Tigers ever since I was a little girl. I used to watch the games with my father. I know this is only your first season as owner, but I think you're going places."

"I hope so. I want to win the Super Bowl, and with a few

strategic trades and the right breaks, I think we'll have a run at it this year."

"I'll be rooting for you."

He grinned down at her as he slipped an arm about her waist and gave her a slight hug. "I'm counting on it."

"Mr. Benedict!" a reporter from the Daily News called him. "Do you have time for a short interview?"

"I have to go," Aaron told Elise. "We'll talk later?"

"I'll be here."

"Good." He flashed her one last, quick smile and moved off to join the eager reporter.

Elise watched him go and wanted to pinch herself, to see if all this was really happening. The comments she'd heard from the guests as she'd made the rounds of the room earlier had made her heart swell. Everyone was enjoying the jungle theme. The waterfall seemed the favorite of many—for cameras were flashing almost constantly as the teams' Tiger mascot passed there with fans for pictures.

Taking a glass of champagne from a passing waiter's tray, she took a deep drink. It felt wonderful to be mixing with the rich and famous, and to be accepted by them. She glanced down at the sleek gown she wore. It was the one big splurge she'd allowed herself, for she'd known she had nothing suitable in her wardrobe for an occasion like tonight. Most of her clothes were practical business suits or jeans for relaxing. She'd never done any work of this magnitude before, but she was ready now. Today, she'd proven she was good enough, and she was glad everything had gone so well, for she'd wanted to impress Aaron.

"Well done, Sis," Rod said as he joined her for a minute. He was wearing a tux and had been overseeing the circulating waiters. "There are TV cameras everywhere."

"When Aaron does something, he does it right."

"I'll say. Wow! I even got to meet Concrete McAllister!"

"You did?"

His eyes glowed as he recounted his conversation with his favorite player for the Tigers. "Zach is going to be so jealous!"

"Zach? He likes Concrete, too?"

"Oh, yeah. Zach's his biggest fan. He thinks Concrete is the reason the Tigers will be a contender this year. It's a shame Zach couldn't come with us tonight."

"Do you think he would have had a good time?" She glanced around at all the people dressed to the nines.

"He would have suffered through it for the chance to meet the players. You ought to see if you can get him invited to some of this stuff. He'd love it."

"We'll see." Elise pictured Zach in his tight T-shirt and jeans, and she smiled. She'd never seen him in a tux and wondered how he would have fit in with the rich and famous. Zach was a down-to-earth guy. He cut right to the heart of any situation and dealt with it straight on. It was one of the qualities she liked best about him—his complete honesty.

"I'd better get back to work," Rod told her. "I've got a real mean boss."

"I know." Elise grinned at him.

"She brings out the best in me, though."

"You sure?"

"Positive." He winked at her as he moved off.

Elise smiled as she watched him go. Rod was turning into a fine young man, and he was pretty good-looking, too, with his dark coloring and quick smile. She knew their parents would have been proud of him.

The rest of the evening went smoothly. It was nearly two in the morning when she found herself supervising the last of the clean-up.

"Superb," Aaron said when he found her near the back of the ballroom.

"I'm glad everything went so well for you."

"For us. We're a great team, you and I."

"We are?"

He'd been holding a bottle of champagne and two crystal glasses behind his back, and he lifted them up now for her to see.

"Here." Aaron handed her a glass and filled it for her, then filled his own. "Congratulations, my dear, on a job well done."

"Thank you," she murmured, enchanted by his thoughtfulness.

She lifted her glass to his and then took a sip just as her eyes met his. For that moment, she was caught up in the power of his blue-eyed gaze. She could easily understand how women fell under the spell of powerful men. Aaron was handsome, wealthy, and sophisticated. What was not to like? She found herself smiling at him, and she barely tasted the champagne.

"To us," he said softly, taking a deep drink from his own glass. He was about to say more when Rod called out.

"Elise! I've brought the van around. Are you ready to start loading?"

His call shattered the intimacy of the moment and jarred her back to reality. "I'd better finish getting things cleaned up." She set her empty glass aside.

"We'll talk next week?"

She nodded. "I'll have the first tentative plans for the big fund-raiser ready for you to go over by mid-week."

"I'll be looking forward to it."

She flashed him a smile and stared to turn away.

"Elise?"

She looked back, and Aaron was still there, his gaze warm upon her.

"Good night," he said gently.

"Good night," she responded, and then hurried off to work with Rod.

Aaron had enjoyed the evening, but he'd enjoyed even more watching Elise pull the entire celebration together. Elise Matthews was a very talented lady.

Rod immediately collapsed onto his bed when they finally got back home in the early-morning hours. It was Sunday night, and he had classes the next morning.

Elise, however, was too excited to even think about sleeping. She'd done it! The media party had gone off without a hitch! She changed into comfortable casual clothes, then went to work on the fund-raiser. It had to be even bigger and better than the media party had been.

"Haven't you been to bed yet?" Rod's sleep-heavy voice jarred her from her work hours later.

"Oh, hi! No, I had a couple of ideas for the next party, and I wanted to get them down on paper." She suddenly realized that sunlight was shining through the windows.

"You must be exhausted."

"I am, but it's worth it. It went great, didn't it?" She turned to look at him.

"It was wonderful."

She beamed at his praise. "I've got to be even better with this next one. That's why I went straight to work on it last night."

"Well, get some sleep today. I'm gonna shower and get out of here. I've got a nine o'clock class," he groaned.

"Do you work tonight?"

"No. It's my night off, but I've got a hot date with Susie Johnson."

"Not too hot, I hope."

"Aw, Sis, you worry too much."

"It's my job," she said with a grin as he stumbled into the bathroom to shower and shave.

Elise watched him go, proud of the man he was becoming.

It was almost noon when she finally decided to rest. She was so tired, she didn't even bother to undress before she fell across her bed. She was asleep almost as soon as her head hit the pillow.

The sound of the doorbell hours later finally awakened her. She buried her head even deeper in her pillow, but whoever was at the door was not going away. Cursing under her breath, she dragged herself from bed and went to see who was so insistent on waking her. She smoothed her hair back and opened the door, not caring that her clothes were rumpled.

"What is it?" she asked, then discovered it was Zach. "Oh... Zach. Hi."

A slow, lazy grin spread across his face as his gaze swept over her. "You were sleeping?"

"Um..." she said, stifling a yawn as she held the door wide for him. "You want to come in?"

"Sure." He moved past her into the small, two-story house. "How did the party go?"

"Just great. I think Aaron was pleased."

"Good. I'm glad to hear that. Is Rod here? I needed to tell him something about work tomorrow."

"No, he had a date tonight. I haven't talked to him since this morning."

"Well, just tell him that I need him to come in as early as possible."

"I'll tell him," she said wearily.

"How late did you stay up last night? You look completely worn out."

"Actually, I didn't get to bed until almost noon."

"Why?"

"I had a great idea for the next event. It's a charity ball, and I promised Aaron I'd have the first plans to him by Wednesday."

"You're not going to get anything to him if you kill yourself in the process. When was the last time you ate?"

She frowned. "I don't know. Sometime early yesterday. I guess. I didn't eat last night at the party because I was too excited."

"How about I fix you something before I go?" He glanced toward her kitchen, knowing she probably had a well-stocked pantry.

It had been so long since anyone had worried about her that she was startled by the kindness of his offer. "What?"

"Something to eat. You're a caterer. Surely, you've got something in the kitchen I can turn into a meal for you."

"But…"

"You're tired, right?"

"Very."

"You need to eat, right?"

"Yes," she agreed with a small smile.

"Well?" Zach grinned at her.

He looked so earnest that Elise didn't know what else to say, so she simply said, "Thanks."

"Go rest. I'll call you when it's ready."

He disappeared into the kitchen, leaving her standing alone in the living room. She wasn't used to the luxury of someone waiting on her. She almost felt a little useless, but she was too tired to worry about it. Taking Zach's advice, she decided to take a shower and freshen up. She knew she must look a mess, and she would certainly feel brighter once she'd cleaned up her act.

While Elise showered, Zach checked out her pantry. He found the pasta he'd sought and then dug through her cabinets for the pots he needed. As he'd suspected she had homemade sauce in the refrigerator. He tested it, searched for her spices and added his own twist to her concoction. A head of lettuce provided the base for a salad, and he added butter and garlic salt to rolls before popping them into the oven. Satisfied that she'd have enough to eat, he sat down at the kitchen table to wait for her return.

As he glanced toward the pantry again, he spied the stub of a candle on the stop shelf. If he was fixing her an Italian dinner, the least he could do was provide the right atmosphere, too...

3

Elise emerged from the shower to find the mouth-watering aroma of Italian cooking filling the house. She threw on jeans and a sweater, then quickly dried her hair. Not bothering with makeup, she headed for the kitchen, more than ready for whatever her personal chef had prepared. To her surprise, the kitchen was dark.

"Zach? What happened? Did you blow a fuse?" she asked as she started into the room. She stopped short when she saw the one and only pitiful candle she kept in case of a power-outage burning brightly in the top of a two-liter soda bottle in the middle of her kitchen table.

"Welcome to Tomaso's Ristorante," he said in a terrible mock-Italian accent.

"Thank you, sir," she responded, playing along.

"We live to please our customers." He bowed and held out a chair for her. "Have a seat."

Elise found herself giggling at his antics as she slipped into the chair. She'd been working so hard for so long that she'd almost forgotten what it was like just to relax and have fun. "It's a good think you have a day job."

"I am sorely wounded." He put a hand to his heart and tried to sound aggrieved.

"Oh, I'm sorry. It does smell delicious, and I'm sure you must have worked hard to achieve this wonderful atmosphere..."

"I would have used a Chianti bottle and been really authentic, but I couldn't find one," Zach joked, dropping his accent. "How hungry are you?"

"Very."

He quickly placed a delicious-looking salad before her. "Do you mind if the hired help eats with you?"

"You mean I'm paying you?" she teased.

"You better believe it."

"How much? Union scale?"

"Better. One smile, and all the pasta I can eat. Deal?"

"Deal. I didn't know you liked to cook," she remarked digging into the salad.

He shrugged. "If there's time, it can be fun, but usually I'm too busy or too tired when I get off work. Fast food can become a way of life if you let it."

"I understand completely."

"So tell me all about your media party. I read the gossip column in the paper this morning, and the columnist was sure singing your praises. I'll bet your phone at the office is ringing off the hook with job offers."

"Good. Job security and a guaranteed income are wonderful things, especially with college tuition and Rod's car insurance." She paused to take a bite. "Ummmm... what did you do to the salad dressing? It's really different."

"An old family secret. My mother was Italian, so I picked up a few cooking hints here and there."

Zach dug into his own salad as Elise told him everything that had happened at the party.

"Aaron even said we made a great team," she finished, remembering clearly his words to her. A thrill shot through her, and her eyes gleamed with excitement.

Zach had been watching Elise as she talked. Her loose dark hair curled softly around her shoulders. It looked silken, and he wondered if it would be that sleek to touch. Her complexion was flawless, and her eyes were dark and expressive. She was his idea of gorgeous. He wondered idly if she had any idea how he felt about her, and realized she didn't. She considered him a good friend, and he'd never done anything to disabuse her of that belief. Any time either one of them had been available, the other had been involved with someone else.

Tonight, however, in the candlelight, celebrating her success with her, his feelings stirred and came fully to life. He wanted her.

"You know, I do have a bottle of Merlot in the basement if you want some," she said, thinking a glass of wine would go well with the meal.

"I should have thought to check your wine cellar earlier."

"I keep my aged stock downstairs."

They both laughed. Her throaty chuckle stirred him even more. "I think I would like some."

"I'll get it, if you'll get the glasses," she offered. "I have some fine plastic ones there in the cabinet by the sink."

"I've always been partial to better plastic," he responded, going to claim the poor man's substitute for crystal while she went to retrieve the bottle from the basement.

He opened it for her when she returned, then poured them each a glass.

"Ah…Candlelight, fine wine, a beautiful woman…" He settled back in his chair as he took a drink. "Not bad."

"You're right. Candlelight, fine wine and a good-looking man make for a great evening," she agreed.

He chuckled. "How did your lottery tickets do last week? The jackpot's really up there."

"You know, I've been so busy, I didn't even check the numbers the other morning!" She jumped up and got the tickets off the front of the refrigerator where she'd left them under a magnet. She grabbed the morning paper and searched for the right page. "Let's see. Maybe I'm a winner!"

Zach watched in amusement as she scanned the numbers in the paper and on her tickets. Her expression when from hopeful to pained.

"Nothing," she complained. "Not even one number matched, and I bought all these tickets! I'm just a loser, with a capital L."

"Aren't we all when it comes to the lottery? I just figured we're donating to someone else's millions."

"That's the truth. But my dad always said I'd be rich one day, and I'm holding him to that."

"Was he psychic?"

"No, but my dad never lied to me."

"It's a happy thought, but in the meantime, I think we both have to keep working."

"There is a connection, isn't there?" She finished off her glass of wine and held it out to him for more.

Zach obliged just as the buzzer went off on the stove. "Are you ready for your next course?"

"It smells wonderful."

He dished up full plates of pasta and sauce for both of them, and put the platter of hot garlic bread dripping with melted butter on the table. They began to eat in earnest then, and her expression reflected her delight in his culinary talents. The look on her face was so rapt that Zach finished off his wine, poured himself another full glass and downed most of it.

"Thank you." She sighed blissfully as she sat back after eating almost every bite on her plate. "I don't usually eat this much, but that was delicious."

"If my shop goes out of business, you can back me in a little Italian restaurant."

"You're on, but we'd have to think of a good name for it."

"You don't like Tomaso's Ristorante?"

"If I'm backing you, I want equal billing."

"Spoken like a true nineties woman. Let's just hope I don't end up cooking for a living. I'm much better with engines than I am with stoves."

"Rod says you do have a way with cars."

"I love them. They're sleek and powerful. There's nothing like the feeling I get when I've been rebuilding an engine, and I finally get it right. When it roars to life." A smile curved his lips at the thought.

Elise found herself staring at his mouth, wondering why she'd never noticed how handsomely chiseled his features were. The shadow of a day's growth of beard darkened his lean jaw. As she lifted her gaze to his, she found his dark-eyed regard upon her, his expression unreadable. Her pulse quickened in instinctive response, and that puzzled her. This was Zach.

"You like the feeling of power?" Her voice was almost breathless as she took another sip of wine.

"I like knowing these hands had the power to bring it back to life," he said quietly.

Elise let her gaze drop to his hands. They were strong hands, powerful, yet capable of the most delicate of touches, she was sure. Otherwise he wouldn't be able to do what he did so well. She looked up at him again, and in that instant their gazes locked.

Time stood still. Awareness of their surroundings faded, until it was just the two of them, alone in the soft, flickering candlelight.

The instinct was older than time, and Zach responded to it. He rose and went to her, taking her hand in his and drawing her up to him. He didn't speak, not daring to risk ruining the moment. There were just the two of them, alone in the semi-darkness.

Zach bent to her, slowly, gently, fearful of breaking the spell that had woven itself around them. Elise was caught up in the moment, aware only of the sensual scent of his aftershave and the warmth of his hand holding hers. When his lips sought hers, she gasped slightly, but did not draw away. Encouraged, he brought her into the circle of his arms.

The wine had cast a warm glow over the moment, and Elise gave herself over to the sweetness of it. Held close to his heart, she lifted her arms to link them around his neck. It felt right to be in his embrace.

Her move was an invitation that sent a jolt of awareness through Zach. He shuddered as he deepened the kiss, his mouth moving hungrily over hers. He had wanted—no needed—her for a long time.

Elise responded to his kiss with equal fervor, enjoying the feel of his hard, muscular body. She moved against him, tangling her fingers in the hair at the nape of his neck as she gave herself over to the unexpected thrill of his nearness.

"What smells so good in here?" Rod called out as he came through the front door.

At the sound of his voice, they moved quickly apart.

"Zach cooked dinner for me," Elise called back. She went to stand at the sink just as her younger brother strode into the kitchen with Susie on his arm.

"You cook?" Rod glanced at Zach where he was sitting in a chair at the table, looking quite relaxed, downing a glass of wine.

"You can't eat pizza every day," he returned easily, revealing none of the turmoil that was churning inside him as he finished off his wine and poured what was left in the bottle into his glass.

"I didn't know you were coming over tonight. If I had, Susie and I would have hurried home."

"I didn't know I was coming by either, but just as I was getting ready to close, three rush jobs came in. I stopped off hoping I'd catch you to tell you to come in as early as possible tomorrow."

"I'll be over right after class."

"Good." Zach drained the glass and stood up to go. "Elise,

thanks for dinner."

"My pleasure," she answered with forced ease. "You did all the cooking."

Her smile was tight, but only Zach noticed.

"Good night. I'll show myself out, and I'll see you tomorrow," he said to Rod.

Zach got in his car, but he didn't immediately drive off. Instead, he sat there, staring sightlessly at the steering wheel. One minute he'd been in heaven and the next... In frustration, he started the car and pulled away from the curb. It was going to be on long, lonely night.

Elise visited with Rod and Susie for a few minutes longer as she finished cleaning up the kitchen, then excused herself and went to her room. She was still tired and would have slept, except the memory of Zach's unexpected embrace was burned into her consciousness. Restless and confused, she sat down at her desk and went back to work. Aaron expected these plans to be on time, and she wanted them to be perfect.

As the hours passed, though, Elise realized she wasn't getting a lot done. Mostly, she'd been sitting there, thinking about Zach. She'd known him for years and had never realized just what a strong, handsome man he was. She wondered what had ever possessed him to kiss her that way and realized it had probably been the wine and the candlelight. It didn't get much more romantic than Tomaso's Ristorante.

Elise smiled and tried to go back to work.

4

"You have reached Catering Elegance. We're out of the office, but will be glad to return your call. Please leave your name and number, and we'll get back to you as quickly as possible. Thanks."

Zach glared at the phone, blaming it for his misfortune in missing Elise again. This was his fourth attempt that day. He hadn't left messages the other times and decided not to leave one now. Sooner or later, he was bound to catch her at her desk. He hung up and went back into the shop.

He started working on a car with a vengeance, wanting to banish the memory of Elise's kiss. It kept haunting him. It had even kept him up most of Monday night, and that was why he wanted to see her again. He needed to find out if she had reacted the same way as he had to their embrace.

He had spoken to her Tuesday morning, but the conversation had been short and stifled. She'd been at the office, surrounded by her staff, working on the plans for the Tigers' charity event that she had to present to Benedict that week. She'd ended their two-minute conversation by telling him to call her the following week.

Here it was a week, later, and he still hadn't managed to get in touch with her. He'd been wanting to ask her out. The fund-raising event was that following weekend, and he was hoping she'd have some time to relax. Things just weren't working out, though.

Earlier in the day, he'd wondered if he was missing a subtle message, but when Rod had come in to work, he'd told him how hard she'd been working on the event all week, putting in fifteen-hour days, and how excited she was about her meetings with Benedict. It seemed they were meeting every day to go over the plans. Zach knew she was just doing her job, but he was finding it difficult to be patient when he remembered the sweetness of her kiss...

"We are switching to our remote at Tigers Headquarters," the radio personality announced, interrupting their scheduled programming. *"Tigers owner Aaron Benedict has called a news conference to begin in three minutes. Reporter Dan Tyler is on site. Tell us, Dan, what's the word on the street?"*

"Rumors have been flying all morning about possible trades, but no one seems to know anything for sure. We'll just have to wait and see what Aaron Benedict has to say."

Both Zach and Rod looked up at the radio in surprise at this news.

"I wonder what's going on," Rod said.

"Hard telling with this new guy in charge," Zach replied.

"Good afternoon, ladies and gentlemen," Aaron Benedict said after coming to the lectern to make his announcement. *"I'm here today to announce some exciting changes we've just made in player personnel. As of today, Ace Knowlen and Concrete McAllister have been traded to the Washington Redskins for Derek Jones and a future first-round draft pick."*

"What?" Zach and Rod both yelled, sharing the same furious expression as they stared at the radio.

"That no-good..." Zach swore.

"I can't believe he'd do something like this!" Rod blurted out. "Trading McAllister! Doesn't he realize how important he is to the team? Doesn't he realize how many fans he's going to alienate?"

"I guess he just doesn't care." Zach was disgusted.

"This is terrible. The season might as well be over."

The announcer came back on as Benedict ended his announcements and left the podium. *"Fan reaction here in town is going to be interesting. Concrete is a favorite. His following is phenomenal."*

The station cut to an interview with a furious fan who wanted McAllister to stay and Benedict to go, and Zach walked over and turned off the radio.

"And Elise likes him? Unbelievable," he said. "The man's obviously an idiot. Trade Concrete McAllister? He's our best player!"

"*Was* our best player," Rod corrected.

Zach shot him an angry look. "How could Benedict get rid of Concrete? And why would he want to?"

"There has to be something going on. Maybe Elise will know when she gets home tonight. I'll ask her."

"It won't make any difference to me. I'll never root for the Tigers again. Not without Concrete."

"You're not going to start rooting for the Redskins, are you?" Rod was aghast.

"You just never know," he answered, still scowling. "I had some hope a couple of months ago when Benedict first bought the team, but now I think he's the worst owner ever. We should get all of Concrete's fans together and run Benedict out of town."

"It wouldn't bring Concrete back," Rod mourned.

"I know, but I'd feel better." And Zach knew he would feel better if Benedict was gone. Elise might have a free minute. Of course, she might be out of a job then, too. He scowled, wanting the best for her, but resenting the rich owner.

The sound of the phone ringing distracted him from his dark thoughts, and he wiped off his hands and went to answer it.

"Collision Plus," he answered in a gruff tone.

"Zach? Thank heaven you're still there!" Elise sounded upset.

"Elise? What's the matter? Is something wrong?" He immediately tensed at the sound of her voice. "Are you all right?"

"Oh, I'm fine, but my car's not. I was just leaving Aaron's office, and it won't start. I tried to get Rod, but he wasn't home. Could you come down and tow me in? I don't know what's the matter with it, other than it's just worn out." Her worry was obvious.

"Where are you?"

"In the high-rise garage right across from Aaron's office building. It's at Sixth and Broadway."

"I'll be there in less than half an hour." He asked her a few more detailed questions about what was wrong with the vehicle and hung up.

As much as Zach was sorry she was having car trouble, at least this presented him with the perfect opportunity to be alone with her. He would have preferred to be cleaned up when he went to see her again and not wearing his dirty work clothes, but if she was having car trouble, she'd be glad enough to see him no matter what he looked like.

"Rod, that was Elise on the phone. Her car's quit on her, so I'm going down now to tow her in."

"I'll go with you." Rod stopped what he was doing, ready to help.

"No, you stay here and keep working. We have to get that car back to its owner tomorrow." He gestured toward the vehicle Rod had been working on. "I'll be back as soon as I can. If anything else comes up, just call me on the radio."

"You got it. Geez, I hope it's nothing too bad with Elise's car. Of the two we've got, hers is the best."

"If anybody can fix it, we can," Zach said confidently. "I'll be back."

He made the trek downtown in record time, considering the near rush-hour traffic, and located the garage she was parked in with no trouble. He found Elise standing next to her dead car on the third level. She looked so downhearted that he found himself smiling as he climbed out.

"It's not that bad. It's not like your best friend died or something."

"It feels like it," she countered, managing a weak smile as she looked at her older, very over-worked car. It had more than a hundred and fifty thousand miles on it, but it was all she had. "The day was going so well and now…"

"Relax. It could be something really simple. Let me take a quick look."

He opened the hood of her car. After getting into her vehicle and trying to start it up several times with no luck, he took one last look at the engine and slammed the hood shut.

"Well?" she asked expectantly.

He approached her solemnly, like a doctor reporting on a life-or-death surgery, but there was a twinkle in his eyes. "It's going to require work—but it'll live."

"Oh, you!" She was laughing now. It always amazed her how Zach could lighten her mood. No matter how bad things seemed to be, he always found a way to make her feel better. A distant memory of how he'd been there for her when her parents were killed returned. He'd been her rock, always there, always supporting her in a quiet sort of way.

"I'm going to have to take it in to figure out exactly what's wrong, but I can drop you by your house on the way, if you want."

"That'd be great. Thanks."

Zach climbed back into his truck and positioned it to hook up to her car. After taking care of all the cables and making sure it was secure, he opened the passenger-side door and spread a reasonably clean towel on the seat. She looked so elegant that he didn't want to risk getting her dirty.

"Want me to help you climb in? We're about ready to go."

"Thanks."

Even though she was wearing her best business suit and heels, Elise didn't hesitate. She grabbed her briefcase and purse and went to Zach. He took her things from her, stowed them safely behind the seat and then offered her a hand up. She took it and allowed him to help her up into the cab. As she settled in, Zach shut the door and circled the truck to climb in himself.

"I really appreciate all your help with this," Elise said as he put the truck in gear.

"That's what friends are for."

"What a mess." She sounded exhausted. "I've got so much work to do with the charity event on Saturday, and now I'm going to be car-impaired."

"So that's the socially correct term for it?"

"Car-less, wheel-less and car-deprived work, too," she quipped.

Zach was laughing as he started to pull away with her vehicle in tow. He was about to swing clear when a limo blocked his way. He slammed on the brakes to avoid a collision.

"What the hell...?" he snarled, angry that the other driver could have caused a wreck right there in the garage."

As he was swearing, the window rolled down in the back of the limo and Aaron Benedict looked out at him.

"Elise! My secretary just told me about your misfortune. There's no need for you to ride home in a tow truck. I'm leaving the office now, and I can drop you by your house."

She was completely caught off guard by Aaron's offer. She'd made the call from his secretary's desk because he'd been in a business meeting, and she hadn't even known that he'd been aware of her problem.

"Well, Zach was going to..."

"I'm sure Zach wouldn't mind delivering your car to you once it's repaired," Aaron said with challenging arrogance as he looked straight past Zach at her.

Zach's grip tightened on the steering wheel. He wanted Elise with him. He'd been looking forward to having a few minutes alone with her for days and now Benedict—

"We can go over those last few details you were talking about earlier," Aaron called out, appealing to the businesswoman in her.

"Zach?" Elise looked to him, to see what he thought. "Do you mind?"

"Do whatever you want to do," he replied nonchalantly. His own acting ability was amazing. "You know where I'll be."

"Thanks," she told him, thrilled that Aaron thought enough of her to offer her a ride.

Gathering her things, she slipped quickly from the truck and hurried to get into the limo.

As she entered the luxury vehicle and settled back on the leather seat, Zach was treated to a quick glimpse of slender thigh before the door slammed shut. He stared after the limo as it pulled away and then looked around himself at the well-used interior of his tow truck. He gave a shake of his head as he pulled out with her car in tow.

Zach knew he couldn't be angry over Elise's decision to ride with Benedict. Who would want to ride with him when they could ride in a limo? He'd known all along how Elise felt about being rich; no doubt riding with Benedict would feel like a dream come true, and he wouldn't want to deny her that chance. She'd have been crazy to pass it up.

He sighed and maneuvered his way out of the parking garage as quickly as possible so he could start working on her car tonight. As he headed for Collision Plus, the only thing that was really bothering him was that she was riding with Benedict.

"I'm sorry about your bad luck with your car," Aaron was saying as he sat back next to Elise in the plush interior.

"Me, too. Car trouble was the last thing I needed with the event coming this Saturday."

"Do you think he'll be able to fix it in time?"

"If it can be fixed, Zach can do it. He's the most talented mechanic I've ever met. He has a way with cars that's just amazing."

"Interesting," Aaron, replied, not really caring. He just wanted to make sure she was taken care of. "Well, if things don't work out right, just let me know and I'll send a car for you."

"That's very kind of you, but I should be all right."

"Do you have plans for the evening?" he asked, changing the entire mood of the moment.

"Only work, why?"

"What do you say we have dinner?"

"Now?" Her eyes widened at the prospect. Aaron Benedict had just asked her out.

"Now," he replied. "I've got a nine o'clock meeting, but I'm free until then. I've been wanting to spend some time with you away from work—to get to know you better."

His statement surprised and pleased her. "I'd love to have dinner with you."

He smiled at her and gave orders to the driver to take them to one of the best restaurants in town.

"At last, we can relax for a while."

"I don't think I remember how," she said with a rueful laugh.

"I'll teach you," he said in a low voice.

His words sent a shiver of awareness up her spine.

Their conversation turned to other topics as they settled into an easy companionship.

"I'm sure my brother Rod and Zach aren't happy with you right now."

"The trade?"

"Exactly. Concrete has been their favorite player for years. Trading him is not going to sit well with them or the other fans. Why did you do it?"

"It was strictly a business decision," he answered, having anticipated the reaction that he knew would be forthcoming from the disgruntled fans. "I'm sure they'll get over it in time."

"Maybe, maybe not," she countered. "Concrete was involved in a lot of charity work around the city, and people really relate to him and like him."

Aaron gave her a benign smile. "Once they see what a great team we're building, they'll get over it."

"I hope you're right for the team's sake. It doesn't pay to alienate the fans."

"If we're winning, they'll be with us. Everyone likes a winner," he answered confidently as the limo stopped at the door of the restaurant.

Their dinner was magnificent. Elise had dined there before when she'd been trying to come up with new and more exciting ways to promote her business. She'd been impressed then and was even more impressed with the standard of service and the delicious food tonight.

"Aaron, this was wonderful. Thank you so much for this evening," she said as she finished dessert.

"It was my pleasure, believe me. What's your calendar look like for the rest of the week?"

"Work, work, and work. Being self-employed is rough. The boss knows exactly what you can get done in any given length of time and expects you to deliver."

"It's not much easier being in the corporate world. At least as your own boss, you have some semblance of control."

"You have control," she countered. "You own the team."

"And that's precisely why I bought them without taking on any investment partners. I want to be the one who makes the decisions—good or bad. It will fall on my shoulders, and I'll take the praise or the flak, whichever comes."

Elise found herself admiring him even more as she teased, "You're going to get a lot of flak about Concrete."

"I just want them to give me a chance. Like I said before, once we're winning, they'll understand why I made the moves."

She lifted her glass of wine to him. "To a winning season for the Tigers."

"Here, here," he seconded, and touched glasses with her.

Aaron had met a lot of beautiful women, but there was something about Elise that set her apart from the others. Maybe it was her willingness to speak her mind with him or just the openness of her personality, but whatever it was, he was drawn to it.

"Elise, I was wondering…"

She looked at him expectantly and realized again just how good-looking he was. His blond hair was razor cut, and the short style was perfect on him. Fierce, competitive intelligence burned in his blue eyes, and she knew he was a force to be reckoned with.

"Would you be my official date for the charity event?"

She blinked, surprised and thrilled by his offer. "I'd love to, but…"

"No buts." He stopped her. "I know you have to supervise everything. I'll be busy with the media and players, too. We'll both be taking care of business all night, but I would love to have you on my arm whenever you can get away from a few minutes. "What do you say?"

"Thank you, Aaron. I'd love to be your date Saturday night."

A short time later they were in the limo on the way to Elise's home.

"I'll see you tomorrow?" Aaron asked.

"I don't know. I'm going to be running all over town taking care of last minute details."

"Well, if you get time, stop by the office for a few minutes. I'd love to see you."

At his words, she looked up at him as he sat beside her, and in that moment, Aaron boldly took her in his arms and kissed her.

It was Elise's Cinderella dream come true. She was in a luxury car being kissed by a rich, handsome man. She turned to him, kissing him back, enjoying the moment as the car came to a halt in front of her house. When he released her, she smiled at him.

"Good night, Aaron."

"Good night, Elise. I'm looking forward to Saturday night."

His words followed her as she left the car, and she stood there on the walk up to her house watching as the driver pulled away. Only when she turned around did she realize that Zach and Rod were standing on the front porch waiting for her.

5

A heated flush stained Elise's cheeks as her gaze met Zach's, and she was glad for the concealing darkness.

"Not too shabby coming home in a limo, Sis," Rod quipped, completely missing the tension between them.

"Aaron decided to take me out for dinner," she returned as she moved to join them. "Hi, Zach. Did you managed to get my car fixed already? I was just telling Aaron how good you were."

"I'd love to tell you that it was that simple and already repaired, but it's not. That's why I came over. I know you've got the big fund-raiser Saturday and you'll need wheels, so I brought you something to drive until I get the part in I have to order for you."

"How long is it going to take?"

"If the distributor has it in stock, I can have it Monday and have your car ready by Monday night. Until then…Well, here are the keys to the car I'll give you as a loaner." He held the key chain out to her.

"Are you giving me the tow truck to drive?" she asked with a laugh. Their hands touched as she took it from him, and she realized how kind it was of him to have taken care of her this way.

"No way, Elise," Rod spoke up. "Zach knows how much that charity event means to you. Take a look at what he parked around back for you to drive for the rest of the week."

She glanced quizzically at the two men, then left the porch to circle the house, leaving them to follow. She was amazed to find Zach's restored '65 Mustang Fastback waiting for her. She couldn't believe he was being so generous. She knew how much the car meant to him, how long he'd been working on it.

"You carriage awaits you, ma'am," Zach said gallantly.

"I can't drive this," she protested.

"Why not?" He was startled by her refusal, and thought for a moment, that since she'd been riding around in limos all night, she didn't want to be seen in such an old car.

"Because it's your pride and joy." She looked at him in amazement. "You've worked hard to restore it. What if something happened to it? I'd never forgive myself."

"It's heavily insured. Besides, if something does happen, I know this guy who does great auto body work…"

She laughed at his good humor. "But Zach…"

"Don't worry about a thing. I want you to drive it. You'll look great in it."

Elise was grinning at the thought of being behind the wheel of the shiny red Fastback 2+2. "I will, won't I?"

"It may not be as classy as the limousines you're getting used to, but…" he began.

"It's classier," she said in all seriousness. "Thanks, Zach. This is so sweet of you." On impulse, she leaned toward him and kissed him on the cheek.

"Ah, Sis," Rod said, lightening the moment. "Zach isn't being sweet. He's being a good businessman. This is just good customer service."

"So you loan your Mustang out to all your customers?" she asked them both.

"Hardly," Zach said with a grin.

"That's what I thought, but you know, it's an idea. They have Rent-A-Wreck. How about opening Rent-A-Hot Mustang? You'd do a booming business on Prom Night."

"You know, you ought to come to the fundraiser Saturday night. It should be fun."

"How dressy is it?"

"Formal."

"I'd hate to pull up in the tow truck wearing a tux. Since you're going to have my best set of wheels, would you want to pick me up?" he suggested, thinking that at last they'd be having a real date and get to spend some time together.

"I would love to, but I can't."

"You're going to be working too much?"

"That, and Aaron asked me to be with him for the evening. I can get you tickets and Rod could pick you up, though—if you'd like to go," she offered, trying to solve his dilemma.

"I'll have to check and see. It'll depend on work," he replied evasively. "I'll let you know."

"Great." She looked back at the perfectly restored car and was thrilled at the thought that she was actually going to get to drive it. There was a twinkle in her eyes as she asked Zach, "You need a ride home, don't you?"

"I could walk, but a ride would be nice."

"Let's go, but there's one condition."

"What's that?" he asked, wondering what she was up to.

"I'm driving."

"You're on."

"Good. Rod, I'll be back in a few minutes." Keys in hand, she climbed into the sports car.

"The lady's driving," Zach shrugged and smiled, managing to sound carefree as he, too, got in.

Elise started the car and grinned at the roar of the powerful engine. She glanced over at Zach and gave him a dare devilish look. "You're really going to trust me with this?"

"Am I making a mistake?" he countered, meeting her regard with a challenging look of his own.

"Let's find out." She gave it gas and they raced from the driveway, turned sharply, and with a squeal of tires disappeared down the street. She glanced only once in the rearview mirror to see her brother running out into the street to watch them drive off.

Neither Elise nor Zach spoke as she drove around town. She was enjoying controlling the muscle car. Occasionally, she glanced over at Zach to see whether she was making him nervous, but he seemed relaxed and happy. They'd been driving for about twenty minutes when he spoke up.

"Turn in at White's." He pointed toward the old circular drive-in restaurant where everyone went to hang out their senior year in high school.

"Think we'll impress the kids?" she asked as she pulled into a parking place.

"No, but I always promised myself that one day I'd show 'em. I'd come here in my hot car and look really cool."

"You did?" She stared at him in amazement.

"Yeah," he said, grinning at her and looking boyish. "But that was over ten years ago. The people I was trying to impress are long gone."

"I never knew you cared about impressing anyone."

"There's only one person I want to impress now…" Zach's gaze caught and held hers. He started to lean toward her, instinct guiding him. He wanted—no needed—to kiss her again.

"Nice car, lady!"

The intimacy of the special moment vanished as a teenage carhop came running up to take their order.

"Had it long?" he asked eagerly.

"Less than an hour," she replied. "It's really his."

"Excellent," the boy, said nodding approvingly to Zach as he checked out the rest of the Mustang.

"Thanks. A lot of work went into restoring it," Zach told him.

"I can tell. Someday, I'm going to have a car like this."

Across the width of the car, Zach and Elise shared a knowing smile.

"What'll you have?" the teen asked, forcing himself to get back to work and quit dreaming about fast cars.

They gave him their orders, surprising each other as they both ordered the same thing—a chocolate shake. When the boy had dashed off to place their order, Elise turned off the headlights, and they settled in to wait. They watched the comings and goings of the drive-in with easy companionship and discovered that it was still the popular place it had been years ago. Their shakes were delivered, and Zach insisted on paying. They devoured them quickly, and Elise groaned as she finished off the last of hers.

"That as delicious," she sighed, closing her eyes in ecstasy. "Thanks, Zach."

"You're welcome."

His gaze was warm upon her as he thought of how beautiful she looked tonight. He was about to tell her that when she sat up straight and started the engine and turned on the lights.

"Are you ready?"

"If you are," he answered, sorry that they couldn't stay longer, sorry that their earlier moment had been interrupted and he'd been unable to recapture it.

"Whether I want to be or not, I have to be back at work first thing in the morning. The closer Saturday gets, the more harried I get."

"It'll be fine. You did a great job on the media party. You'll be great again Saturday."

"I'm glad you think so."

"I know so."

She felt buoyed by his confidence in her and smiled at him just as the carhop came for their tray. She pulled out of White's onto the main street.

"One more stop and then I'd better get you home. It's getting late," she told him.

"You don't have to worry about me. I don't have a curfew."

"So I wouldn't get into any trouble if I kept you out past midnight?"

"None whatsoever."

She pulled into a convenience mart and parked. "I'll be right back."

"What are you doing?"

"I haven't gotten my lottery ticket yet. The drawing's tomorrow night. Every Friday and Monday, you know."

"Well, wait a minute. I'll go with you and get one of my own."

They were back in the car a few minutes later, tickets in hand. Elise had bought ten, Zach only one.

"I can't believe the pot's over forty million, and you only bought one ticket.

"It only takes one ticket to win."

They drove off for Zach's house. Elise pulled into the driveway of the small, brick ranch house.

"I got you here all safe and sound."

"I appreciate it. You want to come in?"

Elise was tempted. They'd been having such fun together, but she knew her job had to come first. Later, when she had money, she would have fun. There was no time now. She had to get back to work first thing in the morning. "No. I've got to get home. I've got too much work to do to take time out for any more fun, darn it."

"Whenever you're ready, just let me know."

"I will, believe me."

Emboldened by the thought that she really would have liked to spend more time with him, he made his move.

"Elise?"

She turned and found herself in Zach's arms, his lips seeking hers in a passionate exchange. He deepened the kiss, drawing her as close as he could. As heady as her embrace was, Zach was silently cursing himself for not having restored a full-sized '60 sedan. He wanted to get closer to her, to hold her fully against him, and it was proving next to impossible in the cramped quarters of the Fastback.

The power of Zach's embrace left Elise's senses reeling. His gentle touch stirred her, and when his hand sought her breast, she didn't draw away. Logic told her to stop, but her desire overruled the logic of the situation. She'd wanted this ever since that night at her house when he'd first kissed her.

"Oh, Zach…" She whispered his name as his lips left hers to trace a pattern of fire down her throat.

She shifted positions then, trying to get closer to him. But the steering wheel and gear shift provided serious obstacles, and she suddenly realized just what she was doing. And she couldn't help herself. She stared to giggle.

"Elise?" Zach frowned as he drew back, wondering why she was pulling away from him and why she was laughing.

"I'm sorry," she told him regretfully. "It just struck me as so funny that we're sitting in a driveway necking like a couple of teenagers. I'm twenty-five and you're how old? Twenty-eight?"

Zach found himself smiling, too, as he gazed at her across the car in the semidarkness. He thought she'd never looked more beautiful. Her eyes were aglow, and there was a slight flush to her cheeks.

"You're beautiful, Elise Matthews." He reached out and touched her cheek.

She savored his caress and then leaned forward to press her lips to his once more. "I've got to go, Zach."

"I know."

He kissed her once more, softly, gently, and then opened the door to get out.

"Let me know about Saturday?"

"I'll tell Rod tomorrow."

"Good night."

Zach watched until she'd driven away, then went inside to his solitary bed.

6

"Yeah, right," Elise grumbled to herself as she sat at the breakfast table on Saturday morning reading the newspaper. Quoting from the paper, she read her horoscope out loud, "'You will be irresistible to the opposite sex.' Hah! That'll be the day."

She thought of Zach, and might have believed a little of the prediction if he hadn't asked Rod for two tickets for Saturday night—one for him and one for the date he was bringing.

Still in annoyance, Elise continued to read, "'Money will come your way in a surprising manner.' Yeah, like a regular paycheck...'cause I sure as heck didn't win the lottery again this week. I can't win if I only keep matching two numbers on a ticket! The good news is, they say it'll be worth fifty-two million for Monday night's drawing. "'The future holds unlimited potential for happiness for you as long as you are honest with yourself and follow your dreams.'"

"Who are you talking to?" Rod asked as he walked into the kitchen, yawning.

"Myself. I'm real good company."

"I know. I like you, too."

She smiled at him and tossed him the sports page.

"How soon are you leaving?" He glanced at the clock and saw that it was just seven.

"I need to be down at the hotel by eight to start setting up. I'm taking my change of clothes with me this morning. Aaron has taken a suite at the hotel, and he said I could use it to change and freshen up tonight."

"So I won't see you again until tonight?"

"Right. You need to be there ready to work at five-thirty. Have you made arrangements with Zach to pick him up?"

"I don't need to. He found another way to get there."

"What's he going to do?'

"I have no idea. He didn't offer, so I didn't ask."

"And he never told you who his date is for the evening?"

"Nope." Rod eyed his sister, wondering why she cared. She and Zach had been friends forever. It seemed odd that she suddenly wanted to know whom he was seeing.

Elise was curious about what arrangements Zach had made for the evening, but she put her curiosity aside. She hadn't had time to talk to him since she'd dropped him off the other night, and he hadn't bothered to call her, either.

"I have to get ready. I want to stop by the gas station and pick up more lottery tickets. Wish me luck."

"On the lottery or tonight?"

"Both."

"I do. It's going to be great. You've done everything right. Tonight is going to be the best night of your life." He tried to sound encouraging.

"You sound like my horoscope." She laughed.

"I hope I'm right."

"So do I." Elise disappeared upstairs to get ready for the long day ahead.

Elise couldn't believe how perfectly everything was going. The Tigers' charity event for cancer had been a complete sell-out. The rich and famous were there in droves. Most of the other professional sports franchises were well represented by their players, and the movers and shakers of the metropolitan area were there in numbers. At last count, the charity event had raised over one hundred and fifty thousand dollars for the Cancer Society. The Tigers had adopted the Cancer Society as their main charity because their legendary head coach, Jim Cutter, had died of it when he'd been in the prime of his life a few years before.

"My dear, you never cease to amaze me with your talent," Aaron said as he handed her a glass of champagne. "The food is magnificent. The decorations are stunning. People are raving about what a success the night has been."

"I'm just glad you're happy with everything."

"If we raise money, I'm happy, and we've already surpassed our goal."

"That's fantastic. Everything has gone smoothly. There were no last-minute emergencies at all."

"That's because you're so organized. You covered every possibility and were ready for any scenario."

As he finished speaking, a photographer from the society page of the newspaper appeared. Aaron slipped an arm around Elise's waist and drew her close to his side just as the man snapped their photo.

"It'll run in Monday's paper," the photographer told them as he moved off in search of other noteworthy subjects.

"I hope I look reasonably intelligent in that. I take a notoriously bad picture."

"I don't know how that's possible," Aaron said in amazement. "You're beautiful."

Suddenly, the opening line of her horoscope slipped into her thoughts—*You will be irresistible to the opposite sex*—and she found herself grinning. "Thank you, Aaron. That's very sweet of you to say."

"And very true," he responded.

"You haven't seen some of my past photos."

"Maybe someday you'll show me."

She looked up at him and saw that he was serious. It surprised her. "You're serious?"

"Very." He gave her a light squeeze, then released her as a business associate summoned him from across the ballroom. "I'll see you later."

To her shock, Aaron pressed a soft kiss on her cheek before he moved off. She was watching him make his way across the room, greeting other guests, when she caught sight of Zach for the first time that night. He was wearing a tux and had his back to her, but there was no mistaking him. Elise wondered why she could never imagine what Zach would look like in a tux before. She knew he did justice to tight jeans and T-shirts, but he was even more gorgeous dressed in formal wear, and he looked as if he were completely at ease, confident and debonair.

As if he sensed her gaze upon him, Zach looked up in her direction and their gazes collided across the room. Zach smiled at her, lifting his champagne glass in silent salute. The petite, seductively gowned blonde on his arm said something. Zach turned away from Elise and concentrated on what his date was saying. When she'd finished talking, he threw back his head and laughed in seeming delight. The woman in turn laughed at his return quip.

Elise watched them move off together, looking to all the world like the perfect couple, and a troubling emotion began to gnaw at her—an emotion she didn't want to name. Her gaze sought out Aaron again, and she spied him working the crowd a short distance beyond Zach. She studied them both as she kept them in the same line of vision. Both men were tall, and each was good-looking in his own way—Aaron blond, wealthy, and sophisticated in manners and dealings; Zach darkly handsome and ever straightforward in his associations. They were both men she admired, but she wondered why, when she saw Aaron kissing another woman and laughing at her witticisms, it didn't bother her at all.

Taking another glass of champagne from one of the waiters, Elise went to check on how things were going. The evening would be a late one, and she wanted to make sure all her employees were doing all right and had everything they needed.

As the charity event came to a close, Aaron asked Elise to stand at his side as he thanked everyone for coming. They stood by the door shaking hands and making small talk with all those in attendance.

"You look familiar to me. I know we spoke earlier this evening, but I don't remember your name," Aaron said honestly as he came face-to-face with Zach.

"I'm Zach Thomas. We met the other day in the garage. I was driving the tow truck."

"Zach. Of course. It's good to see you again. Thanks for coming tonight. Who's your lovely companion?"

"This is Michelle Seton. Michelle, this is Elise Matthews and Aaron Benedict."

"It's a pleasure to meet both of you," she said politely. Then, directing her next comment to Aaron, she added, "But Mr. Benedict, you made a big mistake trading Concrete McAllister."

Aaron grinned. "The trade seems to have been the main topic of conversation here tonight, and most of the crowd wanted to string me up."

"I'm one of them," Zach said drolly.

"Give me a chance to show you what this team can do."

"We wanted to support you, but why trade a fan favorite?" Michelle pressed. "A lot of folks care about Concrete and really like him. He's going to be missed in the community."

"Let's hope a big winning season wins back their loyalty," Aaron said, never conceding that he might have made a mistake in the trade.

"Good night," Zach said, knowing it was a pointless discussion. The deal was done and the man was obviously pleased with it. Then, looking directly at Elise, he repeated, "Good night."

"Good night, Zach. Michelle, it was nice to meet you," she told them, but all the while she wondered where Zach had met her and how they knew each other.

It was nearly an hour later when the last of the guests had departed, and Aaron and Elise were finally alone in the midst of the hotel personnel doing the clean-up work.

"Let's go upstairs to the suite and have a drink to celebrate our success tonight, shall we?" he suggested.

"I'd love to," she accepted, not wanting to think about where Zach and his petite blonde had gone and what they were doing.

Aaron escorted her into the elevator of the plush hotel. She was weary, but exhilarated, for everything had turned out wonderfully. She stepped into the elevator car, and the moment the doors closed and they were alone, Aaron took her into his arms.

"I've wanted to do this all night," he said in a low voice as he kissed her.

For Elise, it was her dream come true. She was in an elegant hotel, being kissed by a millionaire. His kiss, along with the speedy rush of the elevator going up, thrilled her. When they reached their floor and he reluctantly let her go, she was breathless.

Neither of them spoke as he took her hand and led her from the car. They walked down the hall to the luxurious suite where she'd changed clothes earlier in the day. He unlocked it, held the door for her, and went straight to the bar, where an iced bottle of Dom Perignon awaited them. Fluted crystal champagne glasses were on a silver tray next to the ice bucket, and Aaron effortlessly opened the bottle and poured them both a glass.

One entire wall of the suite was a window, and Elise went to stand there and stare out at the skyline of the city. It was perfect…the luxury hotel, the fine champagne, the handsome man…

"To us," Aaron said as he held out one glass for her to take.

She dreamily took it and lifted it to his. "To us."

"Do you realize how great we are together?" he asked as he went to sit on the overstuffed sofa and patted the place next to him for her to join him.

"We do work well together," she agreed as she sat down. "It was a wonderful evening."

"And it's not over yet." He took her glass and set both their glasses aside, then took her in his arms again. "You are one beautiful woman, Elise Matthews, and I want you for my own."

Before she had time to say a word, his mouth covered hers in a passionate kiss. His declaration had left her in shock. *His own? He wanted her for his own?* The thought gave her pause. They barely knew each other. Not that there was anything about him she didn't like. What was to hate? His good looks? His kindness? His money? No, she would be hard put to find anything about him she didn't like— except his trade of Concrete McAllister—but *his own?*

Jolted out of the romantic haze the champagne and his kisses had created, she realized that he wanted more from her than a few kisses. Much more.

"You want me for your own?" she finally said when the kiss ended and she managed to put a little distance between them on the sofa. "Aaron, we've worked together for a number of weeks now, but we really don't know each other that well."

"I know all I need to know about you, Elise, and in case you haven't figured it out yet, I'm a man of action. I know what I want when I see it, and I know I want you."

"But…"

He took her in his embrace again and held her close. "I love you, Elise. Will you marry me?"

She gasped out loud at his proposal, and he saved her from having to answer by kissing her again. She gave herself over to his ardor, enjoying his kiss, enjoying the comfort of being in his arms, but always, hovering just on the edge of her pleasure with Aaron, was the haunting memory of Zach's kiss and touch.

Aaron's kiss became even more heated as he lay back on the sofa and pulled her down upon him. They were stretched out body to body, full length, as he began to caress her and make love to her. She was the woman he'd waited all these years for, and at last he'd found her. He didn't ever want to let her go again, but when he felt her resistance to his advances, he stopped, puzzled, and drew away from her.

"Elise? What's wrong?" he asked as he sat back up and faced her.

"Nothing's wrong, Aaron. It's just that this is happening so fast. I never dreamed you felt this way about me. I need time... time alone to think. I'd better go." She rose and grabbed her purse. "I'll get my other clothes later."

With that, she was gone from the suite.

Aaron stared at the closed door. He hoped she'd change her mind before she reached the elevator. He hoped she would never leave him again. He wanted her with him. He found her intelligence and beauty to be a rare and devastating combination, and he didn't ever want to lose her. He waited quietly, hoping she would return.

But when the elevator came to the floor, Elise got on it.

A short time later, Aaron emerged from the suite in hopes of finding her there. All that greeted him was the empty hall. He turned back into the suite and put away the champagne. Tonight, he would drink the hard stuff.

Elise was trembling as she rushed across the nearly deserted garage, and she didn't feel safe again until she was sitting in Zach's Mustang. The drive home was a blur, and she was still feeling nervous as she let herself into the house.

"It's about time you got home," Rod called out from the kitchen when he heard her come in the front door.

"Have you been here long?"

"No, not too long. Just long enough to get comfortable. How did it go? What do you think?" He went to stand in the kitchen door so he could see her.

Oh, Rod... I don't know."

"You don't know how it went? Everything I heard was that it was terrific. You're making quite a name for yourself."

She didn't answer, but sat down heavily on the sofa.

"Elise?" He could tell something was wrong. "What's the matter?"

"Nothing. Everything..."

"I don't understand."

She looked up at her little brother, who'd come to stand before her sensing that something was troubling her. "It's Aaron."

"What about him?" Rod was instantly ready to go and defend her honor if the man had done something to hurt her. "What did he do?"

"Well, he…"

Rod was expecting the worst. "He what?"

"He proposed to me tonight," she blurted out miserably.

Rod stared at her in complete confusion trying to figure out why a millionaire proposing to her would be so distressing. It seemed to him to be a wonderful thing. "You just got proposed to by a really rich guy, and you're unhappy? I don't get it."

"Ooooh! You men!" She threw a pillow at him.

"What's the problem?"

"I don't know… It's just all so sudden. I've only known him for a matter of weeks."

"Months, now."

"Whatever. It's just that I didn't know he felt this way. I didn't know he really cared about me."

"And this is bad?"

"No, not really. It's just…"

"Do you love him?" Rod knew just the right question to ask.

She looked up at him, her expression serious. "I don't know."

"I guess you'd better find out."

Elise didn't say any more, for she knew he was right. She liked Aaron, liked him a lot. But love him? Want to spend the rest of her life with him? She didn't know.

"I better go to bed and sleep on it. Good night, Rod." She got up to leave the room.

"If you want to talk any more, let me know. I'm here."

"You're a sweetheart. Thanks." She went to hug him. As she was leaving the room, she glanced back his way to ask, "Did you ever find out anything about Zach's date? Her name was Michelle Seton, but I'd never heard of her before tonight."

"Me either, but she sure was pretty."

Elise nodded and went on to bed.

As she lay there in the dark staring up at the ceiling, she realized her dilemma was real. The man she'd always thought was her dream man—a rich, handsome, successful businessman, who drove around in a limo and served her Dom Perignon—had just proposed.

Why, then, was she so miserable?

7

"Got the part in, did you?" Rod said as he showed up for work at the garage Monday afternoon and found Zach working on Elise's car.

"It got here about an hour ago. With any luck, I'll have it ready for her by closing time."

"Great, although I think you might have a fight getting that Mustang back. Elise likes driving it a lot. She took it out for a spin yesterday and didn't come back for hours. But don't worry—there are no big dents in it or anything."

Zach glanced up at him and found that Rod was grinning at him.

"Get to work," he growled good-naturedly.

"Yes, Boss. What have you got for me today?"

Zach pointed to a clipboard with the work orders on them. "Work on the Davenports' car. I promised them delivery first thing in the morning."

Rod checked what needed to be done and went to get the parts it required. As he walked past Zach on the way back, he knew he had to tell him what had happened with Elise. Even though she hadn't made up her mind yet about marrying the guy, which Rod could not understand at all, he thought it was pretty exciting.

"Guess what happened to Elise Saturday night after the charity event?"

"What?" Zach asked, not looking up from where he worked under the hood.

"Aaron Benedict proposed to her!"

Zach went cold inside at his words, and he almost hit his head on the raised hood as he jerked up to look at Rod. "He what?"

"He proposed to her. Said they made a great team and wanted her to marry him," Rod repeated simply as he started to work on the Davenports' car.

"When's the wedding?" The question was ground out of him as he stood there staring at Rod's back. Memories of Saturday night played in his mind—Elise looking as gorgeous as ever on Aaron Benedict's arm. Benedict kissing her there in the midst of the celebration. A society photographer from the paper taking their photo. He realized he should have known what was going on! She had looked happy that night, and marrying Benedict would make all her dreams come true—she'd have the Ritz and her limos and champagne.

"I don't know."

"They haven't set the date yet?"

"No. As of this morning, Elise still hadn't made up her mind."

A surge of hope jolted through Zach at Rod's response, but he fought to remain outwardly calm. "Why the hold up?"

"That's what I said to her. This Benedict guy's good-looking, wealthy, and owns a pro football team. As far as I'm concerned, a brother-in-law doesn't come any better than that, but then, I'm not the one marrying him."

With an effort, Zach brought his raging emotions under control and went back to work on Elise's car. Benedict had proposed...but Elise hadn't accepted yet. There is still time. There was still hope.

Zach paused in his efforts and wondered, hope for what? He frowned, staring down at the wrench in his hand. He couldn't kid himself any longer. He loved Elise. He hadn't said anything before because of her talk about marrying a rich man, and he knew he'd never be rich. He was an honest, working man, born of working-class parents. He'd had to work for everything he'd ever gotten in life, and he didn't expect that to change. There was one other thing he knew would never change, too, and that as the way he felt about Elise. He had loved her for a long time now, and he knew he always would.

With a vengeance, Zach kept working on the car. She hadn't accepted Benedict's proposal yet. He would hand-deliver her car to her tonight and tell her exactly how he felt about her.

It was after eight when the doorbell rang, and Elise got up from her desk to answer it.

"Zach… Hi," she said, surprised to find it was him and glad that it was. He'd been haunting her thoughts. Every time she'd thought she'd made up her mind about Aaron, memories of Zach intruded… his kiss… his touch… his good humor and kindness.

"Your friendly auto mechanic delivering your car on time as promised.'

"Thanks. Come on in."

He walked in and noticed a huge bouquet of roses on the mantel. "Nice flowers."

"Oh, thanks. Aaron sent them to me."

"He has good taste." Zach felt the jealousy rising within him, but kept it under control.

"You want something to drink? A soda?"

"Sure. Thanks."

While Elise disappeared into the kitchen to get their drinks, Zach wandered over to the roses and read the card.

"'Call me—Aaron.'" He read it under his breath and knew what he'd call Aaron if given the chance. Not only had he traded Concrete, now he was trying to marry Elise.

"Zach, I was thinking… " Elise came back into the room carrying their drinks to find him sitting on the sofa waiting for her.

"About what?"

"About our cars. You wouldn't consider a trade, would you? My car for your Mustang?" she asked teasingly, then went on quickly. "Now that mine's running again, it's a real prize. In a few more years, it'll be a collector's item just like the Mustang, and since you like old cars so much…" She left the question hanging, knowing full well what his answer would be.

"That's a tough one. I'll have to think about it for a while."

"How long's 'a while'?"

"About thirty seconds."

"And?"

"I don't think so. Not that I don't think yours s a wonderful vehicle. It's just that I'm fond of the Mustang after working on it for so long."

"Darn. I was afraid you were going to say that."

"If you're serious, I could look around and try to find one to restore for you, but it isn't cheap to do all that work."

"I know. I guess I'll just have to wait until I win the lottery."

Or marry Benedict. The thought crept into his mind as he took a deep drink of his soda, but he didn't say anything.

"So how did everything go Saturday? It looked like everyone had a good time, and I read in the paper that you'd raised the most money ever at one of their charity events."

"It went great. Aaron was most pleased. Did you and your date have a good time? What was her name again? Michelle?" She was bound and determined to find out more about his date.

"Yes, her name's Michelle, and we did have a fine time. She was quite impressed."

"I'm so glad. Where did you two meet?"

"Why do you want to know" He thought he heard more than casual interest in her tone, and it bolstered his hopes. Surely, she did feel something for him. She couldn't have responded to his kiss that way unless she did.

"Oh, I was just wondering." Elise tried to sound nonchalant.

"I've known Michelle for years. What about you and Benedict?"

"What about us?"

"Are you going to marry him?" A muscle worked in his jaw as he asked the question, and he found he was holding his breath as he awaited her answer.

"So Rod told you about Aaron's proposal?"

"Yes. What do you plan to do?" Zach shifted so he was nearer to her.

Elise felt the heat of him as he moved closer. "I haven't made up my mind yet."

"Why not?" he asked, lowering his voice as he slipped an arm around her shoulders and pulled her to him. "He could give you Dom Perignon every night."

He kissed her then, his mouth moving over hers in a devastating, possessive exchange, meant to tell her without words the depth of his feelings for her.

Thoughts of Aaron troubled Elise, but as Zach deepened the kiss and drew her even closer to the hard wall of his chest, all thoughts of the other man were vanquished. She gave herself over to the glory of Zach's embrace. Somehow, they were soon lying on the sofa, their bodies pressed intimately together.

"Is champagne every night what you really want?" Zach asked as his lips left hers to explore her throat.

Elise arched toward him as he continued his sensual assault. When his mouth sought hers again, she gave a soft whimper. His kiss and touch were heavenly, and she felt so safe in his arms. Was this what she really wanted? The haven of Zach's embrace?

"Tell me, Elise," he demanded, drawing away from her a bit, a slightly harsh edge to his voice. "Do you want the champagne?"

"No... I... I don't know what I want."

"Look at me," Zach commanded. He wanted to look into her eyes and see the truth of her emotions. He had to know what she was feeling. "Tell me what you want."

She gazed up at him, her expression confused, the look in her eyes troubled.

Zach wanted to hold her to his heart and never let her go, but she had to come to him of her own free will. She had to come to him because she loved him. He would accept nothing less from her.

"I know what I want," he went on. "I want you. Elise, I love you."

He kissed her again, deeply, thoroughly, putting his whole heart and soul into the exchange.

"But you have to tell me what you want."

He waited, but she didn't speak. She closed her eyes, bewildered by all that was happening. She'd known she and Zach shared something special, but she'd never known he loved her until now.

Her silence as like a knife in his heart, and he moved away from her. Standing over her, he could think only of how beautiful she was and how much he wanted to make her his own.

"Elise," he said her name quietly, though his own passion was hot within him.

She opened her eyes to look up at him.

"When you decide what you want, you let me know. You know where I'll be."

With that, he turned and left her. He let himself out of the house and started up the Mustang using his extra set of keys.

Elise went to the door after him, wanting to stop him, but unsure of just what to say. She wasn't sure of anything right then. A lone tear traced a path down her cheek as she watched him drive away, and she turned back into the living room and sat down on the sofa to try to sort out what she was feeling.

Zach loved her.

She smiled as she thought of his fierce declaration.

But did she love Zach? Was he the man she should spend the rest of her life with?

Elise shook her head, as if that would clear her thoughts. She'd known Zach forever. They'd been friends for years. He was her buddy. She had always known how cute and smart he was. Why hadn't they ever felt this way about each other before? Why was it happening now?

She thought back over the years of their friendship. They'd never dated because she'd gone away to college. When she returned, he'd been involved with other women. There had been one girl a few years back who, she'd heard, Zach had almost married.

Elise found herself smiling at the thought that it hadn't worked out for him with the other woman. Then she frowned, as the possibility that it might not work out for *them* reared its ugly head. The thought of a life without Zach scared her, and it was then that she faced the truth.

She loved him.

As attractive as Aaron was, and there was no denying that he was, money wasn't everything. She wanted the riches loving Zach could bring, even if it meant doing without material things in life. Those things didn't matter—she would have Zach.

The recognition of her true feelings freed her, and Elise laughed out loud.

She loved Zach, money or no money, champagne or no champagne, limousine or no limousine. He might not be rich, but he loved her and he owned one heckuva '65 Mustang. It didn't get any better than that.

Her laughter faded and she frowned. She had to think of a way to tell him. She just couldn't drive over to his house and blurt it out. She had to make this good.

8

It was 6 A.M. and barely light outside.

Zach had been up all night, waiting and hoping that Elise would call or come over. Neither had happened. Resignedly, half an hour before, he'd turned on the television and retrieved his newspaper from the front lawn. He was sitting at his kitchen table now, the newspaper open wide before him, a cup of hot, strong coffee in hand. He smiled to himself and took a deep drink of the potent, steaming brew. It was going to be a long day, and he might as well get ready for it.

His beeper went off, surprising him, and he was tempted to throw it across the room. He didn't want any business. H didn't need any more business. He was tempted to get in the Mustang and take off. He didn't care where, as long as it was anywhere but here. The cold, logical electronic beeper, unaware of his dangerous mood beeped again.

Swearing under his breath, Zach thought about ignoring it, but knew it might be someone in trouble. He pushed back from the table and got up to go to his phone. He dialed his answering service and waited for an operator.

"This is Zach with Collision Plus."

"There's been an accident westbound on Lambert Drive. The nearest cross street is Roosevelt. One car involved no injuries. The driver will remain with the car until you show up with the tow truck."

"Thanks. Did you get the driver's name?"

"No, but the car is a '65 Mustang."

The thought of a '65 in a wreck sickened him. In less than five minutes, he'd closed up the house and was heading for the garage.

Within twenty minutes, he was on the road in the tow truck making his way straight to Lambert and Roosevelt. It took him less than forty-five minutes to reach the site of the accident as reported by the answering service, but when he arrived at the scene there was no sign of a wrecked vehicle anywhere.

"This is Zach with Collision Plus calling back. I've just reached westbound Lambert near Roosevelt, and there's no sign of any accident or broken-down cars. Can you recheck the message, please?"

"One minute, sir." The operator's voice was cool and disinterested. After at least two minutes on hold, the woman came back on. "It was a woman who called in the accident. She didn't leave her name, but westbound Lambert near Roosevelt was the location she gave me."

"There's no one here. She hasn't called back?"

"No, sir. That was our only contact with her."

He gave a snarl of disgust and hung up. A wasted effort and here he thought he was going to help somebody out of trouble this morning—so much for all his good intentions. His mood grew blacker as he returned to the garage. When he got there, it was after seven, and neither of his two employees had shown up yet. He was really angry. Any other day, he might have laughed it all off, but today he just wasn't in the mood.

Feeling positively surly, Zach parked the tow truck, unlocked the garage, and stalked inside. The only light that was on was coming from his office. Cursing his own stupidity in forgetting to turn it off when he'd gone out on the emergency call, he strode toward the light, ready to phone his errant employees and ask them why they hadn't shown up for work.

Or at least he was until he reached his office door and looked inside.

Elise as sitting at his desk, dressed as if she was going to work. She looked up. "Hi, Zach."

"Elise? What are you doing here?" Zach's heart lurched at the sight of her, but he was too afraid to let himself hope about her reasons for coming here.

"There wasn't any Mustang at Lambert and Roosevelt?" she asked, giving him a very seductive smile.

"You called that in?"

She nodded as she stood up and crossed the room to stand

before him. "I had to think of a way to get you out of here. I didn't want to take any chances—

"Any chances with what?"

"With the surprise I have planned for you."

"Surprise?" Zach knew he sounded less than brilliant, but he had no idea what she was up to.

"I even sent Charley and George out for coffee and doughnuts, just so I'd have time to set everything up. You see, I made you something." She moved away to show him what looked to be a pizza box on his desk. "Open it."

He was frowning and smiling at the same time as he lifted the lid. Inside was a heart-shaped pizza made with all his favorite toppings.

"Zach?"

He looked up at her, all the love he had for her shining in his eyes.

"I love you, Zach, and I love pizza in the garage at midnight or at seven in the morning—as long as I'm sharing it with you."

"Elise..."

He opened his arms to her and she went into them. They stood that way, neither speaking, just enjoying the beauty of the moment. Then carefully, gently, he bent to kiss her. It was a kiss of delight and promise, a kiss that told of the loving wonders yet to come.

"Will you marry me, Elise?"

"Yes, Zach. I can't think of anything more wonderful," she sighed, nestling against his chest and listening to the heavy, steady beat of his heart. This was Zach. She loved him. He was hers.

He kissed her again, more deeply this time, as if not really believing what was happening. The last twelve hours had taken an emotional toll on him, but that didn't matter now. The only important thing was that Elise loved him and had come to him of her own free will.

"You're sure?"

"I'm positive."

"I know what Aaron Benedict can give you. That's your dream, isn't it? The Ritz, limousines, and Dom Perignon?"

"For a long time I thought it was, but now I know different. My dream is loving someone as wonderful as you."

"When are you going to talk to him?"

"I already have."

She drew him down to her for a flaming kiss that told him all he needed to know about the truth of her feelings for him.

"I love you, Zach Thomas, and if you want to open a restaurant instead of running a garage, I'll help you with it. I'll even wait tables for you if you want me to."

"We could sell heart-shaped pizzas," he suggested.

"It would probably only be big on Valentine's Day," she said, laughing in delight as she hugged him close.

They both sighed as they stood in the middle of the room, wrapped in each other's arms.

"How soon do you want to get married?" Zach asked.

"As far as I'm concerned, we could go to a justice of the peace today, but I know you have a pretty big family. There's only me and Rod and a few distant cousins on my side."

"We can talk to my parents today and see how they feel about a small, quick wedding and reception."

"Quick, I like the sound of that." She kissed him again. "But I won't be cheated out of a honeymoon. You've got to promise me that we'll have at least a week together. Okay?"

"I don't know if I can afford to take that much time off."

"Oh." She looked momentarily downcast, then brightened. "We'll figure something out. I want you all to myself with no danger of interruptions."

"That sounds great to me," he agreed, remembering how Rod had walked in on them that night at her house. "Uninterrupted, hmmm?"

He kissed her again, then drew away.

"I have something I want to give you."

"What?"

"Just a little something I picked up the other night."

She was smiling brightly, wondering it if was a ring, but instead he pulled out his wallet. She couldn't imagine what he had.

"Here." Zach held a lottery ticket out to her. "This is for us to begin our life together."

"That's so sweet of you. You know how I feel about lottery tickets."

On his desk was a copy of the morning paper. He opened it and handed her the pages with the lottery number listings.

"Check them out."

"Now?"

"There's no better time than the present."

She sat down at his desk to go over the numbers as he took a piece of her pizza to eat. He stood back, watching her expression as she went over the numbers listed. He noticed when her hands began to tremble.

"Zach…" Her voice was hoarse as she looked up at him, her eyes wide with excitement. "You won!"

"I know," he said simply.

"Oh, my God! That's fifty-six million dollars!"

"I know."

And she was in his arms, jumping up and down, kissing him. She was unmindful of the pizza he held, unmindful of anything but the joy of loving Zach. He took her in his arms and twirled her around the office.

"I think we're going to live happily ever after," he said, claiming her lips in a passionate kiss.

"I know we are."

She started to kiss him again when she noticed that Charley and George were standing outside the office door holding a bag of doughnuts and cups of coffee, watching them.

"Good morning, Boss," they said, giving Zach and Elise a curious look.

"It's a very good morning," Zach agreed.

"You're celebrating?"

"Elise just accepted my proposal. We're getting married." He decided to save their other good news until later. This was more important!

"That's great! Congratulations!"

"Come on in. Enjoy the pizza and the doughnuts. I'm taking the day off."

"You?" They were shocked. Zach never took unscheduled time off.

"That's right, gentlemen. You are you own bosses today. I'll see you later."

Grabbing Elise's hand, he hurried off through the garage and out into the parking lot.

The kissed once more right there in broad daylight and then

climbed into the Mustang

"Are you ready to have some fun now?" he asked, remembering how she'd feared taking time away from her work schedule to play.

"Yes, I'm more than ready."

"Let's go."

EPILOGUE

"I now pronounce you man and wife," the minister intoned. "You may kiss your bride."

Zach turned to Elise and kissed her gently.

"Ladies and gentlemen, may I present to you Mr. and Mrs. Zach Thomas."

Applause erupted from the friends and family members who'd gathered for the ceremony. Zach led Elise down the aisle and they left the church, ready to begin their new life together.

The reception was held in the church hall and everyone had a wonderful time. Zach and Elise stayed for most of it, enjoying being with all the people who loved them. Finally, as midnight neared, they slipped away.

Zach stopped on the deserted walk in front of the church to gaze up at the night sky. "It's a beautiful night, Mrs. Thomas."

"It certainly is," she agreed, leaning against him, enjoying the feel of his arm around her.

"I have one last present for you."

She looked up at him in surprise, wondering how he could possible give her any more than he already had. She had his love, and that was all that really mattered. "You do?"

"Here." He reached in his pocket and took out the keys to the Mustang. "The car is my wedding present to you."

"Oh, Zach!" She launched herself into his arms as best she could in her wedding gown. "Is it here?"

"I had Rod park it around back. Can you drive it with that long skirt on?"

"No. I think tonight you'd better chauffeur me."

193

He took the keys from her, and they were soon on their way to the honeymoon suite he'd booked at the hotel near the airport. Their bags were already there awaiting them. They would be flying out in the morning to being their week-long honeymoon in Jamaica.

Zach swung her up into his arms and carried her across the threshold. She looked her arms about his neck and kissed him with wild abandon. He set her from him and hung the "Do Not Disturb" sign on the door. He shut the door and locked it, then turned to his bride. It seemed he'd waited his whole life for this moment, and he could wait no longer.

"I love you, Elise."

Zach needed to say no more, for she was there, in his arms. He helped her shed the dress, glorying in the loveliness of her. Soon they were together on the soft width of their bed, exploring the beauty of their differences.

As his hands traced paths of fire over her sensitive flesh, a fever of need grew within Elise. This was Zach... her love. She gave herself over to the excitement his caresses created in the heart of her. When he moved over her to make her his own, she opened to him like a flower in bloom. Sinking deep within the feminine heat of her, Zach knew the meaning of true bliss. She held him tightly within her, loving the sensation so new and precious. They were one in body. He began to move, and she met him in that sensual rhythm as old as time. Ecstasy was there as they reached the peak of pleasure together. Enraptured, they clung to one another, knowing true love.

"You know, my horoscope was right that day of the charity fund-raiser," Elise said in a soft, sleepy voice as she lay in her husband's arms.

"What did it say?"

"'The future holds unlimited potential for happiness for you as long as you are honest with yourself and follow your dreams.'" She sighed and nestled closer to Zach. "I followed my dreams, Zach, and they brought me you."

He drew her up to him for a soft kiss. He had found his heaven in her embrace. "I like the way you dream, lady."

That simple kiss ignited the fire of their desire again, and all thoughts of horoscopes were forgotten. They came together in perfect union again, giving and taking in love's most sacred way.

They would live happily ever after.

TIME STOLEN LOVE

PROLOGUE

He moved silently and unnoticed through the dark, dank streets of Whitechapel, London's squalid East End. Though he appeared to be one of its residents, he was in truth a predator, prowling courts and alleyways, watching, planning for the moment when he would strike. Only bloodletting could satisfy his hunger, and here he found the perfect hunting ground. The destitute women who walked these streets were more than willing to satisfy his needs for a few pence—until they discovered what his needs really were.

A thrill shot through him at the thought of taking another unsuspecting prey. He stepped back into the shadows. Carriages passed by on the cobblestone street, people walked within arm's reach of him, but no one saw him. He felt omnipotent and immortal.

He thought of the name he'd chosen to sign his letter to the press: Jack the Ripper. It suited him well. They didn't respect his power yet, but they would after tonight. Tonight he would leave his indelible mark of fear upon all of London.

He stepped from the shadows and returned to the hunt, searching the streets for the woman who would quench the fire of his bloodlust.

1

Roni Mitchell walked down Whitechapel's Commercial Street and stopped at a shop window that advertised Jack the Ripper souvenirs. She laughed. In a manner of speaking, Jack had brought her here. For some time, she'd been considering taping an investigative report on serial killers, and these streets, the Ripper's stalking ground, would be her first location.

This morning she had finished her documentary on powerful women in government by taping an interview with Margaret Thatcher. Now, her work done, she had taken her time, enjoying the East End's nineteenth-century charm. Yes, she would definitely recommend the serial-killer idea to her producer.

It was nearly sundown when she reached Whitechapel High Street. A few blocks ahead lay the Underground station, and she quickened her pace, eager to return to her hotel.

She crossed a side street, glanced down it, and stopped. Narrow and shadowed, the street seemed to belong to another age. Half-way down the block, a weather-beaten sign that read 'Antiquities' hung over a small shop.

Intrigued, she turned down the side street. Nearing the shop, she saw the words "Fortune's Treasures" painted on the window, and a battered "Open" propped sign on the sill. A small dark passageway led to the door. It creaked when Roni opened it.

She felt as if she were entering a different world. The air smelled musty, and to Roni's surprise, the shop was quite spacious, its long aisle cluttered with all variety of books and bric-a-brac.

"Good afternoon," a deep voice called.

Roni turned to see a wizened old man perched on a stool behind the counter. He could have been anywhere between sixty and one hundred and sixty. His eyes, bright blue, sparkled with humor and vitality.

"Hello," she said. "I didn't see you sitting there."

"It seems my lot in life is to be missed by the most beautiful women."

She laughed. "Thank you. I'm just completely enchanted. Your shop is wonderful."

"There are those who would not agree with you."

She frowned at his odd comment. "Then they must not appreciate the past." She made her way slowly down one of the aisles.

"My name is Telyur, by the way," the man said.

"It's a pleasure to meet you, Mr. Telyur. I'm Roni Mitchell."

"No 'Mister', just Telyur," he said, smiling. "You're an American?"

"Yes, I'm from California."

"I've never been there, but I've heard it's a lovely place, warm and sunny almost all the time."

"It is beautiful, but then, there's beauty in everything, if you look for it."

"Well said, my dear. Is there anything special you're looking for?"

"No." She paused to examine a stack of leather-bound books. "You never know what you might stumble across. I love the past. There are so many mysteries... I've always believed if I tried hard enough, I could solve them."

She looked up. Telyur was staring at her intently, as if trying to see into her very soul. She smiled uneasily. "You must love history, too, or you wouldn't have this shop,"

"History is my life, my existence."

"Have you been in business a long time?"

"An eternity, I think." He gave an odd chuckle.

"It can't be that bad. You must meet a lot of interesting people." She picked up a mantel clock.

"There are moments when it does seem worthwhile... Are you interested in timepieces?"

"Yes, I always wonder what happened during the hours they were running. I suppose that's why I do what I do."

"And what is that?"

"I'm a TV reporter. I like to discover the who, what, when, where and why of things."

"Sometimes it's impossible to find the truth, you know."

She looked at him. What an odd little man. "Do you really think so?," she asked. "I always think it's best to bring everything out into the light for all to see."

"Perhaps some things should not be seen."

For some reason, his words chilled her. "What do you mean?"

"Pure evil, for instance. Would you want to be the one to set it free?"

She did not know what to say.

Telyur slipped off the stool and walked into a small alcove behind the counter. "I have something here... something you might find interesting."

"Oh?" Roni felt the urge to leave, yet her curiosity held her there.

"Come here, my dear. I want to show you something I have never shown to anyone."

She approached the counter. He began to sort through a jumble of wrapped packages on the counter, studying the inscription on each one.

"Ah!" He held up a small package wrapped in brown paper and tied with a string. "Yes, I think you will be interested in this," he said, brushing a thick layer of dust from the top.

Roni leaned across the counter. "What is it?"

"Let me unwrap it for you." He stopped and looked at her. "Remember, no one else knows of its existence. If word of this were to get out..."

"Then why show it to me?"

His gaze burned with an inner fire. "Because I think it was not by chance that you entered my shop. I believe that destiny has brought you to me."

She said nothing as he untied the string and tore away the brittle paper. Inside, was a plain, lidded wooden box. He pressed it into her hands.

She lifted the lid. Inside lay a gold pocket watch and fob. The watch bore no decoration or inscription. She set the box on the counter and carefully lifted out the watch. The metal felt cold in her hand, and she shivered. Then she looked at Telyur. "Who owned this watch?"

"You won't believe me."

"I'll believe you."

"The watch has been in this shop for as long as I have. I do not remember how it came here, but I do know that it once belonged to Jack the Ripper."

In any other shop, in any other neighborhood, Roni would have laughed aloud, but somehow his declaration wasn't funny. Walking the streets of Whitechapel, she'd seen Jack the Ripper knives, Jack the Ripper deerstalker hats, but this... this was different. "How could you know that?" she asked, her voice a whisper.

"I know. As I have told you, I do not remember how it came here. But I do know that it was found at the scene of one of his murders."

"Whoever found it should have turned it over to Scotland Yard. It's a valuable clue."

He shrugged. "Many things in the past could have been done differently."

"Do you know who the Ripper was?" She had to ask.

"No one knows for sure."

"You don't believe any of the theories the experts have put forth?"

"Each contains some particle of truth, even as each contains a fatal flaw. It is the great mystery of its time, and it remains so today. Perhaps the truth will never be known."

Roni looked down at the watch in her hand. "There's always the chance that some new piece of evidence will be discovered..."

"Yes, there is that chance."

She looked at the watch again. "Does it still keep time?"

"It hasn't worked in all the years I've had it in my possession."

She opened the case and read the time: three o'clock. Then she carefully returned the watch to the box and closed the lid. "I would like to buy it."

"Some things cannot be sold," Telyur said. "They must find the person to whom they rightfully belong." He studied her face. "What did you feel when you first touched the watch?"

In her confusion, she could find no words to describe her feelings.

"You needn't say anything." He handed the box to her.

"I can't just take it," she said. "I must give you something in return." She thought for a moment, then slipped a signet ring from her finger and pressed it into his hand.

"It is sealed, then," he said. "We have made a bargain, you and I. I am glad you came into my shop, Miss Mitchell."

"I am, too," she said, putting the box in her pocket. Then she bid him goodbye and left the shop.

It was dark outside. She turned to look back at the shop and saw Telyur flip the sign in the window to "Closed". Then, without looking up, he turned and vanished into the shadows.

2

Dampness hung in the air, and thick fog blanketed the street. Roni was glad she'd worn her trench coat. She buttoned the top button and hurried toward Whitechapel High Street and the Underground station.

Telyur's strange words still echoed in her mind, but she determined not to dwell on them until she was safely back in her hotel room. She quickened her pace, the fog swirling around her. It seemed to muffle all sound and left her slightly disoriented.

She was about to turn another corner when she heard the faint, muted sound of a chime. She stopped, wondering where the sound had come from, then realized it was the watch in her pocket. Stopping beneath a street light, she pulled out the box. Just as she lifted the lid, it chimed again. Her hand trembling, she lifted the watch out by the fob and held it to her ear. The watch was ticking. She opened the case and strained to read the time in the semi-darkness. Three o'clock.

A gust of chill wind swept down the street, moaning eerily as it passed. At the same time, the street light overhead dimmed, and Roni looked up to see a flickering gaslight. She could have sworn it was an ordinary street light when she'd sought its protection.

It had grown strangely quiet. The sounds of traffic were gone, replaced by an unsettling stillness. Still clutching the watch by its fob, Roni hurried on toward Whitechapel High Street.

Footsteps echoed on the street behind her. She walked faster, knowing that safety was as near as the corner. The footsteps quickened to match hers. Her heart began to race.

Then she laughed to herself. She was being ridiculous, she

thought, and turned to see who was behind her.

She came face-to-face with the man who emerged from the fog. He was far taller than her own five-feet eight inches. His long cape and the clothing beneath it were dark, and he wore a deerstalker hat that shadowed his face, though she could see that he had fair hair and a mustache. Then, for a fleeting second, she caught a glimpse of his eyes. They were cold and emotionless.

She paused, stunned. Then the long blade of a knife gleamed in the distant lamplight. Gasping, she turned to flee.

With lightning speed he grabbed her by the arm, the knife poised in his other hand, his black cape billowing around him.

Her self-defense training told her she wouldn't be able to overpower her attacker, but if she were quick enough she knew she had a chance of getting away. She tried to yank her arm free and run, but he was surprisingly strong. His hand tightened painfully on her arm and he spun her around, slamming her against his chest.

She felt his hot breath on her cheek. Knowing her very life depended on her next move, she reached back to gouge at his eyes, at the same time stomping with all her might on his instep. He let out a grunt of pain, and in the split second when he loosened his grip, she jabbed her elbow in his stomach and broke free, her purse falling to the street.

Cursing, the man reached for her again, but he succeeded in grabbing only the watch she still held in her hand. Releasing it, she turned and ran toward the Underground station and salvation.

"Help!" she cried, running into Whitechapel High Street. The fog was even thicker here, and she wondered what had become of the cars and buses that had crowded the street only a short time ago. Her breath rasped loudly in her ears as she ran, not daring to look back to see if the man was following her.

From out of the fog loomed a horse and carriage. With a cry of panic, Roni tried to dodge the rearing horse. Her foot slipped on the damp pavement and she fell, hitting her head with a jarring thud. Dazed, she lay where she had fallen. The world swam around her, and she closed her eyes.

"Easy, boy," a man's voice said.

She heard the sound of a latch opening. "Bellamy, what the devil is going on?" another man said, this one younger, judging by the sound of his voice.

"It's a woman, sir. She ran right out in front of me. Nearly ran her down, we did."

"A woman? What was she thinking of, running out into the street that way?"

"Is she dead, sir?"

No, thank heaven. She's alive, but it seems she's hit her head. She's going to have a nasty bruise."

Roni felt someone touch her forehead, and she winced with pain. She opened her eyes and saw a man's face hovering near her. Her vision blurred, and suddenly she saw the face of the man with the knife and the stone-cold eyes.

"No! Let me go!" She struggled wildly, striking out at him with her fists.

"What the—" Two strong arms pinned her hands at her sides. "Miss, calm down! I'm not going to hurt you."

"What?" Panting, she blinked several times, struggling to clear her vision and her head. When at last her eyes focused, she realized that this was not the man who had attacked her. This man was young, fair-haired and clean-shaven, his features lean and handsome. His eyes were a deep, smoky gray, and they reflected intelligence and concern, not the deadly intent she'd seen in the other man's gaze.

"I said, calm down," he said gently.

"But you've got to help me! I've got to get away from here!" She imagined her attacker closing in on them even now. The man who held her looked big and strong, but the other man had had that knife.

"Easy now, miss. You've had a bad fall and hit your head." He released her arms.

"But you don't understand! He's after me…" She struggled to sit up and look around. Pain pounded in her head.

"Who's after you?"

"I don't know who he was. But he was right behind me and he had a knife!"

The man went still. "A man was chasing you with a knife?"

"Yes, I had just come out of a shop and he came up behind me. I got away, but…"

"You said you saw him?"

"Yes."

"Did you see him clearly?"

"Yes. His hair was lighter than yours. He had a mustache and the coldest eyes…"

The man lifted his head and looked around, his piercing gaze seeming to take in every detail of the street and buildings. Then he slipped his arm around Roni's shoulders and helped her to stand. "We'd better get in the carriage."

"Carriage?" Now she wondered what in the world this man was doing with a horse and carriage, but she felt too weak and dizzy to ask. She took a step and then the world spun crazily and she clutched at her rescuer for support. When he swept her up into his arms to carry her, she was grateful. She felt safe and protected, and for that moment she gave herself over into his keeping. It was an odd feeling for her; she was so used to taking care of herself.

He settled her in the carriage, then climbed in and leaned his head out the door. "Bellamy, get home as fast as you can!"

"Is she that bad, sir?"

"No… But I think she may have seen him. I must keep her safe." He spoke in a low voice, as if someone were near, listening.

"Yes, Mr. Grayson!"

The man called Grayson shut the door and settled himself beside Roni as the carriage lurched into motion.

3

Though it was dark inside the carriage, Kent Grayson could see that the woman was pale. Yet he could also see she was quite beautiful. Her hair was the color of gold, long and loose around her shoulders. Her features were delicate – her mouth soft and vulnerable, her nose straight and feminine.

Suddenly, she sat up and looked at him, her eyes wide. "That man's a madman! I may have gotten away, but somebody else may not be so lucky! Stop this thing so I can get to the phone and call the police!"

Kent had no idea what a phone was, but he was determined to put her at ease. He must get her safely away so he could question her about what she's seen. "Miss, there's nothing to fear. I am the police."

"You?" She peered at him through the dimness.

"Yes, I'm Inspector Kent Grayson of Scotland Yard."

"If you're an inspector, why on earth didn't you go after him? He had a knife, and the way he was dressed, he looked like some kind of Jack the Ripper impersonator!"

Kent went rigid. He stared at her. There was no way she could have known that name unless she were directly involved in the case. The letter, written in red ink and signed "Jack the Ripper", had arrived at the Central News Agency two days ago on the twenty-eighth, and so far the Yard had taken great care to keep the letter's contents out of the press. The public still referred to the killer as "Leather Apron" because of an apron that had been found at the site of the first murder.

"We'll talk about that later," Kent said. "Right now the most important thing is to get you to safety."

"Just take me back to my hotel, then," she said. "Once I get there I'll be fine."

"Which hotel are you staying at?"

"The Hilton at the airport."

He stared at her in confusion. He knew of no hotel in London called the Hilton. And what the devil was an airport?

He wondered if she was an escapee from Bedlam or some other private institution, come to the East End to play on the police's desperate attempts to catch the killer. Perhaps she had written that letter! Disturbed people often took credit for crimes they hadn't committed. He wanted desperately to challenge her knowledge but decided to wait until they reached his house, where she could not run from him.

"My townhouse is close by," he said. "My driver is taking us there. My physician lives nearby, and I can send for him to come and see to your head."

"My head is fine," she said. "I don't need a doctor."

"I insist."

She eyed him suspiciously. "If you're the police, let me see some ID."

"I beg your pardon."

"I want to see your police badge or whatever you carry around to identify yourself. How do I know you're not connected to that lunatic?"

Kent said nothing as he drew out his identification and handed it to her. She studied it closely, trying to read it in the dark.

"Trust me, Miss... What is your name, by the way?"

"Roni. Veronica, really. Veronica Mitchell."

"I'm pleased to make your acquaintance, Miss Mitchell."

"Look, Inspector, I'm really not in the mood for chit-chat. I've just been attacked. I've lost my purse, the watch... And why are we riding in this thing? Why don't you have a car?"

He frowned. "A car? Do you mean a railroad car?"

She exhaled in exasperation and turned to look out the window. For several moments she was quite still. Then she looked back at him, her face pale. "Where are we?" Her voice was a hoarse whisper.

"I don't understand what you mean..." Kent said. Clearly her injury was serious.

"I mean those people in those old-fashioned clothes and all those other horses and carriages. Is this some kind of tourist thing?"

"Miss Mitchell," he said sympathetically, "you've had a bad fall, and I can see that you're a little confused. Why don't you just rest until we get to my townhouse? After the doctor sees you, I'm sure you'll be as good as new."

"Mr. Grayson, do not patronize me. I want to know what's going on."

He glanced out at the street confused. "I'm sorry, but I'm afraid I still have no idea what you mean."

"I mean everything's changed."

"What is it you're looking for?" he asked. "Perhaps we're in a part of the city you don't recognize."

"I don't care what part of the city we're in! Where are the cars and buses and..." She glanced out the window again and broke off as another brougham went by.

"Cars? Buses?" he repeated.

She turned to him hopefully. "Are we on a movie set or something?"

He shook his head. "I'm afraid, Miss Mitchell, you are making no sense at all."

She stared at him as if he were the one making no sense at all. "Everything looks as though we're in the 1800's."

"But we are."

"We are what?"

"In the 1800's. It's 1888. Really, Miss Mi—"

"You're saying it's 1888?"

"Well, yes, of course!" he said impatiently. Was this some sort of a strange joke, or was she truly daft? Perhaps she had been drinking. He smelled no liquor on her breath. "September thirtieth, to be exact."

"Let me out of the carriage now!" She moved toward the door.

Kent grabbed her arm and pulled her back against the seat. "Please. In just a minute, we'll be at my townhouse."

"I don't want your townhouse. All I want is to find a phone so I can call a cab. I'll take it from there."

"I'm afraid that's not possible."

She stared at him. "Not possible! I don't think so. This is Roni Mitchell you're dealing with. Thanks for your help. It's been interesting. This next corner looks great. Just let me out here." She reached for the door handle.

"I can't let you do that, Miss Mitchell." He spoke in a low voice, but his arm held her back firmly.

She gave him a look of panic. "What are you talking about? You can't let me do what?"

"I can't let you leave."

"Why not?"

"Because you've seen the killer."

"The killer?"

"As you said, you saw Jack the Ripper. No one else has ever seen him and lived to tell about it."

"You're saying the man who attacked me was Jack the Ripper? First, you try to convince me it's 1888, and now... You're out of your mind!"

"No, Miss Mitchell. I'm quite sane. You have seen the killer, and therefore he has seen you. The only safe place for you is with me. You will remain under my protection until I discover what connection you have to all this." He looked out the window. "Ah, here we are now," he said, and the carriage drew to a halt.

4

"Shall I carry you inside?" Kent asked as he helped her descend from the carriage.

"No. I am perfectly capable of walking now," Roni said irritably and moved past him. She looked up at the three-story townhouse and paused. Once again she felt that something strange was happening.

As if sensing her hesitation, Kent took her arm. "Let's go inside. Bellamy, you can put the carriage away. And then I'd like to see you."

Roni froze. "I told you. I'm not going in that house with you. Why don't you take me to the Yard and we can talk there?" She tried to pull away from him.

"Miss Mitchell, I think it would be more prudent if we went inside and discussed things privately." He tightened his hold on her arm and propelled her straight up the steps. As they reached the door, it opened, startling her. Then she saw an elderly, kindly-looking man in a butler's uniform and breathed a sigh of relief. At least she wouldn't be alone with Grayson.

"Good evening, sir," the butler said.

"Good evening." Kent released Roni's arm as soon as they were inside. "Hargrove, this is Miss Mitchell. She'll be staying with us, and I'd like to you tell Mrs. Randall and Mrs. Reilly and anyone else who asks that she is my American cousin who's come to visit."

"Very well, sir," Hargrove replied.

"I never agreed…" Roni began, but Kent shot her a quelling look.

"Hargrove, I suggest you prepare the front guestroom."

"Yes, sir. Let me take your coats," Hargrove said, and waited as Roni removed her trench coat. Both men stared at her. She frowned.

She knew her outfit was current and fashionable. The fuchsia wool jacket over a white silk blouse and black slacks had been perfect for her day's outing in Whitechapel. Why were they looking at her that strangely?

"You're dressed like a man..." Kent said.

Roni had had enough. "If you think for one moment I'm buying this 1880's act of yours, think again!" Exasperated, she marched out of the foyer and into the front room. Once she found Kent's TV and VCR, his telephone, and newspapers with the date June 2, 1994 on them, she would tell him he was full of it and get the hell out of here.

But there was no TV, no VCR, and no telephone. The furniture was heavy Victorian, and tiny flames flickered in the Tiffany lamps lighting the room.

At that moment, the truth hit her, shattering her anger and leaving bewilderment in its place as she tried to grasp the magnitude of what had happened to her. She knew that a lesser woman would have panicked. But Roni was not given to panic. On the contrary, if she had achieved the impossible and traveled through time, then this was truly the challenge of a lifetime, terrifying but also fascinating.

"Damn, it really is..." she murmured. But how had it happened?

"It really is what?" Kent asked, closing the door behind them.

She faced him with as much bravado as she could muster. "I'm hoping you have some liquor in the house, because when I finish telling you, we're both going to need a drink."

"Telling me what?"

"We need to have a talk... a long one. I don't think you're going to believe much of what I have to say, but you have to hear it anyway. Since you're a detective and I'm a reporter, maybe together we can figure this out. You got any whiskey?"

"Whiskey? Well, yes."

"Good. I'll take a straight shot. This has been a long day, and I've got the feeling it's going to get even longer before it's over." She dropped onto the sofa.

Kent crossed to a small liquor cabinet, returned with two shot glasses and handed one to her. Then he sat down at the other end of the sofa. "You say you're a reporter? Are you with the Central News Agency?"

"No. I'm a TV reporter. I live in California. I flew here to do an interview with..." She could see from his face that he was completely bewildered.

"Why don't we start at the beginning," he said. "Suppose you tell me what you were doing in Whitechapel tonight?"

"That's what I was trying to do," she said in exasperation. "I'm here in London on business. I finished my project early and decided to go sightseeing in Whitechapel."

He stared at her. "No one goes sightseeing in the East End."

"In 1994 they do."

"Nineteen ninety-four?" he repeated, scowling.

For the first time, she smiled. "Good. I'm glad to see you looking so perplexed. Now you're as confused as I am. While I was walking around the East End, I found this antique shop run by a very interesting man named Telyur. I bought a watch from him, left the shop, and the next think I knew I was being chased by a wild man with a knife. The rest you know."

"You actually want me to believe that you came here from the future?"

"Look, you're the detective. Figure it out. I sure can't. All I know is that one moment I was in Whitechapel chuckling over Jack the Ripper souvenirs and the next minute I was running for my life in 1888. If you can give me a logical explanation as to how I got here, I'll be glad to listen to it."

Kent downed the rest of his whiskey in one gulp, then got up and poured himself another.

Roni watched him, sensing his doubt. "Look, I know it sounds wild. I know it doesn't make sense. Lord knows, I had no great desire to be whisked back in time like this. I feel like Michael J. Fox with the car. At least, he could get back to the future."

Kent returned to the sofa. "Michael who?"

"Never mind." She signed in frustration, seeing the uncertainty in his eyes. She sipped her whiskey and enjoyed the fiery effect. "Look…" she began again. Then she remembered something. Setting her glass aside, she stood up and shoved her hand into the pocket of her jacket. She almost shouted for joy when she felt the five-pound note she'd stuffed there earlier after paying for her taxi.

"I know my words aren't convincing you, but this should!" She pulled the bill out of her pocket and handed it to him. "Look! Queen Elizabeth's picture is on it. That'll prove I'm not out of my mind."

"Queen Elizabeth has been dead for years," Kent scoffed, taking the note from her hand and staring down at it. He frowned.

"Not Elizabeth the First. This is Elizabeth the Second!"

"Elizabeth the Second?"

He studied the bill for a long moment and then glanced up at her. His face had grown pale, and she could see undisguised amazement in his eyes.

"Now, check the date," she said.

He did, and she heard him draw a sharp breath. "Nineteen ninety-two," he murmured. "This is incredible."

"I know."

His gaze met hers, searching, questioning, and finally believing. She gave a little smile when she saw the acceptance in his eyes. "I don't know how this happened to me, but it did. The question is, what do we do now?"

"I think the first step is to pour you another whiskey." He retrieved the bottle and refilled their glasses.

They drained their drinks in silence.

There was a knock, and Kent rose and opened the doors. He stepped out into the foyer, and Roni could see him speaking to Bellamy. Kent reentered the room and pulled the doors closed. He sat down on the sofa again and studied her.

"If you're from the future, how do you know about Jack the Ripper?" he finally asked.

"*Everyone* knows about him in my time. The Jack the Ripper murders are one of the greatest unsolved mysteries of all time."

"Unsolved?" he said, clearly shocked.

"No arrests were ever made. Let me try to remember what I've read. I think he murdered a total of five or six women. On one night he actually killed two. I wish I could remember the dates..."

Kent shook his head in wonder. "So far he has killed only two... The letter he wrote to the press hasn't even been released to the public yet. No one knows the name 'Jack the Ripper' except those only directly involved in the investigation—and the killer himself."

"And someone from the future," she added simply.

"Yes, and thank heaven you're here with me. You heard what I told Hargrove to tell my cook, Mrs. Randall, and my chairwoman, Mrs. Reilly. And I have given the same instructions to Bellamy, so there will be no uncomfortable questions about you, and I can keep you here safe until we catch him."

"But you won't catch him," she pointed out.

"Yes, I will. If it's the last thing I do, I'll see him pay for what he's done."

"And will do," she said. "You can't change history, so what do you want to do now?"

"I want you out of harm's way until the Ripper is in custody. Just because there's no record in your time of his being caught doesn't mean he wasn't. Perhaps over time, facts about this case and the Ripper's arrest were lost. If so, I wouldn't be changing history after all. Nevertheless, when we have him locked up, I want you to see him so we can be sure we have the right man."

"Now, hold on a minute. There is no way I'm going to sit in this house like a prisoner and wait for you to find the Ripper. Look, let's assume for a moment that your theory is right and that you will catch him. I can help you with the investigation. I'm trained to uncover information. It's what I do for a living."

"Miss Mitchell…"

"Roni."

"Roni, I don't want you to leave this house. I… I've seen what the Ripper does to his victims. You'll stay right here where it's safe."

She shook her head. "I'm going to help you. Have you gotten any fingerprints or blood samples? Any skin or blood under the victims' fingernails?"

"What are you talking about?"

She stopped realizing she was over a hundred years ahead of herself. "Never mind. Look, I want to help. Tell me what you have."

"I don't want you involved."

"I'm already involved. I became involved the minute the Ripper attacked me. I am going to work with you."

"No, you're not."

"Why not?"

"Because you're a woman."

"Oh, really," she said, amused.

"Yes, and it's a man's duty to protect a woman from the ugliness of life."

"But I'm the only real witness you've got."

"Not if you're dead, and that's exactly why I want you to stay here. What if he came after you again? You'd be helpless against him."

"No, I wouldn't. I can take care of myself."

"Of course you can, my dear, but…"

"But nothing. Try me." She stood, ready to demonstrate her prowess after seven years of Tae Kwon Do.

He looked at her in dismay. "I have no intention of trying to harm you."

"I didn't say you were going to. I said you should try. Come on. Try to grab me."

"This is ridiculous."

"Are you afraid?"

Reluctantly, Kent followed Roni into the foyer.

"Now," she said, "pretend you're the Ripper and you're after me. Come at me." She motioned for him to charge her.

"This is pointless. I'm bigger and stronger than you are, and I don't want to hurt you."

"You won't. I thwarted Jack's attack on me, didn't I?"

In a lightning move, Kent charged Roni and tried to grab her. She was ready for him. Timing her move perfectly, she shifted her weight to the side, grabbed him and tossed him. He was heavy and it wasn't easy or pretty, but she had proven her point. He might not be unconscious, but he was on the floor, and had he been the bad guy, she would have had time to escape.

"Satisfied?" she asked, feeling slightly more in control of her situation.

"I don't think I'd like living in the 1990's," he muttered as he got up.

"I'm working with you on this case," she said. "You may be right that you will catch the Ripper but that we will never learn of it in my time. There is also the possibility that you will not only catch him, but once his identity is discovered, a massive cover-up will occur – another reason why there would be no record of the case being solved in my time. Either way, he must be stopped.

"Here's how our partnership will work. I'll tell you everything I can remember, and you'll share your information with me. It's fifty-fifty. Have we got a deal?"

"I don't like it."

"I didn't ask you if you liked it. I asked you if we have a deal. Well?"

"All right, but on one condition. You are not to go roaming the streets looking for him, and you will confine yourself to discussing theories and whatever clues I might find. Besides," he added, smiling, "I can't have you hunting him down with me. How would I explain you to the Yard?"

5

"Mr. Grayson?"

Hargrove's soft call, accompanied by his knock at the bedroom door brought Kent instantly awake.

"Yes? What is it?" Kent sat up in bed as Hargrove entered the room and lit a lamp.

"One of your associates from the Yard is downstairs, sir. It seems there's been more trouble."

Kent swore violently under his breath. Quickly, he got out of bed and pulled on his pants, then at a run he grabbed a shirt and suit coat and hurried from the room. When he reached the top of the staircase, he saw his friend Rod Davidson, waiting for him downstairs in the foyer.

"What happened?" Kent tucked in his shirt as he descended.

"It's horrible, Kent. He's struck again, and not just once this time... He murdered two tonight!"

Kent reeled. Roni had known about the double murder before it had even occurred. Any doubts he had had about her story vanished. "Let's go," he said, shrugging into his suit coat and then his overcoat.

"It is gruesome, sir," Rod said.

"I didn't expect it to be otherwise." Kent followed his colleague into the predawn darkness.

Roni sat in the parlor of Kent's townhouse, trying to occupy herself. When she'd awakened early this morning, Hargrove had informed her that Mr. Grayson had gone out during the night. After the huge breakfast Mrs. Randall had prepared, Roni had read the newspaper, marveling at the events of October 1, 1888. Since then, however, she had been at loose ends. She wondered where Kent had gone and whether his sudden departure had anything to do with the Ripper. He had made no mention last night of having to go out.

It was midday when she heard him come in, and she hurried to the foyer, eager to see him. He was handing Hargrove his coat when she reached the parlor doorway. When he turned to her, his face was grim and haggard.

"The Ripper again?" she asked.

"It was just as you'd said. He struck twice just before dawn."

"Oh, God…" Agony filled her as she thought that if she had remembered more, she might have been able to prevent the killings. "Did you find anything?"

"Nothing. It's as if he disappears into thin air."

"What are we going to do?" she asked.

He glanced at her, dressed in her own clothes, and gave a little smile. "The first thing we'd better do is buy you something to wear. Those clothes would draw too much public attention."

"In the future a lot of women will be running around in slacks, but I guess you don't want me to be a trendsetter."

He couldn't help laughing. "No, not right now."

"But I don't have any money."

"I'll pay for them."

"I appreciate your generosity. I'd like you to keep track of everything you spend so I can pay you back." But even as Roni spoke, she wondered how she would ever be able to do so, stranded here with no career prospects and no way of returning home.

"It's not necessary," he said.

"I insist. It's the way we do things in my time."

"Very well. I'll order the carriage and join you in a few minutes."

Kent went upstairs to wash before his outing with Roni. He felt contaminated by the ugliness he had just seen. He yearned to get away from the case for a while, and today was the perfect opportunity. He would take Roni to buy an appropriate wardrobe, and then they would dine out. She was a breath of fresh air in his life – something he needed now. The long hours he had spent working on the murders had tarnished him, dulling his heart and soul. Roni, he hoped, would bring the shine back to his life.

After washing up, Kent donned a dark suit and waistcoat and descended the stairs to the foyer.

Roni was waiting for him in the parlor, and when he joined her, she smiled at him. "Are you ready to go?" he asked.

"If you are."

The dress shop was a short carriage ride away.

"These clothes are wonderful," Roni said, looking through the window at the display of hats, bustles and parasols. She laughed. "What great antiques!" Abruptly her smile vanished. "You really think it's necessary for me to wear these things?"

"Yes, if you want to move around freely and go unnoticed."

She nodded, but her expression was doubtful as she gazed at the selection of bustles.

A short time later, Kent watched as Roni emerged from the fitting room at the back of the dress shop to model yet another outfit for him, a visiting dress of dark green wool. Demure in style with its high neck and long sleeves, it fitted her to perfection, the skirt nipping at her waist and then flaring out over the bustle in back.

He smiled broadly. "You look lovely."

"Do you really think so?" She tugged at her corset. "I feel like a sausage."

"You'll get used to it," he said, then he turned to the proprietress. "We'll take it. And the lady will also need something for evening wear."

The woman frowned. "While some of our day dresses are ready-made, I'm afraid our formal gowns are still sewn to order." She paused, then smiled. "I do have something in back that just might fit… The gown was made for another customer who cancelled the order at the last minute. I think with a few alterations, the gown just might do. Come with me my dear…" She ushered Roni into the fitting room.

A half hour later, Roni emerged from the back again, this time wearing a low-cut gown of lace and royal blue velvet. Kent stared at her, mesmerized, as she walked slowly toward him. The seamstress had helped her arrange her hair in a sophisticated style, and although he had thought her lovely before, he now thought her positively ravishing. The color of the gown suited her fairness, bringing out the blue of her eyes and the highlights of her upswept pale-golden tresses.

Kent's gaze dropped to the décolletage and his breath caught in his throat. The gown was obviously made for a much smaller-busted woman. Roni more than filled out the bodice, her breasts swelling temptingly above the lace. As much as he enjoyed the view, he reminded himself that the proprietress thought Roni was his cousin and he forced his eyes away from the enticing display.

"As you can see," the shop owner was saying, "I'll need to let the seams out at the bodice. Otherwise, it fits beautifully."

"How soon can you have it ready?"

"By the day after tomorrow."

"That will be fine. We'll take it."

Kent met Roni's eyes and knew while he was with her he could put the ugliness of the murders out of his mind. He was pleased that the current fashions suited her so well, but he'd had little doubt. Her figure was slender yet womanly, and her manner, for all her strange ways, was ladylike. He had never met anyone like her, and he doubted he ever would again. She was the perfect combination of beauty and intelligence, and he grew more intrigued with her every minute.

"As soon as the alterations are completed, deliver the packages to my home," he instructed the proprietress as he paid the bill.

"What would you like us to do with her other clothes?" the woman asked, eyeing the parcel. She had barely concealed her shock at seeing Roni in men's trousers when she and Kent had arrived.

"I'll take them with me," Roni said as she emerged from the fitting room, where she had changed into the dark green visiting dress. To Kent she looked every bit an 1880's woman.

But clearly the clothes did not feel as right as they looked, for as Kent escorted Roni from the shop, the parcel containing her old clothes under his arm, she chafed uncomfortably.

"Incredible," she muttered as she struggled to climb into the carriage.

"What is it?" he said.

"This corset! In my time, we would burn the damn thing. What evil sadistic person created it? No doubt it was a man. How's a woman supposed to breathe in it, let alone move?"

"I've never given it much thought."

"You should. This is cruel and unusual punishment. How could a woman run in this if she were in trouble? It would be next to impossible for her to protect herself."

"Why would a lady need to protect herself? Her husband would protect her."

"Some women don't have husbands to protect them. The

women in Whitechapel, for example."

"You're right," he said grimly as he helped her into the carriage. All thoughts of the murders dissipated as he caught a glimpse of her shoes, and realized they had to make one more stop.

"Bellamy, take us to the women's shoe shop," he directed as he settled himself beside Roni.

"Yes, sir."

"I guess I do need shoes," Roni remarked as she glanced down at her practical, low-heeled pumps.

"After we get them, we can dine out, if you like. If you're hungry?"

"I'm famished, and, yes, I'd love to eat out." Roni smiled at him, then turned to gaze out the carriage window.

To Roni, nineteenth-century London was even more fascinating in the daytime than at night. As strange as it was for her to be here, she was determined to enjoy every minute.

But why was she here? She thought back to her actions the previous night, just before she had realized she was standing under a gaslight. She remembered hearing the watch chime, opening it, and hearing it tick. Then the fog had come up and she had found herself still holding the watch in the gaslight's dim glow.

Her heart pounded and she felt a sheen of sweat break out on her forehead. It was the watch that had caused her to travel in time! But her realization brought her no relief, for she knew that without the watch, she could not go home.

And another thought assaulted her. Even if she had the watch, would she want to leave?

Kent glanced at Roni as she peered out the window, and again he was struck by her beauty. He had found her attractive when she had worn trousers, and, now, dressed in the current fashion, she completely entranced him. Though she had been with him less than a day, the thought that she might leave him someday made him uneasy. She captivated him, and didn't seem to possess the flirtatious artifices he'd suffered through with most of the unmarried women he knew. Despite their bizarre meeting, he was strongly drawn to her, and was actually looking forward to having dinner with her—after they bought her shoes.

Two hours later, after finishing their meal in the quiet establishment Kent had chosen, they finally took up the subject of the murders, reexamining everything they knew about Jack the Ripper, trying to find the clue that might reveal his identity.

"Who were you considering the most likely suspects in your time?" Kent asked.

"You may not want to hear this…"

"Go ahead," he encouraged.

"History has focused on five suspects. One was a poor, single man from the Whitechapel area. One was a lawyer from a good family who was rumored to be insane. One was the queen's physician, and the last two…" She hesitated, knowing that what she was about to say was close to blasphemy. "The last two were the queen's grandson, Prince Eddy, and a friend of his, J.K. Steven."

Kent nodded. "We're investigating all those leads," he said noncommittally.

She understood his discomfort that one of the royals might be involved. If one of them was, then that would explain a cover-up in this time. "All I know is that the last murder will occur sometime in early November—around the tenth, I think, but I'm not certain."

"Early November… So we have about a month's reprieve," he said.

She nodded. "If you're going to catch him, you'll have to do it between now and then. If we could save that one woman's life, all this will have been worth it." She looked down at the table. "His last murder… was his most savage."

"I'll do everything in my power to stop him before then," Kent promised.

"I believe you."

In the soft, muted light of the restaurant, she met his gaze across their secluded table. She could see the fierceness of his determination in the depths of his gray eyes, and her admiration for this special man grew. She knew that his dedication to solving the case wasn't motivated by a desire for fame or accolades, for he knew now from what she had told him that he would get no recognition for his success. He wanted to catch the Ripper for only one reason—to save lives.

There was a long pause as they gazed at each other enraptured, as if seeing each other for the first time… as if their coming together had been destined.

"Let's speak of something else," Kent said at last. "Tell me about your life… about you…"

She was relieved to be distracted from thoughts of the murderer. He haunted her every waking moment as it was. She began to tell Kent about her life in California. She told of how she had built her career, and of her desire to become the best investigative journalist in television news.

"Do you have any family?" he asked.

"My mother lives in Chicago. Whenever I can, I fly out to see her, but—"

"Fly?"

She smiled. "We have airplanes… jets, actually. We can fly from coast to coast in a matter of hours."

"Amazing. What about your father? Is he dead?"

"No…" Roni paused, remembering the pain of her parents' divorce when she was twelve. "He and my mother were divorced. I rarely see him anymore."

"Oh."

She heard the shock and surprise in Kent's voice; she knew that divorce was practically nonexistent in his time.

"And you have no husband or fiancé?" he asked.

"No. I guess I'm too busy to think about romance. There's not much time for a relationship with all the traveling I do. Plus, I'm not really sure I want to get married."

"Why not?"

Her expression was tinged with sadness as she looked at him. "My mother loved my father with all her heart and soul. Her entire life was centered around him, and when he left her… Well, she was never the same after that. I don't think I want to put myself in that position…to give a man that kind of power over me."

"But marriage isn't a matter of one partner having power over the other. A husband and wife should complement each other, not dominate each other. A marriage is sharing both the good and the bad, with complete and total trust. What man wouldn't want to come home to a loving wife?"

"Plenty of them," she said with a hint of bitterness, thinking of all the nights she'd listened to her mother cry herself to sleep. "That's why I'm determined to be independent. I don't need a man to take care of me. I'll take care of myself."

"So you never want to marry? Surely you want to have children someday."

"Who says I need a husband to have children?"

He stared at her, aghast. "Have things changed so much in the next hundred years?"

"Well, there was the sexual revolution in the sixties. Women are no longer repressed as they are in your time. They no longer believe they exist only to satisfy a man's desire."

Kent chuckled. "Repressed is a hardly a word I would use to describe the women I've known. I've never met a woman yet who thought she existed simply to satisfy my desires, unless you'd like to be the first." There was a gleam of wicked amusement in his gaze

"I'll pass, but thanks for the offer," she countered.

"Most of the women I know would be insulted to think that you considered them less than their husband's equals. What could be more important in the world than raising children and keeping a warm, loving home for a family? Family is the most important thing in the world, you know."

Roni sensed that Kent meant every word he was saying, and she was touched by his ardent devotion to marriage and family. She found herself wondering what it would be like to be married to a man like him...a man who truly believed in the vows he would take, a man who would put his wife and children first in his life, and she decided it might not be so bad. "What about your family?"

"My parents are both dead, but I have a brother who is happily married with three sons. I see him at the holidays."

"No fiancée?"

"No. I suppose I'm like you. I'm wedded to my job. There is satisfaction in knowing that I'm helping people… But tell me more about the 1990's. What else is exciting?"

Roni paused, not sure where to start. "Well, we have cars-horseless carriages is what they used to call them, and they run on gasoline. We have television- it's an electronic device that projects a picture with sound, so instead of relying on newspapers for information, you can just turn on the TV and get all the news you want. We have highways, skyscrapers, air conditioning, electricity…"

"Do you miss it all?"

She paused to consider his question. Of course, she missed it. That was her life. But she was here for whatever purpose. "Yes." She heard the loneliness in her voice.

Kent reached out to cover her hand with his. She was surprised by her reaction to his touch. She felt drawn to him, and knew instinctively that she could trust him with her life.

"Could you be happy here?" he asked.

"It's a slower-paced, more romantic time, but…" She found herself wondering about her life… if she could ever find the watch, which seemed impossible… if she was destined to stay in the 1880's. The whole situation was strange, so unlike anything she'd ever experienced, that she was uncertain how to answer him. The question that flitted through her mind was whether she could spend the rest of her life here with him. She could form no definitive answer. "I'm not sure."

"Perhaps I can convince you that you could be happy here," he said warmly, and lifted his glass to her. "To the future…"

6

Later that night, Kent bid Roni good night and she started upstairs. Halfway up, she paused. "Kent?"

Heading for his study, he stopped and glanced up at her.

"Remember the night you found me, I told you I lost my purse and my watch? Well, the Ripper took the watch from me during the attack, and I have finally figured out it was the watch that brought me here. Without it, I can't get home…"

He heard the vulnerability in her voice, and it touched a deep chord within him. His determination to protect her became a burning need. Despite her objections, he would keep her safe—for however long she decided to stay with him.

"We'll take everything a day at a time, Roni. I will be with you for as long as you need me."

"Thank you," she said, smiling tremulously.

He returned her smile. "I'll always be here. You needn't worry."

She hesitated, as if intending to say more, then seemed to change her mind. "Well, good night."

"Good night." He watched her climb the stairs and wondered if she was real or if he was caught up in some kind of dream. If it was a dream, he had to admit that he was enjoying it. And it comforted him to know she would not disappear from his life. Only the knowledge that the Ripper was still out there and might be looking for her tempered his good mood.

He entered his study and settled himself at his desk, intending to go over his notes on the case. Instead, he found himself staring out the open doorway at the stairs. Thinking of Roni and what they could do together tomorrow. He wanted to show her London, wanted to show her more of life in his time. Most of all, he just wanted to be with her. The idea surprised him, for his work had always been his obsession. It had been his life, his reason for being, and now… Despite that he known Roni for only one day, he would miss her terribly if she were to go.

The weeks that followed passed in a sweet, steady rhythm of discovery for them both.

At first, while Kent was working, Roni passed much of her time reading. She eagerly devoured the London newspaper every day and then started on the books in the library.

Kent met her for lunch as often as he could, and he did take her to see the sights, but there were still long hours when he was gone and she was alone with the servants. Eventually, reading wasn't enough to keep Roni occupied, so she started to pitch in and help Mrs. Reilly and Mrs. Randall with their work. Both ladies protested that she was a guest and, as such, shouldn't assist them, but Roni was so persistent that they ultimately capitulated.

As Roni worked with them, she listened to them sing Kent's praises. It seemed he was invariably kind and generous with those he cared about, having taken good care of both women through the years they'd been in his employ. Roni came to like and respect him even more.

There were days, though, when Roni longed for her home, her work, and her own time. She wondered if anyone missed her and if her mother, friends, and colleagues were looking for her. Some nights, she would lie in bed, trying to figure out what she was going to do. Certainly, a career of her own was out of the question in this time period, but she wondered if Kent might let her help him with his cases. Roni was certain that her abilities could aid him in solving crime. All she had to do was convince him to let her work with him behind the scenes.

Sometimes at night, the thought of how truly alone she was in this strange world haunted her. Then Kent would slip into her thoughts and somehow calm her fears. There were even some nights when she drifted off to sleep trying to imagine what it would be like to be married to him. The idea was not unpleasant.

For his part, Kent put in long hours on the job, but he grew increasingly frustrated by the department's failure to catch the Ripper. Despite his dedication to his work, he always found time for

Roni. He enjoyed their sightseeing almost as much as she did, for experiencing the city through her eyes renewed his love for it. In the evenings when he came home, they would discuss the case and any new information he had learned that day.

One evening, Kent arrived home to find Roni at his desk in his study, reading the newspaper. Her concentration was so intense that he was curious to find out what she was reading.

"Is something troubling you?" he asked.

"Hmmm?" She was surprised to see him, for she hadn't heard him come in. "No, no, nothing's bothering me. It's just that..." Abruptly she laid the newspaper aside in frustration.

"That what?"

"There's a picture of Prince Eddy there... As you know, he is considered a suspect in my time, and I was trying to see..."

"Is he the one?" Kent tensed as he awaited her response.

"What if he is? Even if you arrest him, he will never be punished, and the public will never know what he's done." She gave him an agonized gaze.

"Is he the one who attacked you?"

"You'll be ruined if you try to do anything about it..."

"I don't care. Nothing is more important than finding the Ripper before he strikes again."

Roni picked up the newspaper once again and concentrated as she stared at the likeness of the prince. "I can't be sure. I wish I could be, but I can't... There's so much difference between a picture and seeing the real man who attacked me that night. What I mean is that the Ripper wore a hat and his features were shadowed. I just can't be certain. I'm sorry."

"There's nothing to be sorry for. The whole department is just as frustrated as you are. We've tried everything from bloodhounds to decoys to catch him, without success."

Roni sat perfectly still, then lifted her gaze from the newspaper to him. "Kent, what about using me?"

"I have been. Your knowledge of the Ripper had been extremely helpful."

"That's not what I mean. You said the Ripper might be after me because as far as we know, I am the only person to survive one of his attacks and I can identify him. So, why don't I make myself conspicuous? You could use *me* as a decoy. I'm more than willing to go to Whitechapel and help you trap him."

"No."

"Why not?"

"Because as I told you before, you could be killed, and I won't allow you to be deliberately set up for that to happen. I simply won't be a party to it. Besides, even if I were willing to go along with your idea, I would need my superiors' approval to use you in a stakeout, and they would never give it. You're going to stay right here where Hargrove or I can protect you should the need arise."

"Do your superiors really have to know?" she asked. "I mean, if we catch him, you don't have to tell them of my involvement. You also forget that I wouldn't be alone on the street. You'd be there, watching me."

"All right, forget my superiors for the moment. What if I was watching from a distance and he proved to be faster than I was? You'd end up dead."

"You have very little faith in my ability to defend myself. Didn't I prove to you I could do it?"

"You proved that you could defend yourself from a man who attacked you head-on. But what if he came upon you from behind? What if he stabbed you before you knew what was happening? No, it's best to leave things as they are."

"But Jack did grab me from behind, and I escaped," she persisted. "And just to be safe, I could carry a gun. Don't you have one?"

"Certainly, but what good would it do you? You must have time to aim and fire. If he surprised you…"

"You're determined to keep me out of this, aren't you?"

"I'm determined to keep you alive, and if that means keeping you in this house out of harm's way, then that's what I'm going to do. So leave it alone. Now, for a change of topic, would you like to go for a walk tonight? It's clear out and the weather's mild."

Though Roni was tempted to keep arguing with Kent, she conceded good-naturedly. In the few weeks she had been with him she had learned to gauge his moods, knew just how far she could press him. As much as she wanted to help capture the Ripper, she realized that Kent was probably right. His superiors would never go for the idea of using her as a decoy.

She smiled at him. "I'd love to go for a walk with you."

Outside, walking beside Roni, Kent found himself as enchanted as ever by her witty conversation. Well-versed in many subjects, as he had discovered from their many conversations, she was stimulating, and he told himself again that she must be a dream, for no real woman could have fit so perfectly into his life. But then, whenever he touched her, he knew she was no figment of his imagination. He did not know why she had come into his life, but he would always be grateful that she had.

He felt her gently squeeze his arm and looked at her.

"You're so far away," she said. "Is something wrong?"

He smiled, slightly embarrassed at the direction of his thoughts. "No. I was thinking about you."

"Me? Why?"

He stopped walking and reached for her hand. She felt vibrant, alive. He wished he could keep touching her for all eternity. "I was just telling myself that I'm here talking to a woman who hasn't, by all right, been born yet."

"If that's the case, then I'm talking to a man who had been dead for a number of years. Do you realize how old you would be if this were my time?"

He thought about it and laughed. "Old. Very old."

"I'm glad you're not. I don't usually date older men." She was laughing, too.

"I don't know how all this has come about, but I'm glad you're here, Roni…"

"I am, too." Her reply was a whisper on the gentle night breeze.

They stood still on the quiet street, caught up in the intimacy of their confessions.

Kent studied her upturned face in the moonlight. She was everything he'd ever wanted in a woman. He longed to take her in his arms and hold her close. He wanted to kiss her, to keep her near and never let her go. With an effort, he maintained a grip on his desire, determined to continue his role as a gentleman. It wasn't easy. She was so lovely… He wanted her with a passion that surprised even him.

Roni gazed up at him and she knew in that moment that she wanted to kiss him, to be in his arms. At times she had found his protectiveness almost smothering, for she wasn't used to anyone keeping tabs on her. But during their time together, she had come to appreciate his concern for her and her safety. She had to depend on him for her very existence, yet he had never tried to take advantage of her in any way. No man she had ever met could match him.

Ever one to go after what she wanted, she closed the distance between them. Without a word, she looped her arms around his neck and drew him down to her for a kiss.

Kent was momentarily shocked. No woman had ever taken the initiative with him. He'd been battling his own need for her, and she had come to him. After his initial disconcertment, he quickly decided he was delighted that she had. As he lips sought his, he embraced her, his arms encircling her and bringing her against him.

Their lips met, and in that dark London night, they shared their first kiss. It was a passionate blending of desire and restraint as they tasted the sweetness of their newfound feelings for each other. The world around them faded.

Kent wanted to crush Roni to him and claim her in all ways. Just this one kiss sent heat flooding through his body, settling in his loins, urging him to claim her, to make her his own. Only a last shred of sanity saved him. As much as he thrilled at having her in his arms and feeling her soft curves pressed against him, he knew it couldn't be. She was a lady. He had her honor to uphold. He could not and would not take advantage of her.

With a fierce effort, he broke off the kiss and stepped back. Staring down at her once again, he could see passion's flush on her cheeks and he knew she was as deeply affected by the embrace as he was.

"I'm glad you kissed me," she said in a low voice, wanting him to know that she had enjoyed every second of it.

"We'd better go…" he said, feeling a little awkward as he faced the truth of his feelings for her. She was becoming important in his life… so very important.

"Are you sure?" Her tone was inviting.

"No. I'm not sure at all. That's why we're going," he admitted. Then, unable to bear the thought of not touching her, he took her arm and linked it through his.

Roni smiled contentedly as she walked slowly at Kent's side. She felt right, as if this was where she was meant to be.

They strolled quietly for some time, before he turned to her. "Do you like opera?"

She nodded.

"Good. I'll get tickets and we can go this weekend."

When they returned to the house, Roni bid him good night. With all her heart she wanted him to kiss her once more, but he did not.

Sleep was long in coming. She tossed, remembering every blissful moment of being in his arms. She fantasized again about being married to Kent, and smiled. He was compassionate, gentle, devoted, and caring, not to mention handsome, sexy and intelligent. As she closed her eyes, she thought Kent wouldn't rob her of her independence after all.

In his room, Kent lay awake, staring at the ceiling. His thoughts were of Roni. By some incredible happenstance, she had come to him through time. He didn't know how or why, but he did know that he didn't want to lose her. Images of coming home to find her waiting for him appealed to him, yet even as he pictured sharing his life with her, he worried about what the fates had in store for him. As always, the specter of the Ripper hovered in the back of his mind. The realization that November would soon be upon them gave him a nagging sense of dread. He feared that something terrible was going to happen, and that he would be unable to stop it.

*

She'd actually done it! Roni smiled as she stared at the perfectly set dining-room table with its white linen tablecloth, highly polished silver, sparkling crystal, and delicate china.

That morning, right after Kent had left for work, she'd decided to fix a special dinner for him, since it was the cook's day off. Now, a great sense of feminine pride filled her as she stared at her handiwork.

Roni's heartbeat quickened as she realized Kent would be coming home soon. She hoped he would enjoy the dinner she'd prepared. She knew she would. It seemed an eternity since she'd last had pizza, and she'd labored all afternoon making the dough and trying to find the right ingredients. It hadn't been easy, and she still wasn't certain just how it was going to taste, but the pie smelled delicious in the oven.

Taking such pleasure in cooking for Kent gave Roni pause.

Domesticity had never been her strong suit. Some nights when she'd been working late, there had only been time for a microwave dinner or a peanut-butter sandwich. Roni frowned as she mentally debated the merits of eating a microwave dinner alone in her apartment after a hard day at the TV station or having a homemade pizza here with Kent. She was considering that revelation when she heard the front door.

"You're home…" she said brightly as she hurried to greet him in the foyer.

"Finally." Kent had passed another frustrating day following up on the endless and ultimately useless leads in the Ripper case, and he had been more than eager to head home to Roni. Seeing her now, smiling in warm welcome, he had to fight down the urge to take her in his arms and kiss her. "What smells so good?"

"I cooked dinner for you tonight."

"You didn't have to do that. Didn't Mrs. Randall leave something? She usually does on her day off."

"She did, but I wanted to make something special for you. I cooked my favorite meal for you. I hope you enjoy it. I don't think you've ever had anything like it before. Everything's just about ready. Come sit down, and I'll get you a glass of wine." She took his hand and led him into the dining room.

"Roni, the table looks lovely. You must have spent hours preparing for dinner." He was impressed. As he took his seat, she poured a glass of wine and handed it to him.

"I did."

"You mean to tell me you actually enjoyed doing a domestic chore?" he teased.

"I have to admit, I did. I wanted to do something special for you."

"You have, just by coming into my life."

His words left her breathless and she smiled at him tremulously as her gaze met his. For a brief moment, the universe narrowed to just the two of them. There was no past or future. There was only now—the time that they shared.

"Thank you," she said.

"Have some wine with me?" he invited.

"Just as soon as I get the salads and the pizza."

"Pizza?"

"You'll see."

A short time later, Roni was watching with pleasure as Kent devoured the last slice with gusto.

"Your pizza was delicious."

"I'm glad you liked it. I was worried that it might not turn out right. I've never made it from scratch before."

"You did a marvelous job. What other recipes do you know? I may fire Mrs. Randall."

"Don't you dare! She's a wonderful cook, and after pizza, there's only tacos and hamburgers from McDonald's left in my repertoire."

"McDonald's?"

"A fast-food restaurant." At his quizzical look, she said, "When I don't have time to cook, I go through the drive-through grab some burgers to take home."

"You actually drive through a restaurant?"

She laughed. "No, there's a window you drive up to, and after you pay, they had you your food in a bag."

"I think I like this kind of dining better," he remarked thoughtfully.

"So do I," she admitted, thinking how wonderful it was to be sitting with him, sharing an intimate dinner. "Well, I'd better start washing the dishes."

"We'll do the dishes together." He stood up and picked up his plate and glass.

Roni was startled by his willingness to help. Every man she knew high-tailed it when it came time to clean up after a meal.

"Thanks."

"My pleasure."

Later, after Roni had bid Kent good night and had gone upstairs to bed, she couldn't help wondering if being married to him would be as wonderful as this evening had been. His conversation had been interesting and intelligent. He'd helped with all the housewifely chores without complaint, and he'd even liked her cooking. She had to admit he was close to being the perfect man. She was smiling as she drifted off to sleep.

The following Saturday evening they attended the opera. As they took their seats, Roni was pleased that they had a good view of the stage and the rest of the theater. When everyone stood and began to applaud, she noticed Kent kept gazing at something across the theater.

"What is it?" she asked.

"His Royal Highness is here." He nodded toward the box where Prince Eddy stood with his entourage.

The prince acknowledged the audience's welcome, and when he was seated, the audience sat. Roni stared at him, trying to discern if he was the man who had attacked her on that dark night, if he was the one whose violent use of a knife would mark him as the killer of the century. If he was, that would certainly account for the necessity of a cover-up.

As if sensing Roni's gaze upon him, the prince suddenly glanced in her direction, frowning slightly. Roni quickly looked away, unnerved by the thought that he might have known she was watching him. Now she felt even more confused as to the Ripper's identity.

After the opera, Kent took her to a fine restaurant.

"This place is wonderful," Roni told him as she sat across from him at the candlelit table.

"After your pizza, I felt I owed you a special night out."

"The opera was special enough. You didn't have to do this."

"But I wanted to."

The waiter came to take their order then, and after he'd left them and their wine was served, Kent lifted his glass to Roni.

"To us," he said with quiet intensity.

Roni lifted her glass to his, and they drank to the toast.

"Do you think you could be happy here? Can you accept our way of life?" Kent asked. He knew she would be remaining in his time if they couldn't find the watch, and he wanted to protect her, to keep her safe.

"I don't know," she answered hesitantly. "I've tried to change my way of thinking, to come to grips with the fact that I may never go back... but everything is so different. I'm used to being independent and taking care of myself."

"Could you be content without your career? Could you be satisfied being a wife?"

"I've learned so much from you in just the short time we've been together, and I realize that I was wrong about a lot of things about marriage. A marriage doesn't necessarily have to be the way my parents' was."

"No, it doesn't. It can be a wonderful thing... two people

working to make a life together. It's a challenge, and not an easy one, but worth the effort, I think—if there's love."

"There has to be love," she agreed as she looked up at him.

"Without it life means little." He gazed at her, wondering if love was the elusive emotion that was filling him, keeping visions of her dancing softly through his mind.

"I know I watched my mother try to exist without my father after he left her."

"But that won't happen to you."

"No. I won't allow it to. I'm firmly convinced we're each responsible for our own happiness. We can choose to be happy or we can choose to be miserable. I choose to be happy. Life's too short for anything else."

She smiled at Kent as the waiter served their first course.

It was hours later when they returned to the townhouse. Hargrove had already retired for the night, so they were alone in the foyer.

"Thank you for a lovely evening," she said as Kent took her wrap.

"It was my pleasure." He put her cloak away with his own. "I had a wonderful time."

"So did I." She turned to him as he came to her.

"Did I tell you that you look lovely tonight?" His deep voice was a velvet caress to her senses.

"Thank you." She lifted her gaze to his and in that instant saw a flare of desire in the depths of his eyes. She stood poised and motionless, wanting him to kiss her, wishing she could once again know the pleasure of his touch. She had come to care about him deeply, but except for that one kiss she had given him, he had made no move to touch her again. He had been the perfect gentleman, and it was driving her crazy.

Her wish was granted, for Kent could no longer deny the need that had been building within him. She haunted his thoughts by day and his dreams by night. He had never felt this way about another woman, and the power of his feelings for her surprised him. Logically—his whole existence was built around logic and good, methodical police work—she shouldn't even be here with him. And yet...

"Kiss me..." She finally whispered, unable to bear being so close without touching him.

It was all the invitation he needed. He took her in his arms and held her. His mouth found hers, and Roni gave a soft sigh as she instinctively nestled against him. She arched with need for him.

The kiss sparked a flame inside Kent that quickly grew to a raging fire. He was lost in the glory of her embrace. It was heaven to hold her, and he realized almost painfully that if he didn't let her go now, he never would. With a Herculean effort, he ended the kiss and held her slightly away from him.

"Good night, Roni," he said, the regret in his voice unmistakable.

Roni understood, for she, too, was ready to cast all common sense to the wind and love him. She stood on tiptoes to give him one last quick kiss before moving away from him

"Good night, Kent."

She started up the stairs. Kent remained downstairs, feeling the need for a drink before retiring. He watched her until she was out of sight, then stepped into the parlor and poured himself a shot of whiskey.

7

Roni entered her room and turned up the lamp on the dresser. She walked to the bed and turned back the covers. Something metallic gleamed on her pillow, and puzzled, she leaned closer.

It was the watch Telyur had given her, the watch the Ripper had taken from her the night he'd attacked her.

Her heart lurched in her breast and she backed away from the bed.

He had found her.

"Kent!" she screamed, and ran out into the hallway.

He came bounding up the stairs. "What is it?"

"He's been here!"

"Who?"

"The Ripper!" She pointed through the doorway into her room, and he stepped inside. "There," she said, "on the pillow."

Kent crossed to the bed and looked down at the watch. He picked it up and studied it, then looked at Roni. "This is the watch he took from you?"

She nodded. Revulsion shuddered through her. She felt violated.

"He found me, Kent. He was here in my room. This is his message to me…"

Kent came back out into the hallway and took her in his arms. "Are you all right?" he asked. "You're as white as a ghost."

She looked up at him sharply. "Oh, God, Kent, he may still be in the house!"

He muttered grimly, "Come with me."

They went down the hall to Kent's bedroom, where he took the keys from his pocket and unlocked the chest at the foot of the bed.

Inside were two pistols. He handed her one and grabbed the other.

"Be careful. It's loaded."

As Roni took the weapon she felt great relief. She wanted to be prepared when they faced the Ripper.

Kent led the way first to Roni's room. He made a thorough search while she waited at the doorway.

"He's not in here. Stay with me while I check the rest of the house."

"You don't have to worry about that," she told him, shadowing his every step.

Hargrove appeared from his quarters on the third floor. "What's happened, sir?"

"Someone's been in the house, Hargrove. Did you hear anything usual tonight?"

"Nothing, sir."

Hargrove joined them in their search. At the back of the house they found that a window looking out on the alley had been forced open.

It took them the better part of an hour to ascertain that the intruder was not inside.

"Even so," Kent said, "we're going to have to be extra careful from now on. In the morning, Hargrove, I want a second set of locks installed on all the doors and windows."

"Yes, Mr. Grayson, I'll see to it first thing. Is there anything else tonight? Would you like some tea?"

"No, thank you, that'll be all for tonight."

Hargrove climbed the stairs to his room, and Kent and Roni went into the parlor, still too shaken to retire. Kent could tell that Roni was fighting to be brave, trying to put up a good front for him, but her trembling hands betrayed her.

"Would you like something a little stronger than tea?" he asked.

"Definitely," she answered gratefully.

He poured her a small whiskey, but didn't fix one for himself. After what had just happened, he had no intention of dulling his senses. He would take no chances with Roni's life.

Roni finished her drink and set the glass aside. She looked at Kent sitting close beside her. She didn't want him to think badly of her, but she couldn't face the prospect of being alone in her room tonight.

"Kent, would you stay with me tonight?"

He touched her cheek in a gentle caress as his eyes met hers. "Don't worry, my love. I'll keep you safe."

Bending to her, he kissed her with infinite care. Then he rose, taking her hand and drawing her up with him. He picked up both of the pistols and led her from the parlor and upstairs to his own bedroom. There he placed the guns within reach in the nightstand drawer, then turned back to the woman he loved more than life itself. When he had heard her cry out his name earlier that night, the terrifying thought that something had happened to her had shaken him to the depths of his soul.

"I love you, Roni," he said, standing before her. "I don't know what will come of our time together, but I can't deny what I feel for you any longer."

She smiled at him tenderly. "I feel as if I've known you forever. It's almost as if you're a part of me..."

"I want to be a part of you," he said, his gaze darkening as he lifted her into his arms and kissed her passionately. He looked into her eyes. "I want to be with you every minute. I want us to be together always."

"So do I." She linked her arms around his neck as he carried her to the wide, inviting softness of his bed.

He lay her upon it and stretched out beside her. "You're the most beautiful women I've ever known."

"I want to be beautiful – for you..." She reached out and rested a hand on his chest, feeling the solid, heavy beat of his heart beneath her palm. "What we have is so precious... Kent, I'm afraid I'm going to lose you..." The words were agony for her to say.

He cradled her to him. "Don't be afraid, love. I'll be with you always."

"But what if..." She rose for a moment to look down at him, committing to memory the manly beauty of his features. She was giving her heart and soul to this man, and the fear that the Ripper could hurt him and that Kent might be taken from her filled her with pain.

He silenced her with a kiss. "I'll never let you go," he vowed. "No one will ever take me away from you. No matter what, we'll be together..."

For now, they would forget everything else—the uncertainty of their lives, the cruelty and violence of the Ripper. For now, it was just the two of them, giving of themselves as neither of them had ever given before, pledging their devotion with words and caresses.

Kent helped Roni to undress, stripping away the many layers of clothing that he now cursed for their inconvenience. His frustrated muttering drew a sensual chuckle from her as she helped him with the many ties and buttons. She had worn her hair up tonight, and he took great pleasure in freeing her golden mane. As the pale curls cascaded down her back, he raked his fingers through the silken length. Gazing upon her unclothed for the first time, he knew she was feminine perfection. Her breasts were high and firm, her waist slender, her hips round and inviting.

Unable to deny himself any longer, he stripped off his shirt and went into her arms. His mouth slanted across hers in a possessive exchange that left them both breathless with the promise of what was to come. There would be no stopping this night. Driven by desperation, fear and love, they would come together, pledging with their hearts the truth of their devotion. They were one and would be one forever.

He shed the rest of his clothes and then moved over to claim her in love's most perfect way. She whispered his name and then their bodies melded in rapturous union. They moved together, their sole reason for being to love each other.

A spiraling crescendo of desire took them higher and higher until ecstasy exploded within them, sending them both to heaven and beyond. They drifted in love's aftermath, joined in body and spirit. They had given each other their most cherished gift, and they knew paradise.

They did not speak, but lay together, their limbs entwined, their hearts beating in union. They had no future and no past. They celebrated the moment and cherished each touch and caress. Theirs was a love that had been stolen out of time.

"I love you, Kent."

He drew her closer and kissed her deeply. "And I love you."

There was no need to say more as she felt the heat of him deep within her again.

Kent had wanted and needed her for so long that just having her near aroused him. This time setting a slower pace for their lovemaking, he savored every moment of having her silken body beneath him. He caressed and kissed her, teaching her of love's delights and encouraging her to learn more.

She proved an apt pupil, and she eagerly experimented, touching him as boldly as he had touched her. Her boldness won her his passion, and he began to move more quickly inside of her, his pace frenzied in his need to claim her once more.

The crest came upon them in a rush of glory, and they clung together, mindless in the pleasure that had swept over them. They lay sated, neither of them having known a love so sweet.

After that night, Roni did not return to her solitary bed. Each day that followed held new delights as they learned more about each other, and each night was idyllic as they lay in each other's arms.

Time passed far too swiftly for them. They wanted only to be together. Roni never even thought of testing the watch to see if it would send her back to her own time. She had decided that she belonged to Kent. He had shown her the beauty of true sharing and devotion. Any doubts she's had about committing herself to a relationship were gone. In all of time, there would be no other man for her.

But as November neared, the final murder loomed closer, and Kent had to force himself to leave Roni more and more often. He worked from dusk to dawn, prowling the streets of the East End in his constant search for the vicious murderer. Kent and Roni both knew this was his last chance to catch the Ripper.

Prepared to be away from Roni tonight, Kent arranged for Hargrove to keep watch. He also left one of his pistols close at hand for her, in case she should need it. He hated leaving the paradise of her arms and going out into the dank, filthy streets, but the Ripper had to be stopped before it was too late.

Night after night, alone in his bed, Roni turned restlessly as she anxiously awaited Kent's return. She feared for him and ached to have him back with her, safe from the bloodthirsty killer.

Seven days and seven long nights passed during which Kent worked the streets in his search. Roni found she couldn't even rest in her bed. Nervous and worried, she paced late into the night. She didn't know why she was so upset, but instinctively she felt that something was wrong.

She had avoided going into her own bedroom since the night of the break-in, but for some reason she was drawn there now. She entered and lit a lamp. Nothing had changed. Hargrove had put the watch the Ripper had returned to her on the dresser. From where she stood in the doorway, she could see the gold glimmering in the semi-darkness. Instinctively, she went to the dresser and picked up the watch.

When she'd held it in Telyur's shop, it had felt cold. Now, as it lay in the palm of her hand, the watch felt warm, almost hot. The change startled her. Nervously, she opened the case and found that the watch had stopped.

And as she stared down at the watch, remembering Telyur and his strange shop, a date suddenly came to her mind. November 9.

That was today.

Sometime before dawn, the Ripper would kill again.

Her hand closed around the watch as she turned and fled from the room. She must find Kent and warn him!

She hurried back to Kent's room and dressed quickly, pausing only long enough to get the pistol her had left her. Then she crept from the room. Sneaking past Hargrove would be the hardest part.

She made it to the foyer without waking the butler and donned her cloak. It was well past midnight when she slipped from the townhouse and headed for Whitechapel and the stakeout area where Kent had told her he'd be. In the pockets of her dress, she carried not only the gun, but the watch as well. Not only had it sent her back, it had also brought Jack the Ripper to her. Perhaps it would do so again tonight.

The trek to the East Side took a while, but finally she arrived. Her nerves stretched taut, she moved off into the darkness of the narrow, deserted streets.

Several drunks staggered by, but no one paid any attention to her, and she was relieved. Walking quietly, she searched for some sign of Kent but found no trace of him. A fine misty rain began to fall, adding to the night's chill.

It seemed she had been walking for hours when she heard heavy footsteps. The memory of the first time she had heard footsteps in the night was alive and terrifying, and this time she wasn't sure whether to stop and confront whoever was behind her or continue moving at her steady pace. Slipping a hand into her pocket, she gripped the pistol. As the steps came closer, she tensed. The man drew alongside of her and with her heart pounding she turned to him.

It was a bobby, walking his beat.

"Evening," she said.

"Good evening, ma'am." He looked puzzled to see her there but continued walking disappearing down a side street.

Roni realized she was shaking. It hadn't been the Ripper. It had been a policeman. She almost laughed at her overreaction and was glad to move into the dim glow of a gaslight.

"I knew you would come."

The sound of that deep voice shattered her momentary calm, and she spun around, pulling out the gun as she faced the man she knew to be a cold-blooded murderer. Viciously, he knocked her arm aside, sending the gun flying.

She turned to flee, but he grabbed her around the neck and yanked her back against him. She screamed, the echo reverberation through the streets and alleyways.

"Why you..." he hissed. He tried to throw her to the ground, but knowing she was fighting for her life, she kicked and clawed at him. His arm at her throat was choking her, and she was thrashing wildly in his grip, trying to break free of his deadly hold, she could feel her strength ebbing as darkness closed in on her.

"Roni!" Kent yelled, running from the side street where he had kept his vigil. He charged toward the Ripper. He wanted to use his gun, but he didn't dare while the murderer was holding Roni.

The Ripper saw Kent coming and threw Roni aside just as Kent launched himself at him. Roni went sprawling to the cobblestones but recovered immediately when she realized that Kent was in danger. She screamed for help as she got up and searched frantically for the gun she'd dropped.

Meanwhile, Kent and the Ripper struggled wildly. In the scuffle, the Ripper's deerstalker hat flew off, clearly revealing his face. Kent stared at him in amazement.

"You bastard!" he cried, attacking again in a mindless frenzy, wanting to make this man suffer for the pain he'd caused.

The Ripper still held his knife, and he struck swiftly as Kent lunged at him, the blade finding its mark in Kent's side.

Roni saw the Ripper stab Kent and screamed just as two bobbies came running toward them. The Ripper let out a blood-curdling laugh as he watched Kent fall, then gasped as the two policemen came at him from behind and knocked him off his feet.

"My God…" they said, staring down in disbelief at the man they held to the ground.

"Kent!" Roni ran to where he lay clutching his shoulder. She fell to her knees, tears streaming down her face. "Are you all right?"

"Roni…did they get him?" he asked hoarsely, then shut his eyes in pain.

"Yes, they got him…" she answered, sobbing. "We've got to get you to a doctor… You're bleeding and…"

From her pocket came the muffled sound of the watch's chime. She snatched it out and opened it. "It's working again…" she said in wonder.

"What is?" he asked, looking at her.

As she handed him the watch so he could see it, the wind picked up, moaning as it rushed down the street.

"Kent…" She grasped his hand, knowing what would happen and fearing it. A sudden heavy fog swirled around them, obscuring the world and sweeping them away through time… together.

Roni clung to Kent, refusing to be parted from him, knowing that her life would be empty and pointless without him.

Then, in an instant, it was over.

They were beneath a streetlight in Whitechapel, and Roni could hear the sounds of traffic and see the lights in the windows of houses. She still knelt beside Kent.

He struggled to sit up. "Roni… what happened? Where did they go?"

"It's all right. Be careful with your shoulder… Let me help you." She put an arm around him and helped him to his feet.

"Miss, are you and the gent all right?" an elderly man asked as he emerged from a building nearby. "Good Lord, he's bleeding!"

"Yes. Please, would you call an ambulance? I've got to get him to a hospital."

"Straight away!" The man hurried back inside the building.

"Roni…" Kent's face was pale as he stared down at her. He felt a little light-headed, but he knew it wasn't from his wound. He looked around in awe. "It was true… everything you said…"

"Everything," she confirmed, as the blare of sirens grew louder.

"Was it the watch?' he asked.

"Yes… I never told you *how* I knew it was responsible for my traveling through time. The first time I heard it chime and then opened it was the night Jack attacked me and you found me. Tonight was only the second time I've heard it chime and opened it. Now the watch has brought us back to my time. Do you remember we talked about making a future together? Well, we're going to live that future now. Trust me."

She kissed him softly just as the ambulance turned down the street and came to a halt in front of them.

EPILOGUE

Clad in casual slacks, a polo shirt, and loafers, Kent sat on a chair in the hospital room, eagerly anticipating his release after three weeks of confinement. Within the hour they would have the doctor's signature and he would be free to go… free to explore a whole new world with Roni. So far he had been fascinated by modern inventions and the marvelous convenience of electrical gadgets and machines. He remembered wondering—it seemed so long ago—if he would want to live in the 1990s, and he decided now it wasn't such a bad place after all.

Roni stood at the window, staring out at London's skyline. She couldn't imagine everything having turned out any better. There had been a few awkward moments in the ambulance when she had had to explain their clothes to the attendants by saying they had come from a party and had been robbed. That white lie explained Kent's having no currently dated identification. From that moment, all had gone incredibly smoothly. Though Kent had lost quite a bit of blood, and had developed a serious infection that had required intravenous antibiotics, he had completely recovered, and today they were ready to begin a new life.

"I have only one regret," Kent said.

She turned to him smiling. "What's that?"

"That there's no record of the Ripper's arrest."

His gaze met hers across the room, and they both knew what he meant. She had brought him all the books she could find about the Ripper, and he had been angered by the lack of information they had contained—especially regarding the Ripper's real identity. When Kent discovered that many files had been destroyed in the hundred years since the murders, his anger had escalated into outrage and disbelief.

Later, when he had finally calmed down, he had realized that Roni's theory of a cover-up of Jack's arrest had indeed been true.

"I've been thinking about that," Roni said. "You've been wondering what to do for a living now that you're here with me. Well, I'm sure I can get you a job at my station. You're certainly a qualified investigator—although it might take you a little while to catch up on the new techniques. I've been wanting to do a documentary about serial killers, starting with Jack the Ripper. Interested?"

"Most definitely. I want the truth told. This is one secret that's been kept too long."

"I agree, but we're going to have to have factual proof. Believe me when I say our eyewitness testimony won't carry any weight with the network. All it would do is get us both locked up somewhere."

He frowned at the thought that no one would believe them, but then, he hadn't believed her when he'd found her. He smiled. "I can't think of anything I'd like more than to spend the rest of my life working with you..."

He went to her. He winced a little when as he moved, but he knew that the wound was not serious and that the soreness would be gone in another week or so. "I told you I would never let you go, and I meant it."

Roni put her arms around his neck and pulled him down to her for a kiss. "I'm glad you're here, Kent Grayson. Without you, I wouldn't even have a life."

He raised his head and smiled gently. "Will you marry me, Roni? Will you be my wife, my life, my love for all time?"

She returned his smile and kissed him again. "Oh, yes, Kent. For all time..."

ABOUT THE AUTHOR

After working as a department manager for Famous-Barr, and briefly as a clerk at a bookstore, Bobbi Smith gave up on career security and began writing. She sold her first book to Zebra in 1982.

Since then, Bobbi has written over 40 books and 6 novellas. To date, there are more than five million of her novels in print. She has been awarded the prestigious Romantic Times Storyteller of the Year Award and two Career Achievement Awards. Her books have appeared on numerous bestseller lists.

When she's not working on her novels, she is frequently a guest speaker for writer's groups. Bobbi is mother of two sons and resides in St. Charles, Missouri with her husband and three dogs.

You can follow Bobbi on Facebook in the group Bobbi Smith Books.

13Thirty Books
Exciting Thrillers, Heart-warming Romance,
Mind-bending Horror, Sci-Fantasy
and
Educational Non-Fiction

Bad Attitude & Diamond In The Rough

Bad Attitude
Meet bad boy, undercover state trooper Reid Cameron.
Meet Polly Sweet, the woman who is about to be his downfall.
In order to catch a jewel thief, Cameron wants to use Polly's house, and he comes up with a plan, whereby they play at being lovers. But when the first play-acted kiss happens, neither one is ready for the feelings that kiss ignites or for the consequences that ensue. Has this bad boy finally met his match? How Bad is Too Bad?

Diamond In The Rough
Detective Dan Murdock is on a dangerous stakeout, when advice columnist, Millie Gordon unwittingly shows up on the scene, putting them both in danger. To save her from possibly being shot when the mobsters arrive, Murdock jumps into Millie's car and throws himself over her to protect her, little realizing that the real danger starts when their bodies come together.
Both of them try to deny their undeniable desire for one another, but when Millie decides Murdock would make a great "unsung hero" for her upcoming book, she maneuvers him into letting her ride along with him as his partner. How long will they be able to resist the obvious smoldering sexual attraction between them?

Romantic Times: Vegas

The Excelsior Hotel and Casino. Built in Las Vegas in 1960 by mobster Louis "The Lip" LaFica. For decades the towering hotel has been the subject of incredible stories and rumors that have kept it in the public eye the world around. Why have so many lovers been mysteriously, magically, magnetically drawn to this magnificent edifice? And why now have so many bestselling authors at last come together to reveal the adventures of these lovers who have stayed at the glorious Excelsior?

The Third Hour

The Third Hour is an original spin on the religious-thriller genre, incorporating elements of science fiction along with the religious angle. Its strength lies in this originality, combined with an interesting take on real historical figures, who are made a part of the experiment at the heart of the novel, and the fast pace that builds.

Ripper – A Love Story

"Queen Victoria would not be amused--but you will be by this beguiling combination of romance and murder. Is the Crown Prince of England really Jack the Ripper? His wife would certainly like to know....and so will you." - Diana Gabaldon, New York Times Best Selling Author

Heather Graham's Haunted Treasures

Presented together for the first time, New York Times Bestselling Author, Heather Graham brings back three tales of paranormal love and adventure.

Heather Graham's Christmas Treasures

New York Times Bestselling Author, Heather Graham brings back three out-of-print Christmas classics that are sure to inspire, amaze, and warm your heart.

Zodiac Lovers Series

Zodiac Lovers is a series of romantic, gay, paranormal novelettes. In each story, one of the lovers has all the traits of his respective zodiacal sign.

Never Fear
Shh... Something's Coming

Never Fear – Phobias
Everyone Fears Something

Never Fear – Christmas Terrors
He sees you when you're sleeping ...

Never Fear – Tarot
Coming Fall 2016

More Than Magick
Why me? Recent college grad Scott Madison, has been recruited (for reasons that he will eventually understand) by the wizard Arion and secretly groomed by his ostensible friend and mentor, Jake Kesten. But his training hasn't readied him to face Vraasz, a being who has become powerful enough to destroy the universe and whose first objective is the obliteration of Arion's home world. Scott doesn't understand why he was the chosen one or why he is traveling the universe with a ragtag group of individuals also chosen by Arion. With time running out, Scott discovers that he has a power that can defeat Vraasz. If only he can figure out how to use it.

Stop Saying Yes – Negotiate!
Stop Saying Yes - Negotiate! is the perfect "on the go" guide for all negotiations. This easy-to-read, practical guide will enable you to quickly identify the other side's tactics and strategies allowing you to defend yourself ensuring a better negotiation for your side and theirs.

13Thirtybooks.com
facebook.com/13thirty